D0948912

The Greek Generals Talk

ILLINOIS SHORT FICTION

A list of books in the series appears at the end of this volume.

Phillip Parotti

The Greek Generals Talk

Memoirs of the Trojan War

UNIVERSITY OF ILLINOIS PRESS

Urbana and Chicago

*Publication of this work was supported in part
by grants from the National Endowment for the Arts
and the Illinois Arts Council, a state agency.*

This book is printed on acid-free paper.

"Diomedes at Aulis," *Southern Humanities Review* 17, no. 4 (Fall 1983):
  343-48.

Library of Congress Cataloging-in-Publication Data

Parotti, Phillip, 1941-
    The Greek generals talk.

    (Illinois short fiction)
    1. Trojan War—Legends. 2. Troy (Ancient city)—Legends.
3. Greece—History—To 146 B.C.—Fiction.
I. Title. II. Series.
PS3566.A7525G7 1986   813'.54   85-27516
ISBN 0-252-01304-2 (alk. paper)

for my father

The Greek Generals Talk

A Note on the Trojan War

In the haze of myth, Peleus fell in love with Thetis, a beautiful nymph from the depths of the sea. Zeus, Lord of the Thunderbolt, also coveted the Nereid but cooled his ardor when warned that she would bear a son mightier than his father. With Zeus's blessing, Peleus and Thetis enjoyed a lavish wedding attended by all of the gods, but through an oversight, Eris, goddess of strife, was lamentably excluded from the invitation list and snubbed. For spite, Eris made a clandestine appearance anyway, remaining just long enough to roll a golden apple across the floor, where it finally came to rest between the guests' feet: clearly inscribed on the apple were the words "For the Fairest." As soon as the apple was noticed, Hera, Athena, and Aphrodite each laid claim to it, but their ambitions led to such an unseemly squabble that the three goddesses almost instantly called upon Zeus to determine who most deserved the prize. Wisely, with shrewd diplomatic style, Zeus declined to make such a decision, referring the matter instead to the judgement of Paris.

Before Paris was born, Hecuba, queen of Troy, was frightened by a nightmare in which she dreamt that she would give birth to a burning brand. Warned by seers to expect a child who would cause Troy's ultimate destruction, King Priam exposed the boy at birth. Sadly for Troy and the House of Dardanus, the matter did not end with Paris's exposure; rather, a shepherd discovered the boy on the slopes of Mount Ida, rescued him, and unwittingly raised him as his own son. There, on the mountain, in his late youth, the three goddesses found Paris and besought his judgement. In her way, each goddess attempted to bribe

Paris: Hera offered him power in return for the prize; Athena offered him wisdom and military victories; but Aphrodite offered him the most beautiful woman in the world. In the heat of youth, Paris awarded Aphrodite the apple.

Helen, the daughter of Zeus and Leda and the wife of King Menelaus of Sparta, surpassed all other women in charm, grace, and beauty. Indeed, her attractions were so irresistible, so powerful, that virtually every king in Greece had sought her hand; when she finally chose the red-haired Menelaus as her husband, each of her other suitors swore a joint oath to protect her and her marriage in honor of their commitment to her beauty. In the meantime, Paris found his way home to Troy, enjoyed his city's welcome, and, at Aphrodite's urging, departed on an embassy to Sparta. Menelaus showed Paris every facet of gracious hospitality, but after nine days, when Menelaus departed on a diplomatic mission to Crete, Paris betrayed his host by first seducing and then abducting Helen and taking a sizeable portion of the Spartan treasury with her as he sailed away for Troy.

Stung by such an unpardonable breach of the laws of hospitality, the Greek kings rallied to Menelaus's cause, allying themselves for war under the leadership of Menelaus's elder brother, Agamemnon, king of Mycenae and overlord of all Achaia. Their forces gathered at Aulis on Greece's east coast, but, once there, the loss of favorable winds prevented their sailing for Troy. While hunting, Agamemnon had inadvertently shot an animal sacred to Artemis, goddess of the hunt; as punishment, she had caused the winds to fail, and the Greek fleet languished. Called upon to read the signs and recommend a course of action, Calchas divined that only by sacrificing a virgin could Agamemnon appease Artemis. Faced with such an extreme form of atonement, Agamemnon took the responsibility on himself and sent to Mycenae for the youngest of his daughters, Iphigenia. In order to ensure the maiden's arrival, Agamemnon lied to Iphigenia and to her mother, Clytemnestra, telling them both that he had arranged for the girl to marry Achilles at Aulis. Upon receipt of this news, Iphigenia was quickly dispatched to Aulis, and when she arrived, Agamemnon summarily put her to death. Immediately Artemis relented, the winds were restored, and the Greek fleet sailed for Troy.

Prior to assaulting the Plain of Ilium, the Greeks attacked and reduced the offshore island of Tenedos; then, using the island as a base, they moved on to Troy. As the Greek fleet appeared, the Trojans swarmed to the beaches, hoping to repel the invasion. Protesilaus, the first Greek ashore, was struck down by Hector, but his death inspired the Greeks, and soon they had accomplished their landing and were fighting their way upcountry toward Ilium. Pressed hard, and then harder, by Achilles, the Trojans steadily gave ground, finally withdrawing behind the city's walls. When a Greek embassy failed to recover either Helen or the Spartan treasure, both sides settled into a nine-year war of siege, stalemate, and attrition, punctuated by frequent vicious raids.

During the war's ninth year, when Agamemnon insulted Achilles by taking away the lady Briseis, the war prize awarded to him by the army, Achilles angrily withdrew from the fighting, taking his Myrmidon army with him. Achilles' mother, the sea nymph Thetis, interceded with Zeus on her son's behalf; as a result, Agamemnon was made to feel the swift-footed warrior's absence, and the war approached a crisis. Sensing the ripeness of the moment, Hector and the Trojans again took the field, attacking the Greeks in a fierce counteroffensive. Hard pressed, the Greeks fell back and, recognizing his error, Agamemnon relented, offering Achilles full restitution and compensation for the insult. But the proud Achilles rejected Agamemnon's overtures, and the military crisis intensified as Hector and his Trojans stormed the Greek camp, breached its wall, and set fire to more than one of the Argive ships. At the last possible moment, when most of the Greek generals were already wounded and the situation seemed hopeless, Achilles seemed to relent; but in place of rejoining the battle himself, he chose to remain aloof and sent instead his best friend, Patroclus, who took his place at the head of the Myrmidons. The Myrmidon counterattack struck the Trojan flank like a thunderbolt, and for a while Patroclus enjoyed unprecedented success, driving the Trojans back, killing Sarpedon, and even attacking the walls of Ilium. But in the moment of his greatest triumph, Apollo stunned Patroclus, allowing Hector to kill the luckless squire and rob his body of Achilles' armor. Infuriated by the death of his friend—a death that he himself had helped to

precipitate—Achilles finally rejoined the battle with the expressed purpose of killing Hector, knowing full well that if he succeeded his own
death would shortly follow. Numbed by what he had done to Patroclus
and fully accepting his own tragic destiny, Achilles butchered his way
across the Plain until, after chasing Hector three times around the walls
of Troy, he killed him in full sight of the city that Hector had fought so
hard to defend. Days later—after Achilles had tried and failed to defile
Hector's body—at night and guided by Hermes, Priam made his way to
the Greek camp, entered Achilles' hut, and attempted to ransom his
son's body. As Achilles looked at the old king, he finally faced the full
effect of his wrath, the full measure of pain his pride had caused; for a
moment, he perceived something of the suffering his own father would
experience. In that moment, Achilles relented, returning Hector's body
to Priam for burial.

The war entered its tenth year during the weeks that followed. Commanding a huge army of Amazons, Penthesilea joined Priam, but Achilles killed her in battle, and the Greeks defeated her army. King
Memnon of Ethiopia also reinforced Priam, but, following another
fierce battle, he, too, fell victim to Achilles, and once again the war
dissolved into stalemate and siege. At this moment, Achilles ceased to
be a factor in the war: guided by Apollo, who joined him atop the
Trojan wall, Paris shot an arrow at Achilles, struck him in an exposed
heel, and killed him. In the wake of Achilles' death, Odysseus and Aias
contested the possession of the great man's armor, which had been a
gift from the gods; when he failed to obtain the prize, Aias committed
suicide.

As the siege dragged on, Helenus, the seer-son of Priam, fell into
Greek hands and subsequently revealed that Troy could fall only when
the bowman Philoctetes reentered the battle in company with Neoptolemus of Scyros, Achilles' son. By means of trickery, Odysseus and
Neoptolemus managed to coax an embittered Philoctetes back from his
involuntary exile on Lemnos. There, early in the campaign, he had
received a festering snakebite that had led the Greeks to abandon him to
ten years of suffering. Using the bow of Heracles, Philoctetes shot and
killed Paris, who had ceaselessly taunted the Greeks from the heights
of Ilium. Thereafter, wearing disguises, Odysseus and Diomedes stole
into Troy at night, removed the sacred statue of Athena known as the

Palladium, and carried it from the city. Once the Greeks had taken the Palladium—an idol considered to be the source of Trojan strength—everyone expected the city to fall. Hopeless or not, Ilium still stood, resisting all efforts to bring the war to an end.

Having tried all other means for successfully concluding the war, the Greeks finally resorted to a deception. Urged on by Odysseus, Epeius built the wooden horse. Filling the horse with the strongest of their warriors and leaving it on the beach, the remaining Greeks sailed away as though departing forever. In fact, the fleet went only as far as Tenedos, where it remained out of sight behind the landmass, waiting for the signal to return. Meanwhile, as the astonished but joyful Trojans poured onto the beach to examine the horse, Sinon was discovered, captured, and brought before the Trojan elders. Sinon told the Trojans a strange tale, reporting that he had been abandoned by Odysseus in order to prevent him from giving evidence about a murder the Ithacan was supposed to have committed. Sinon explained that the horse had been left as an offering to Athena, that its construction had been undertaken as an act of atonement for the theft of the Palladium, and that its huge size had been designed for a specific purpose: to prevent the Trojans from dragging it into Ilium, where its mystical protective powers might replace the Palladium as the source of Troy's strength. Despite Laocoön's warnings to the contrary, the Trojans became convinced that Sinon had told them the truth, that the massive horse would in fact protect them from further attack. By nightfall they had breached their own wall and pulled the horse all the way across the Plain and into Troy.

Thus Troy fell. At midnight, after the Trojans had celebrated their victory over the Greeks, after they had retired to their homes and fallen asleep, the Greeks swarmed from the horse, recalled their fleet by means of a signal fire, and went over to the attack in a vicious night of fire and sword. By the time the sun rose, Troy was in ruins and all but a few of her citizens were dead.

The Greeks did not linger before Troy; by mid-morning they had divided their spoils and set sail for home. Some, like Nestor, Diomedes, Idomeneus, Philoctetes, and Neoptolemus, reached Achaia swiftly and safely, but others experienced varying degrees of difficulty or outright failure in their attempts to return to the Greek homeland.

Separated from the remainder of the fleet by high winds encountered in a severe storm, Menelaus and Helen were driven all the way to Egypt; seven more years passed before they again set foot in Sparta. King Agamemnon arrived home with dispatch in company with Priam's daughter, Cassandra, whom he had taken from Troy as his concubine, but at the precise moment when he stepped from his ritual bath, Clytemnestra and her lover, Aegisthus, stabbed him to death. Locrian Aias, the half-brother of Telemonian Aias, committed an act of blasphemy following his escape from the sea; for this, Poseidon dashed him back into the depths, where he drowned. Having also angered Poseidon, Odysseus required ten full years en route, and when he did reach home he found his kingdom, his household, and his family beset by the forces of political chaos. Odysseus was the last Greek to reach home, but his trials continued even after he had set his house in order. Following a brief sojourn with his family, he moved again into the unknown, seeking to placate Poseidon. As he disappeared into the hinterland, Achaian Greece entered the autumn of its years.

Historically, if something like the Trojan War was actually fought, its focus was probably economic, and it probably took place between 1250 and 1185 B.C. Within two generations of the war's end, the Dorian invasions from the north had overrun most of western Greece: the result was a dark age that lasted for more than four hundred years.

Map I   Achaia

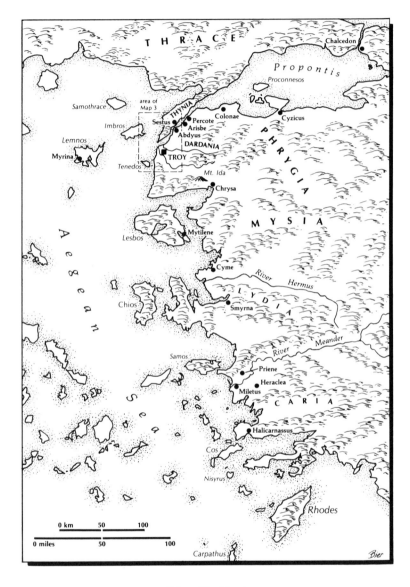

Map II Troia

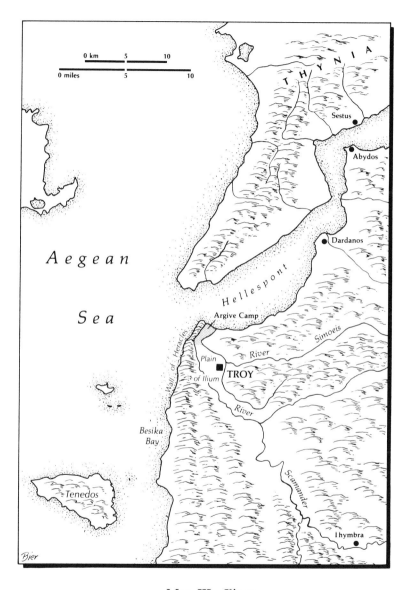

Map III   Ilium

But now, seeing that the spirits of death stand close about us
in their thousands, no man can turn aside or escape them,
let us go on and win glory for ourselves, or yield it to others.

Sarpedon to Glaukos
Homer *Iliad* 12.326-28
Richmond Lattimore translation

Diomedes at Aulis

Tros? Tros has been with me for fifty years; he's a good servant. He was just a boy when I brought him home, small, frightened, undernourished; his eyes were horribly diseased, and it was weeks before he could see clearly. I found him in a blue house, in a street behind the Palladium; he was squatting on the floor of a long hall, beside an overturned statue of Ilius, crying, and speaking frankly, I think he was too weak to move. They didn't eat well during the last year, you know. We'd cut the roads leading in from Phrygia; for all practical purposes, we eliminated their food supply. Oh, occasionally something got through—a few goats, a cart of grain, some fowl—but never enough to do more than give them momentary hope. Once, during the last harvest, right before we went in, the Mysians tried to bring a relief convoy down the river. If they'd succeeded, it would have prolonged things by a year, perhaps more, but we got wind of what they were up to and sent three companies up to stop them. Antilochus, I remember, was in charge, and he did a good job; nothing, not even a barley corn got through, but the river ran red for four hours. That's where he was killed, the brave Antilochus, just east of Thymbra, multiple arrows through the neck. Someone said Paris was leading the Mysians, but that was never confirmed. A few weeks later, we were inside the city, and that's when I found Tros. He's been a good servant; I offered him his freedom over twenty years ago, offered to set him up on a small farm just south of Nemea with cattle and a new wife, but he preferred to stay with me, and now that the veins stand high on my spear hand and now that I can no longer drive my horses with any assurance, I'm grateful that he stayed. Loyalty is a good thing in a man, an even more admirable thing in a slave; frankly, I don't know what I'd do without him. It's at times like this, you know, that I'm glad my Lord Nestor's dead. Now you know what I mean by that, of course: I loved that old man more than any other officer I ever served with; he was like a father to me, but can't you just imagine what he'd say if he could see me now, as I am here today? We'd never hear the end of it.

   Not that way. Over here, here, where the path turns north and runs up along the edges of the cliffs. There were olive trees here in those days, great leafy things that branched out over the path and made it seem like a long cavern. Thersites didn't remember those either, did he? I thought not. You've got to remember two things about Thersites. First, he was the most blatant braggart who made the invasion: I've heard a dozen stories about him since we came home, and not one has contained a single grain of truth, not a grain. The first thing he did when he got home was set himself up as a storyteller, a *storyteller,* mind you, not a poet: he didn't have the class for that. Somehow, you know, he managed to get home before all of us, and then, when we did get home, there were more false stories floating around than flies over carrion, and in most of them, Thersites had managed to put himself forward as Achilles' right-hand man. When Meriones got back and heard what was going on, he made a special trip to the mainland, caught up with Thersites in a gully at the base of Parnassus, and flayed the skin off his back with a rawhide whip. Thersites deserved it. Demodocus, you know, spat on him at Cnossus, and when the fool tried to enter Pylos, my Lord Nestor threatened to sell him to the Egyptians. And that's my second point—about Aulis, I mean; Thersites wasn't there. He and some of that Theban rabble that kept him company weren't even present; they had crossed over to Euboea and were sitting down there in Chalcis, in a wine merchant's shop, too afraid and too drunk to attend.
   —I don't blame Thersites' fear: I don't blame that at all. I've been a judge to my people for many years, and fear is an inescapable condition. It's not that, then; it's the giving in to it that's contemptible, and the lies, the endless lies he told for his own glorification. But not the fear. I remember the fear; it was in the air like a pregnant tempest. We

came up here at noon, and the whole sky was black as night. The darkness beneath the trees was so intense that we lighted torches to see our way, and even then you had to be careful. Nireus, a prince of Syme, took a wrong turn somewhere on the path and remained lost for more than two days. It was like crawling through a cave. And all that time, the girl was silent; she didn't make a sound, not a whimper, not a moan, not anything. She wasn't far ahead of me on the trail, but in the darkness, I only saw her once, when her father had stopped and the flames of his torch outlined her face. She had, I think, the greatest composure of any woman I have ever seen, and as long as I live, I will never forget the expression on her face, the serenity of her resignation. I can't speak for the others, but as you know, we went to the war for Helen; at least in my own case, after Aulis, I think I finished it for Iphigenia.

—There, that's the stone; this is the spot. Tros, open the basket; hand me the jar of fine wine from Samos and that little sack of white barley that we've carried here from home.

And so, you intend to call your poem *The Cypria.* The plan is admirable. I have heard Demodocus, of course; he sang intermittently for three days when I attended the funeral of King Idomeneus in Crete, and in my lifetime I've heard none better, but still, I would like to see a chronological treatment of the war that would take into account its causes and effects, that would give it shape and leave for posterity a record of the event with a sense of order. Demodocus, you know, is splendid with individual episodes, absolutely splendid, but from what I remember—and please understand that I am not a literary man with Demodocus's gifts and talents—still, from what I recall, his recitations at Crete lacked form a little; I'm not sure that form is the right word—unity, perhaps. Somehow he failed, I thought, to capture the immensity of the event. Excuse me, please, if I offend the prestige of your profession; I admit what I am: a grey-headed old man whose tongue and tact have become as lifeless as his spear arm and whose uncultured, old-fashioned ideas must seem more than a trifle foolish. Perhaps the immensity of my recollection dwarfs the reality of the event; such aberrations are possible, I know, and, in truth, much of my reason for making this trip is for the purpose of restoring my own perspective on

the past to something as close to the truth as possible. We, each of us—
those of us who fought there, I mean—has judged and will judge himself and the others; such judgements are inevitable, and I've made
mine over and over again through the past fifty years, but not long, I
think, remains for me to make that judgement final, and before I retire,
finally, from the field, before I give over to the arrows of Smintheus, I
want to be as accurate about myself to myself as I can. Thus, I am
making this journey, but when it is over, when I am home again in
Argos after having seen this stone of Aulis, after having journeyed
again to the Plain of Ilium and, the gods granting, again returned, when
I am home wrestling with Smintheus, who will interpret me to the
children and grandchildren I never had?

—I no longer express myself well, and this is the tragedy of my
years. It is, I think, the function of old men to think, and about this
business of Ilium, I have thought long and hard. There was more to it,
you know, than the mere going, the mere fighting well, and still, how
are the numberless children of Argos to know of the thing beyond the
mere going, the mere fighting well? My memories are my memories,
and not, after all, terribly significant, but for our ¡ uple, the war *was*
significant. Demodocus knows the story of the great horse, but a
greater story by far lies in a simple quarrel that took place between the
great Achilles and my Lord Agamemnon, and still, after fifty years, no
one sings of it. And Odysseus—Odysseus is gone again, gone, this
time, thirty years, crushed, no doubt, at last by the hand of Poseidon,
although he was much beloved of Athene and I hesitate to count him
dead yet. I would like to see proof. Penelope? Penelope is dead. Telemachus is dead. The younger Laertes rules: a good man—a *good* man,
mind you—but not Odysseus, not even Telemachus. The boy is a first-
rate judge and administrator, but by his own admission, he cannot draw
the bow. Helen's granddaughter, Lykia? Beautiful, *beautiful,* but not
Helen, not even Hermione; beside those women and another—say this
one of Aulis—Lykia is pure but plain. And that's the thing I'm talking
about, the thing that's gone.

—Fifty years ago, on the black day when I first came to Aulis, it was
like the womb of the earth. But look at it now: the olive trees are gone;
nothing is left but rocks, a faint sea breeze, and a few dry blades of
grass. The stone is cold, the lady of Aulis is gone, and only a seer and

a craftsman like yourself has the power to restore them. It is true that I still have the vision, but without your craft, those images fall like autumn leaves.

Yes, you are right, of course; the picture was seared across my brain, and I can never forget it, but the image you mention is absent. I could not watch. I saw her face once, on the trail coming up here, and, as a result, she has lasted me a lifetime. I don't want to seem maudlin; for fifty years I have never thought of myself as maudlin when I thought of her, but, all the same, I could not watch. When the Argive princes circled the stone, I managed to stand behind Aias; I turned my back to the stone and faced the sea.

—The moment Calchas uttered his prayer to Artemis, I knew the stroke had been made. That fool Thersites promoted some story about Artemis having spirited her off miraculously to the land of the Taurians; god, how I wish that were true, but facts are facts. The sky simply exploded with a storm so dense that I had to turn back and touch Aias to make sure he was there, and then, with a blast of thunder that sounded like the crack of doom, the Cloud Gatherer set the sky on fire, and there, in the bay, silhouetted against Euboea, I saw one thousand black ships stretching away into the storm as far as the eye could see.

—The storm lasted for hours. Exactly how long we were up here, I can't say, but when we finally got back down to the beach, true night had fallen, the storm clouds had blown away, and the stars were out. We conducted her funeral right down there, built her pyre right down on the beach. Her father and uncle sprinkled the ashes with wine just before sunrise, collected her bones, packed them in a decorated urn filled with honey, and buried her at the foot of the cliff. We celebrated her funeral breakfast at sea.

Here, please—permit Tros to pour you another cup of wine; we have more than enough, and these autumn afternoons are cool. The wine will warm us.

—I dreamed of the ships again last night, their long black hulls scudding through the waves, their great bows shining like polished shields in the early morning sun. North of Scyros, my lords Agamemnon and Menelaus tacked on extra sail, put out all oars, and made a race that lasted more than ten leagues. The elder Atreus won but cheered the younger when, after shipping oars, he allowed the red-haired Menelaus to catch up. They were like that, those two; they were both good men, but Menelaus, I think, a little weaker, a little more happy-go-lucky than his brother. I could never understand why Helen preferred Menelaus over Eurypylus, Odysseus, or Idomeneus, although Idomeneus, I admit, might have been a little too old for her. I mentioned this to Odysseus once, and he merely laughed, said she had gone to Paris for the same reason, said she went where she was most needed. That's a curious answer for a man like Odysseus to give, don't you think? But he gave it. I visited Neoptolemus once, many years ago, and Hermione told me the same thing. Perhaps there's something to it; perhaps not. I don't think I'll ever really be able to fathom the idea.

—The return was nothing like the going out. We went out with a thousand black-hulled ships, but when we came home, we came like shadows. I took eighty ships to Troy; my Lord Nestor took ninety. As you may know, we sailed home together, but between the two of us, we commanded fewer than twenty black hulls, and two of those really belonged to Euryalus of Tataus. No matter how one remembers it, it was a hard war, but the going out—the going out was a wonder, a dream. All day long, on either side, those slender black hulls sliced the waves like the swiftest dolphins, and then, in the night, when the lanterns were hoisted on the masts, the sky seemed lighted by artificial starlight.

—On the sixth day, the king detached me and half of my force, and, together with my Lord Nestor, we sailed past the Plain, up the Helles-pont, and raided Sestus for provisions. We brought away one thousand cattle, many slaves, and a quantity of copper. We were four weeks before Sestus and lost two hundred men.

—I liked serving with Nestor; he was a good commander, and he anticipated things. He was the first of us, I think, who realized that the days of individual combat were coming to an end; he was the first of us to integrate chariots with infantry and make them fight as a unit. There is no question, of course, about the fact that Achilles was the best fighter in the field, no question at all. But Nestor was a general, and that was the difference. As far back as that first raid, he told me that a day would come when we would have to lead by direction rather than individual, physical example—when we, as commanders, would be too sick, tired, or wounded to do the fighting ourselves—and then, we'd have to learn how to give orders rather than mere exhortations. He was right, you know; by the time Hector attacked our ships in the ninth year, we were all out of it, all wounded. But that's when we began to win, when we formed the men into disciplined units and gave them coherent direction. That was nine years after Sestus, nine years. Nestor knew what was coming; my Lord Nestor was the best general of the lot. When we reached Argos on the return voyage, we parted friends, and I never saw him again.

If these old eyes do not deceive me, Hyperion is racing hard now toward the land of the Ethiopians, and we are going to have to go back down to the plain, and our chariots, and the house of Nisyrus, who is treating us with such unparalleled hospitality. We sail tomorrow, you know, for Euboea, then next week for Scyros, Lemnos, and the Plain of Ilium. Come with me, my friend, as my guest. I will bear all expenses for your trip, and if it won't sound presumptuous of me to say so, it will be something of an education for you when, together, we tour the dusty Plain of Troy and drink the clear, fresh water of Xanthus. No matter that your sight is failing; I will take you over the field myself, foot by foot. A poet, I think, ought to know his ground as well as a general, and by sheer accident, I am one of the last generals to survive. Perhaps you will be the last poet to know the field truly. Where my legs are weak, you and Tros will be my staffs; where your eyes will not see, Tros and I will change vision to word and answer all your questions. Thus I will show you the outlines of the towers of Troy, the spot where the great Achilles fell, and the wide, brown stretch of empty land where once, in my youth, I contended with the gods.

—Tros, the evening wind grows cold; bring me my cloak, please. And Tros, a spear; let me walk down from Aulis once again with a spear in my hand, to finish it for the lady.

Thoas at Pylene

Friend, I am a man of plain speech, an old sea captain with nothing more than years of fighting behind me, but, still, I can see that your amphorae are particularly fine. Your craftsmen show talent and a clear ability to marry strength with grace. Obviously, they understand the wheel well—as well, I think, as the artisans of Cnossus, where the clay is firm, and white, and turns so very smoothly under the skilled hand.

—Have you your tablet and a stylus? —Good, make your marks: I wish to order forty of the vessels, with caps, for the storage and transportation of oil, a wedding gift for young Laertes of Ithaca, the grandson of my friend. And decorate their sides with fish and fowl, especially fowl—especially the owl of bright-eyed Athene, daughter of the Cloud Gatherer: she always showed affection for my friend—now gone—and for his son, too, and if Pylian Thrasymedes speaks the truth, she favors also the young Laertes, high on his rocky throne amidst the orchards of meadowless Ithaca.

—Yes, the owl, I think, should be the main motif, with large grey eyes, with centers that penetrate, conveying acumen and prescience. Forget the fish. Let each show forth an owl, perched in an oak, vigilant and wise. And when they have been formed and fired, send them to my compound by the sea at Chalcis; there, my men will fill each pipe with new pressed oil from the Calydonian olive groves and then transport them over the sea to Ithaca. The gift, I think, will be fitting and not displease the son of the son of my friend.

—Nay, Friend, permit *me*. Let's sit outside, there, beneath your fig trees. My wallet is filled with bread, and soft white cheese, and a jug of sweet, dark wine from Elis; and Melanippus, my oldest slave, still pours with a steady hand.

Yes, Friend, that is true: in those days, I commanded all of Aetolia. High-hearted Oeneus was dead by that time and so, too, the red-haired Meleager on whom kingship over the Aetolians had devolved, and from my citadel at Olenus, I ruled the land.

—My, but that was long ago, in difficult times. Not like now, when all we face are those crude barbarians to the north. The Encheleans, they call themselves. Bah. Who are the Encheleans? A rabble—no more. But the Troad? The Troad was different.

—I took forty ships to the Troad, and each ship carried fifty men. There was great energy in the going out, Friend, and strength, and high spirits like the courage of a fierce pride of lions in the night, when first they plunge into a sheepcote, before the guarding shepherds give alarm and men come rushing from their huts with brands and spears. That was what the going out was like: more than a thousand black-hulled, high-beaked ships cresting the waves, racing before the wind, plunging into the sea's salt spray, their great sails billowing against the sky, their long pine oars flashing in the sun; and my men—my warriors, bronzed and glistening with oil and sweat—pulling together over each new mountain of foam, chanting their deep sea hymns, low, to my Lord Poseidon, the Earthshaker, the Master of the Sea. Oh, let me tell you, Friend, we had great energy in the going out, great strength.

—On the fifth day, as Helios reached his zenith, we slid in under the lee of Tenedos and beached. Ashore, a hard battle was still being fought. Earlier that morning, at sunrise, my Lord Idomeneus had assaulted the island in force, and, as our ships beached on the clean white sand, we could still see his noble Cretans advancing upcountry against retreating parties of Trojans. I cannot remember whether the citadel had been taken by that time, but it fell before nightfall, and then, as we ate a meal and rested beside our ships, we saw the funeral pyres beginning to burn upcountry and knew that the battle had ended, that our Cretans were already beginning to bury the dead.

—We rose early on the sixth day, and sailed, and, with favorable winds, entered the Hellespont. There, the Atreides detached my whole command, and, together with illustrious Nestor and the great

Diomedes, we raided Sestus for provisions. We brought away one thousand cattle, many slaves, and a quantity of copper. We were four weeks before Sestus and lost two hundred men. But then, when the Pylian general withdrew with all his forces, and Diomedes with them, he commanded me to guard the straits between Thynia and Dardania, all the way up the swift currents of the Hellespont, beyond Abydus and Percote to wide Propontis, where the dolphins swim and Thracian Boreas makes his home.

—You have never been there, have you, Friend? —I thought as much. It is a distant place, indeed, harsh in the whirl of its currents, treacherous in the solemnity of its shores. The Hellespont flows southwest, down from Propontis like a dark, mighty river, ominous and swift, then narrows between the hostile citadels of Sestus and Abydus, turning due south and racing ahead until the southern rocks draw up like a fishhook, forming a small natural harbor beneath the enemy stronghold of Dardanos. Beyond Dardanos, the channel turns gradually southwest again until, as it passes the Plain of Ilium, it flows toward Achaia and opens into the sea.

—Here, Friend, with this stick I will draw you a map in the sand beneath our feet.

—Yes, that is the fishhook, and from the harbor that it forms below Dardanos, where we captured eight of Priam's broad-beamed ships, a curving road runs up beside the high rock walls of the citadel and then inland, southwest along the coast until it bends south, crosses the river Simoeis, and, bending back, enters windy Ilium from the east. Mind you, Friend, we did not know all of that in the beginning. When we first sailed up to raid shadowed Sestus, we saw only the exposed portion of the road, the rocky, winding stretch that climbed up from the shore to disappear behind the towered citadel. My Lord Nestor marked this path, and later, at Sestus, after our victory, deduced that topknotted Thracians would try to use it. "Princely Thoas," he said, "it is a road to Ilium; it must be: in this corner of the world, all roads lead there. Mark you this: the Thracians are now alerted to our presence. After all, we have just sacked one of their precious cities, and I do not think they will wait for long before they gather a fleet and try to force a passage down the channel. They will want to anchor in the lee of that fishhook of land and reinforce Dardanian Priam over that same rocky supply road, and that, at all costs, must be prevented. You, my Lord, you, and your forty ships, and your bronze-armed Aetolians *must* prevent it. But fight at sea, Thoas; fight at sea."

—Well, Friend, as events showed, my Lord Nestor appreciated each important detail of the situation. Diomedes and I were young then, and far less knowledgeable about the strategic importance of the straits, but fortunately, owing to my Lord Agamemnon's foresight—and, Friend, I admit this freely—he made us no more than lordly Nestor's lieutenants for that raid. It takes time, you see, to learn the craft of war: in our youth and in our haste and with our enormous inexperience, we wanted to attack and capture Dardanos at once. Had the great Achilles been there, with all his wonderful intensity, I think he would have attacked Dardanos first, without ever having gone near Sestus. But, Friend, from the distance of my years, and even behind these dull grey eyes that shine no more, I can still see that such an attack would have been a mistake: there were no cattle in the expanses behind Dardanos, no slaves to be taken, and no copper for making bronze, only the long, dusty road to Troy and plenty of Priam's infantry, both inside the fortress and bivouacked across the surrounding hills.

—Certainly, my Lord Nestor's decision proved to be the right one. Rather than seek a fleeting glory, he elected to content himself with the attack on Sestus; conserve our army; supply our main body on the Plain with ample quantities of beef, labor, and shining copper; and shut down one of Priam's own vital supply routes by holding the channel and squeezing Dardanos off at the neck. Thus bypassed, the strong point became useless, impotent, lifeless. In time, near the end of the ninth year of the war, when Argive forces finally began to cut off other supply roads into Ilium, the fortress of Dardanos—which had itself to be resupplied along the road to Troy—ceased to be a stronghold. Instead, it became a weak point in the city's defense, a liability, a drain. When Hector concentrated the whole of the Trojan alliance around the high grey walls of Ilium and prepared for his last great assault against us, Dardanos was finally abandoned, its garrison withdrawn.

—I still remember that day, Friend. I brought my Aetolians down the channel then, strong in their high-prowed ships, left three of those ships to guard the fishhook and a small blocking force of infantry, for surety, to occupy the citadel. Then, with the remainder of my men, I

joined the Argive armies massing on the Plain and took my orders,
there, from the Atreides. We formed our battalions behind Nestor and
the brave Antilochus, who died so young. We were a smaller force by
that time—fewer in number, worn down and scarred by our years in the
straits—but that was long ago, long ago when, still, men might contend
with gods.

—Melanippus, the artisan's cup grows empty, and yours. Pour out
more wine and, from the wallet, sprinkle barley on its surface. Helios
grows strong overhead, but here, beneath these fig trees, old men may
sit, and drink, and speak of yesterdays, refreshed.

Yes. —Yes, that is true: we were nine full years in the straits. I do
not mean, of course, that we were always underway. By the hand of
Apollo, good Sir, no man could withstand so long a term behind the
oar, even where the sea is smooth. And in the Hellespont—where Lord
Poseidon always dipped, and whirled, and stabbed his hand, sweeping
and dashing the currents swiftly toward the sea—an hour there was like
a day, and a day like a week, and my seamen groaned, straining and
sweating like bullocks before the plow.

—Friend, within the time of seven days after we withdrew from
shadowed Sestus, within the time of seven days after my Lord Nestor
and the great Diomedes removed to the Plain, my Aetolians were
spent, finished, exhausted, hanging on their oars. Rightly judging the
limits of my men—knowing they were on the verge of collapse, as they
were—I dispatched my red-haired Euenus, my lieutenant, in one of our
high-prowed ships, sending him with a message for the Atreides, and
on the morning of the following day, lordly Agamemnon sent us
relief—twelve ships, just enough to hold the channel in the event of an
emergency. Blue-eyed Nireus of Syme was in the van with three trim
ships, and, following him, bold Tlepolemus sailed with nine long ships
of lordly Rhodians.

—We hailed them as they beat up into the narrows, and then I gave
commands. On my order, six of the black-beaked vessels hove to in the
lee of the fishhook and dropped their anchor stones, but each remained
well out from shore, safe from any attack by the Trojan archers at
Dardanos. At the same time, at bold intervals in column, the other six
ships began to ascend the narrows, each lordly Rhodian straining hard

at his oar, pulling mightily toward that boiling neck of foam that cleared the race between Sestus and the high Dardanian citadel at Abydus. We watched them go, and cheered them, and then my Aetolians slipped the fishhook, caught the current, and, before Helios could even reach his zenith, beached our ships without loss near the clear, white mouth of ever-flowing Scamander. Reunited there with their fellows, my exhausted warriors threw themselves onto the sand and slept, and later ate, and then slept again. I gave them two long days to regain their strength, and then, at the urging of the Atreides, returned them to their oars.

—Pardon? —Oh, no, my Friend, we had learned a lesson by that time and went over to a scheme of rotation. Having seen the condition of my warriors when they first dropped from the sides of our ships, collapsing onto the sand like an army of new-felled trees, my Lord Odysseus sought me out, and lordly Nestor, too, with sound advice. "You can't find safe harbor anywhere but here," said my Lord Odysseus. "The fishhook is far too small for such a fleet as this, and all the rest is rock or cliff, whipped by the swiftest currents. Go over to rotation." I looked then to greying Nestor, and he in turn gave me an encouraging smile. "The Man of Many Turns is right," he said. "Go over, Thoas. Launch ten ships each day: five in the morning when Aurora flushes her cheeks and five in the evening when my Lord Helios descends to the land of the Ethiopians. Good advice is well followed, and such a rotation will conserve your men. It reminds me of a plan I once used to patrol the Gulf of Messene." He told us a tale then, wonderful for its powers of description, about a sea war he had fought in his youth against tall, walleyed raiders from the west. He had commanded, I think, discovering the enemy only after ten of his ships inaugurated a rotation patrol which kept some of them always at sea.

—To make a long story short, Friend, I followed well his good advice. In time, we learned that we could maintain twenty ships within the channel—fifteen at intervals beating up, five racing down while the other twenty rode at anchor before the Plain or beached beside the broad white mouth of Scamander for refit or repair. This gave my Aetolian seamen two good days ashore to rest, eat, and gather their strength for every two-day period they spent behind the oar.

—The plan was sound, you see; the system worked well. And as weeks passed and then months, my Aetolians came to know every twist of the shore, every drift of the current—how to steer in close beside the Thynian cliffs below Sestus so as to avoid the strength of the race, how to hug the Dardanian coast above Abydus, even to Percote, under full sail after prayers and splendid offerings to Zephyrus. But in the winter, when Zephyrus retired and Boreas roared down from Thrace, tearing and slashing with his icy blasts like an enraged lion, wounded, cornered, that springs upon a hunter to devour his face with fang and claw, when ice formed on our oars and biting sleet gnawed at our faces, then we knew much pain and reduced the size of our squadrons from five ships to two, sailing once only, every ten days. It was hard, arduous duty, that, and even here, beneath the summer fragrance of your orchard, I can still almost feel the sharp winter pain of sea salt freezing on my hands, against my face, in the corners of my aging eyes.

—Ah, your cup, my Friend, is empty. Melanippus, break bread for the artisan and fill his cup. And place before us, too, some of those tart, ripe olives that we bought this morning from the Phokian.

Did you say *where?* —Ah, yes, that is what I thought you asked me. Above Percote, in the broad finger of Propontis, where the dolphins swim and Lord Poseidon smooths his ruffled beard with milder hand. Forgive me; my hearing is not so clear now as in my youth.

—Yes. In the autumn of the second year, when the leaves turned, and fell, and floated dry upon the edges of broad Propontis, above Percote where the neck of Thynia is long and slender, the Son of Cronus sent down the demon Strife and Ares, Butcher of Men, who swung his mace and unleashed the dogs of war. And there, for the length of a day, we fought a deadly battle at sea and came away much changed.

—Athena of the bright eyes warned us that the time was ripe. All things had fallen into the sear, and when the midnight Archeress reduced her crescent orb and Thracian Boreas groaned from the depths of his high mountain caves, the Man of Many Turns came to me on the beach beside my own long ship. "My Thoas," he said, "I swear by the bright-eyed daughter of Zeus that the time to strike has come. One of my people is upcountry in Thynia; all along the coast, the Thracians are pregnant with purpose."

—I understood our danger then and called up my fleet. Blue-eyed Nireus joined me again, and bold Tlepolemus with all his lordly Rhodians, and my Lord Meges, the warrior son of Phyleus, with forty black ships from high Dulichium and the sacred Enchinades. We launched our ships on the instant and bent our backs to the oars, and Zephyrus blew us a steady breeze that swelled from the west to send us sailing over the waves like a company of hawks. Black against the wine-dark sea, we raced the Hellespont: first to the tip of the fishhook, then on through the narrows between Sestus and Abydus until finally we skimmed into the long, broad finger of Propontis. I gathered eighty of our high-beaked ships in line abreast there, placed twelve in crescent screen far out ahead, and sped on toward Proconnesos.

—Alkmaon, Thestor's son, was first to sight the enemy and report. High-hearted Meges chose the man for his keen eyesight, and we were not disappointed. From his advanced station far out in the screen, he sent back word that Thracian ships were under sail north of rocky Proconnesos. I prayed then to the Lady of the Flashing Eyes and to Lord Poseidon, and offered sacrifice, and neither failed me.

—My Friend, I had to act quickly then, for time was short. My Lady Athena bade me leave the screen to serve as decoy, but with the remainder of my fleet, I altered course so as to hide their mass under the lee of Proconnesos's western cape. There, hidden by rocky cliffs, I arrayed the fleet again in line abreast, each of their high-prowed beaks pointing northwest, and readied my men for battle, and waited, watching like a hungry eagle when, perched on a crag of high, sharp rock, he searches the ground below, hungering for the unsuspecting hare.

—I had not long to wait. Before great Helios even unveiled the shadows over our ships, our decoys scudded by, bending on every foot of sail from their holds, smiting the sounding furrows hard with their long pine oars, in unison, like racing crews well trained and fresh in breath and arm. Moments later I gave the signal, and all ships hoisted sail. Then, my Friend, was energy, and strength, and the deep, low chant of our sea hymn. With each man mightily dipping his oar into the wine-dark sea, we shook with power and speed, and fell upon the Thracians like a shattering storm just as they sailed into sight past the cape in pursuit of our decoy.

—They had a larger force than we by thirty ships. Eioneus, king of Thrace, had gathered them from all around Propontis, from Cyzicus, Selymbria, and Chalcedon, and even beyond the Channel of the Wavering Rocks from Heraclea, and Sinope, and Thracian Istrus. He planned, I think, to force the Hellespont all the way down to the fishhook, relieve the impotence of Dardanos, and send arms and men over the high narrow road to reinforce the Troad, but he reckoned not on the strength of our blow. We fell upon him like eagles, bolting out of the sun, while his men turned white with panic.

—I was the first that day to kill my man, Grondius of Chalcedon, who was standing in full armor high in the stern of his ship. With my first cast, I struck the man on the ear piece of his crested helmet. My spear-point cut clean through the shining bronze and pierced the bone behind; darkness swallowed him, and he crashed to the deck like a falling mast.

—Then was much killing, Friend, as our high-beaked ships thrust in alongside, snapping the shafts of Thracian oars with the impact of our prows, our men grappling, and boarding, and hacking with sword and axe, or standing off to bring down the enemy with bronze-tipped arrows or the sharp, thick points of boarding pikes forged in the furnaces of far away Achaia. We disabled half their fleet with the first impact. The others, trembling with fear, chattering like terrified squirrels when, from the skies, the Lord of Lightning shatters their homes with his thunder—the others fled. But their ships were slower than ours, broader in beam, heavier, less seaworthy, less built for speed, and, straining hard at our oars, my Aetolians thrust past them, pulled beyond their van, and turned them. I gave commands then, and leaving my Lords Meges, Nireus, and Tlepolemus to finish off the disabled, my brave Aetolians drove the remainder of the Thracian fleet against the rocks, along the neck of Thynia, where their broken keels disappeared beneath the foam.

—Some seven or eight of their vessels survived, I think. I counted two drawn up on a narrow patch of sand north of Percote, and three more above Sestus. Later, eagle-eyed Alkmaon reported seeing two or three sails escape to the east. But most—more than fifty—broke apart on the rocks.

—For hours, Friend, the sea virtually foamed with men. Some few managed to swim ashore along the barren Thynian neck; others hugged the rocks, looking like gripping white spiders, but most, panic-stricken, lunged for the nearest piece of wood—broken oars, masts, beams—and clinging to them floated hopelessly with the currents. For days after, we plucked them from the sea like half-drowned dogs, white, limp, some still clinging to life, a few as far south as the fish-hook, one all the way down near the mouth of Scamander. But most perished, struck down by the hand of Poseidon, and in the days that followed, their bodies washed ashore along every mile of the Thynian and Dardanian coasts, food for vultures and the thin, hungry dogs that came out of the hills, and He, the Courier, led them down through the chambers of decay to Hades.

—Know you, my artisan, that we captured thirty broad-beamed ships before Proconnesos and nine hundred men, and killed many, many more. The ships we later used for transport and supply, but that was not until Argive expeditions led by men like the swift-footed Achilles and Aias of the great shield began reducing Dardanian coastal cities and the far-away trading ports of Phrygia. We sold the nine hundred Thracians as slaves, some at Scyros but most at Myrina on rocky Lemnos, where they brought us good return in grain and wine. The wine, though, as I recall, was not as good as this that we import from Elis.

—I wonder, may Melanippus replenish your cup? A barley cake, perhaps, to ease your hunger?

That is an astute observation, Friend. You are right, of course: the Thracians never regained their strength, never again seriously threatened us. We broke their backs in the deep, dark seas west of Proconnesos. In the ninth year of the war, I'm told, Rhesus, son of Eioneus, finally—finally managed to lead a small contingent into the Troad, but measured by former strength, this army was a very small threat, indeed. And they did not reach Ilium over the Dardanian road.

—No, the men of Thrace never tried the Hellespont again, in numbers. Instead, they sailed east, under the safety of their own coast, all the way to the Channel of the Wavering Rocks. There they reversed course, hugging the southern shore, and sailed west into the fortified

Phrygian harbor of Cyzicus, where they disembarked. Eventually, I suppose, they reached Troy over inland roads, arriving on the Plain only days before Hector's great counterattack. According to my Lord Nestor, the Man of Many Turns and lordly Diomedes neutralized them as a fighting unit by completely demoralizing them. Shortly after the Thracians arrived, you see, and even before they had gone into action, Odysseus and Diomedes raided their camp at night, killing Rhesus and twelve of his staff as they slept. In the morning, when the rank and file became aware of what had happened, terror petrified them. They ceased to be of use then as a unit, and later, I think, their companies were broken up and parcelled out to other Trojan commanders for use as reserves. I know that I met and fought some on the Plain, recognizing them by the heightened gloss of their topknots. But as a major force? No, they did not fight again, convincingly: our victory off Proconnesos proved too conclusive.

—Now understand, Friend, I do not mean to imply by such words that the men of Thrace never again tried to shoot the Hellespont. They did, of course, in trickles, always at night, in single small ships or tiny barges. Some got through, landing unimportant numbers of men and supplies on the stone-hard beach below Dardanos, but we captured many, destroyed more, and some—owing to pitiful seamanship—were lost beneath the waves, dashed against the rocks by the strong, dark current of the race. Their losses far outweighed their gains, and in the eighth year even the trickle stopped, and the Hellespont became secure. It was an Achaian, an Aetolian stream: fast, powerful, open only to my clansmen's ships.

—So you see, Friend, by the ninth year our control of the seas was beyond dispute. When Hector launched his great offensive on the Plain, the Atreides called us in then, brought us ashore, and placed us in a deep fighting formation behind the Gerenian charioteer and masterly Antilochus. That was the crisis, you see, Troy's last sharp thrust, but after Achilles returned to the battle, Troy was finished. Hector was the only real general Priam had; when Achilles killed him, it was all over.

—Oh, the war dragged on, of course, for nearly a year. And we fought again on the Plain, too, twice, throwing back the savage Amazons and forceful Ethiopians, but after Hector died, the issue was never in doubt. Had it not been for the ruse of the horse, starvation would have finished them soon enough, probably by the end of the tenth year. By that time, you see—by the time of the horse—our grip around Ilium was tight; all roads in and out had been squeezed shut at last. When we did get into the city, the people of Priam were everywhere weak with hunger, starving in their homes.

—Here, my friend, take a piece of this fine white cheese. I always find it very satisfactory with the wine.

The Plain? The Plain was vicious, Friend—deadly, dusty, and hot. The Butcher of Men roared with rage there, and the men themselves dropped like swatted flies or locusts mashed beneath one's feet.

—I lost many good men on the Plain: Diores, son of Amarinceus; Alkmaon of the strong, bright eyes; Haimon of Pylene, my kinsman. . . . And I lost friends, too, . . . great Medon of the high ox shield . . . and my strong right arm, lordly Tlepolemus, rider of the sea, son of mighty Heracles, who sailed with me at Proconnesos and won. Somewhere, I think, in Rhodes, his grandson survives. There is a story afoot in Achaia that my Rhodian was murdered by his friend, long-haired Prothous of Magnesia, in an argument over spoils, but the story is a great lie, one of many spawned by that sea slime that calls itself Thersites. Know you, Friend, Thersites—the greatest ugliness in Achaia—cast everywhere about him slime and lies, and this lie in particular disserved a noble man. My Lord Tlepolemus died a heroic death in combat and was mourned by all of us, long-haired Prothous most of all. Sarpedon killed him, but not without receiving the point of Tlepolemus's own spear so deep in his thigh that his Lykian henchmen had to drag him, fainting, from the field like a wounded boar.

—Indeed, I, too, fought before Troy, and led my warriors in battle, and killed my man—again, a bold Thracian spearman, Peiros, who came from Aenus wearing a long black topknot on his head and silver greaves on his shins. And once, amidst the deafening din of battle, where dust rose above our steaming bodies like the swirling thick smoke of a funeral pyre—once, I faced great Hector; I faced him, and cast my spear, sinking it in his shield, but failed to wound him, and he disappeared among the Trojan host.

—I lost many fine men beating back Hector's offensive. When the battle was over, my Aetolians numbered only enough to man twenty of our ships, no more.

—Well, my friend, I see we reach the last of the wine. Enough remains for half a cup, I think. Let Melanippus pour it for us and sprinkle its dark surface with the remains of the cheese.

Oh, Friend, you are too generous, too *too* generous by far. Please, I am no more now than a very old soldier, a sea warrior without a ship. You yourself can see how much I've fallen into the sear: my beard is white, my spear arm soft, my eyes no longer clear. I have even given over command to my sons and grandsons. Know you, Friend, I can put to sea no more on the raiding voyage: the roll and pitch unsettle me, and with these ears I am not even able to hear the sea hymn when it is chanted low by our bronzed, young men, my Aetolians who joy behind the oar.

—No, Friend, all that I have told you was long, long ago when still I might accomplish work of noble form. I am content now to remain at home, content to tend my vines and trees, and eat ripe olives in the evening sun. If the northern threat proves real, if those barbarians beyond Dodona have strength, even then, I am still too old to go and once again stand my ground in the field. No, soon, I think, the Slayer of Argus will guide me in the night to the chambers of decay.

—Artisan, you are a generous man. I will accept the gift, but, please, expend no special effort on it. A jug, a krator—a vase, perhaps: something that will show your skill but save you time for more important work.

—Yes, I like your plan, indeed—a smoothed, finished vase showing forty high-beaked, black-hulled ships scudding like dolphins over the wine-dark seas.

Meges at Dulichium

Ha! —That is the story that was given out, assuredly. But pardon, please, my amusement in this matter: I do not laugh at you, but at myself, and now, after all these years, at the man . . . no, that would not be the right word . . . at the creature, let us say, who fabricated this tale.

—Oh, let me tell you, my friend, at the time it was no laughing matter. When we finally beached our long-beaked ships here on the sands before Dulichium, we found no songs or flowers of welcome, no happy laughter of wives and children, only a long, low mound marked at intervals with memorials to our passing. Then, as we climbed the hill, there, toward our citadel, we were forced to defend ourselves— from our own people. Thinking, you see, that we had all perished at sea off the Euboean coast, the people's newly elected leaders mistook us for sea raiders and gave the alarm. Let me tell you, my friend, for several hours, it looked as though we had survived ten long years against a bitter enemy in the Troad only to be attacked on our doorsteps by our own friends and neighbors. Thersites, you see, had preceded us.

—Of all who went, Thersites was the least erected warrior on the Plain. —No, I misspeak myself: to apply the word *warrior* to an ass like Thersites is a corruption of language, and in this case, all corruption belongs to the man. A warrior he was not. An ass, even, may exceed him in the nobility of its nature. What he was—and this I can say without equivocation—what he was, was the ugliest braggart, the most blatant liar Achaia ever produced. Somehow—and in my visits with Gerenian Nestor and blue-eyed Menelaus, He Who Awakes the

People, we have never determined how—somehow, that cretinous
whelp reached home before any of us—weeks before the first of us, if
my information is correct, which means that he deserted the army even
before we sacked Ilium. At any rate, as I say, he reached home before
any of us and put himself forward as the hero of the piece, proclaimed
himself my Lord Agamemnon's herald.

—You can imagine, I'm sure, what that produced: Thersites was
everywhere welcomed, everywhere applauded, everywhere sanctified
and worshipped as the darling of the army. These things alone might
have done little harm, but not content to hear his praises sung—and
this, I think, is native to the beast—he began to sing them himself, and
then much harm was done.

—He landed, we think, near Phthia and there, among the Myrmidons, advanced himself as Achilles' right-hand man. From Trachis he
went down to Athens and announced himself as the field commander
who had led Menestheus's infantry against great Hector's counteroffensive, and in Argos he let loose a story that Diomedes had been killed
during a raid on Sestus early in the war. From there he went on to
Pylos, reporting that my Lord Nestor had lost his leg in the fighting,
and in Pylos, too, he cast the rumor that brave Antilochus had been
killed by King Memnon, son of Tithonus and the blushing Dawn. He
was smart, you see; he kept on the move, never staying too long in a
single place, never quite wearing out his welcome, but he hadn't reckoned on Nestor's swift return, and at Pylos Lord Nestor nearly caught
him.

—From what I've been told, the fool was sitting at his cups when the
men of Pylos sailed into the bay, but some minutes passed before anyone realized who they were. You see, my Lord Nestor had sailed for
the Troad with ninety ships. —He returned with less than twelve, and
from the fleece-lined benches on the porch of the palace, Nestor's
arrival, like my own here in Dulichium, gave the appearance of a raid
or the entry of a small merchant fleet. No one apprehended its meaning
until the ships beached and armed men began to leap from their sides,
casting helms and shields in all directions onto the sands, thus revealing their true identities. Then, I believe, the talebearer took to his
heels. Upon learning of the man's presence and the enormity of his
lies, my Lord Nestor sent the raven-haired Pesistratus in pursuit with a

party of his fellows, but they were young men, all of them, unskilled in war and late, very late, in starting. They lost Thersites' track in the mountains north of Thryon. They had orders, I believe, to bind him, flog him, and sell him as a slave to the Egyptian traders at Kalydon.

—And so, you see, Thersites found his way here to Dulichium, to my people, and remained with them ten days, reporting that I had gone down with my whole fleet near Caphereus in Euboea. My people mourned twelve days. On the thirteenth, they erected this mound in memory of me and my men, and on the fourteenth day, following a festival of games, they met in council and elected new leaders. Two months later, we returned.

—I had gone out to Ilium with forty black ships, and when four, only, sailed into our harbor and my men—wearing full battle dress, expecting to be welcomed home like heroes—leapt onto the beach, the alarm bell was sounded. We were met on the road, first by a party of archers and then by the massed armed force of our sons, grown to manhood. As Helios passed his zenith and began his advance toward the land of the Ethiopians, both forces stood facing one another, here where we stand.

—Oh, my friend, we were not prepared for such a greeting, and the surprise of our reception made us burn with shock and frustration. Our sons, thinking to defend their mothers, their sisters, and their absent fathers' properties, refused to give ground; and we, shot through with conflicting pangs of pride and pain—we, too, refused to give ground; and then, I think, the issue would have come to blows had not the bright-eyed goddess interceded and made us shout our names, one at a time, man by man, all the way across this sloping plain where we had drawn up in a line in sight of our homes. Then, at last, our wives and aged parents heard us calling, came forth across the rocky ground, removed our helms, touched our hair, and our faces, and our hands, and, lifting their voices like sweeping sea hawks, pierced the air with cries of joy.

—The event ended pleasantly enough, but not, I'm sorry to say, without some blood: three of my men were wounded by the archers who came out as advance guard while the remainder of our sons were arming themselves. I hold Thersites responsible for that blood, and, like my Lord Nestor, I, too, sent my own strong son and many others after him, but he was long gone, and again he escaped. Eventually, I understand, great-hearted Meriones cornered him in the foothills below Parnassus and flogged him publicly, but that is rumor. Whatever the case, the damage was done: today, no matter where you go in the land of the Achaians, you are bound to hear one or another of the apocryphal stories that upstart contrived.

—Let us walk this way. This path is not so rocky as the other, and often at this hour a soothing sea breeze rounds the cape, offsetting the inland heat. There, to the northeast, if you look deep into the mists, you can see the island home of the Man of Many Turns.

The truth? It would take days to reveal all of it, and that, I'm sure, is beyond your patience. And besides, the spurious tales fathered by that dog are as numerous as the leaves on the trees, or so experience indicates, if that may pass your test. Consider, if you will, the lies he fabricated about the brave Antilochus, my Lord Nestor's son and second heir. When first he came among my people, Thersites, that father of swine, contrived some swill that the steady Antilochus was exposed at birth on Mount Ida and later suckled by a bitch. —Yes, well you can see why my Lord Nestor was angry, can't you? But that isn't half of it. Oh no, he wasn't content to stop there, with a little lie, but, true to form, he compounded it by ten, suggesting that Antilochus had only joined the expedition late, much against the Gerenian's wishes, and, though of inferior ability, he had used his father's influence to gain high place in the command. Fie! *Blasphemy!*

—Please, my friend, pardon my heat: lies such as these would stick in the mouth of a goat, and for a man—a human being, no matter how low—to have uttered them is a transgression against our kind, a wanton malevolence performed without motive, something detrimental to all of us. My Lord Nestor, know you, sent for Antilochus in the fourth year of the war. Before that time, you see, Antilochus had remained in Pylos, a youth completing his military training under the auspices of his elders, but when he arrived on the Plain, he was already a man— tall, broad, bronzed like the blade of a sword—and his qualities as warrior and leader were beyond dispute.

—He did not begin as a major field commander at all: he became one in less than three years, certainly, but his father's influence had nothing to do with his high place in the army. He earned that place through hard fighting, and intelligent leadership, and an iron refusal to give ground before the enemy. He was very aggressive, you see, but never ambitious, and he was quiet outside of battle, sometimes almost reclusive. But the moment he took up his spear and shield and put on his helm, he was like a dark wind blowing up from the Argive camp, and the Trojans gave way before him like leaves before a storm. Achilles spotted those qualities in him while the man was still in the ranks and urged my Lord Nestor to promote him, and in the moment Antilochus was placed in a subordinate position with the Myrmidons, accompanying the great Achilles on raid after raid. He captained one ship and fifty men in the attack on Lesbos and again in the sack of Colophon. During the raid on Cyme, he commanded three ships, and when Achilles struck Smyrna with more than fifty of our high-beaked hulls, the brave Antilochus shared subordinate command with lordly Patroclus. Thus, and only thus, did Pylian Antilochus earn his place in the army—always by excellence, always by leading, always by being at the forefront, by urging his men forward across the length and breadth of the Troad.

—In the seventh year, after three hard years of fighting, when he had proved himself before all men, both Trojans and Argives, before even his noble brother, Lord Thrasymedes, the Atreides brought him in and with his father's blessing made him a field commander on the Plain. My Lord Nestor himself divided his own command, giving over to his son sole responsibility for the men from Arene, Thryon, and handsome Aepy. Sacrifice was made, then, to Father Zeus, my Lady of the Shining Eyes, and Ares, Butcher of Men; and, Nestor assisting, my Lord Agamemnon made much ceremony to mark an event that our entire army found pleasing, and fitting, and just.

—Perhaps, my friend, we should sit for a moment, here, beneath these olive trees. The path is steeper than I remembered, and the spear wound in my thigh, though old, retains its twitch. These are my son's groves; this is the fifty-third year since he and I planted them in remembrance of my homecoming.

No. Absolutely not! And in some ways, I think, that lie dwarfs all the others. Not only did it foster a litter of ugly untruths, but, by telling it,

Thersites completely obscured the actual facts, and those, my friend, deserve to be known. Brave Antilochus died a soldier's death, a death in its way so heroic, so true to the man that we should tell the facts about it to our children, and to our children's children, and to their children until the truth is known to all Achaians. It was a hard death, you see, but it was the death of a soldier who did his duty and the death of an officer who stood by his men.

—The pure fact is that King Memnon and his Ethiopians never came anywhere near my Lord Antilochus. Late in the ninth year of the war, the great Memnon did succeed in bringing a strong force of Ethiopians into the battle. By that time, you see, we had destroyed Hector in his last major offensive, destroyed the bitch Amazons commanded by that fierce Penthesilea, and nearly succeeded, finally, in bottling up the city. Assuming that the end was in sight, we were ripe for the unexpected, and the unexpected is exactly what struck us.

—For nine years, throughout the entire war, we had always maintained a strong naval patrol south of the Isle of Tenedos; but when the Amazons smote us with such force, across land, in the late summer of our ninth year, the Atreides called in the fleet, which instantly released six thousand more warriors to bolster our men on the Plain. My Lord Nestor advised against this move, urging King Agamemnon to leave at least twenty of our black-hulled ships at sea, patrolling and vigilant; but in a moment of doubt Lord Agamemnon made what was, perhaps, a hasty decision, brought all the ships ashore, and committed the crews to battle. Well, as events later showed, the Amazons were not so numerous as the Atreides thought, and we could easily have afforded to have kept the entire screening force at sea. To our sorrow, we did not.

—Once the men of Crete and Aetolia were ashore and once the Amazons had been defeated, most of us—my Lord Nestor excepted—saw no reason to return the patrolling forces to sea. Overconfident, no doubt, believing we had destroyed the last external threat to our enterprise, secure in our ignorance, with the odor of victory blunting our senses, we turned our whole attention to cutting all inland supply routes and starving Ilium into submission. Operations proceeded apace, and each day some small command or another would go off upcountry on an independent operation designed to interdict this or that

supply column trying to reach the Troad from one of Priam's allies—
the Phrygians, the Mysians, the Maeonians. . . . On a dark night in
early autumn, just as the leaves were beginning to fall and the nights to
turn cold, lordly Memnon, son of the blushing Dawn, brought more
than one hundred and fifty ships up past Tenedos, beached them on the
white sands circling Besika Bay, and, after a forced march through
shadows cast by those coastal hills that men call the Walls of Heracles,
attacked us at dawn with nearly eight thousand men.

—We were totally unprepared. Most of us, myself included, were
sitting before our breakfast fires watching rose red spread across
Aurora's cheeks. The Ethiopians were disciplined: they made no sound
during their approach, and they were among us before we knew what
hit us, and there, after nine long years, Memnon's men succeeded in
doing what Hector's had never been able to do: they fired more than
ten of our ships. I remember well, Friend, those great plumes of black
smoke drifting toward the sky, obscuring the dawn with darkness and
death, and I remember, too, the sensation of fear that ran through my
bones. But we had not warred so long for nothing. Absorbing the initial
shock with much damage, we turned and fought, and stood, and held
our ground.

—And now, my friend, the point I want to make is this: the brave
Antilochus was never approached by lordly Memnon. When the Ethiopians struck, they struck the right side of our line—first the Myrmidons
and Achilles, then Podarkes and the men of the North, then Menestheus's Athenians, and finally my islanders. Eight thousand men make
a great army—of that, you may be sure—but still, all of Memnon's men
could cover only about a quarter of our front. Some, I think, may have
spilled over into the camp of the Lokrians to my left, but the four
armies on the right absorbed most of the shock. The brave Antilochus,
fighting beside his father, was among the Argive forces to the left of
center, four armies away, contending with other Trojan companies that
had made a sortie from the city, rushing to sustain their Ethiopian allies
by hitting the opposite side of our line. As you have heard, Achilles
killed Memnon with a spear thrust, shortly before Hyperion reached
his zenith. By mid-afternoon the attack was spent, and, as the sun
dipped and then fell, the remnants of the Ethiopians gave ground and

retreated inside Ilium's walls with their allies, leaving thousands of dead behind them. It was a brave effort—brave but luckless; had it come during Hector's great offensive, it might have finished us.

—Hyperion's curls grow warm, do they not? Here, Friend, my wineskin is full, and this wallet contains figs and new white cheese. There— look carefully in that direction: you can see the pinnacles of Ithaca quite clearly, now.

As I said, the brave Antilochus died a hard death—hard, dutiful, and, to my mind, heroic. Thersites could not even have known about it; Antilochus died mere weeks before we sacked the city, and by that time, if my information is correct, the braggart had already deserted, had already returned here, to Achaia, was already as far south as Athens, possibly Argos . . . possibly—I shudder to think of it—possibly already on his way to sandy Pylos with the sick lie about Antilochus that he would pour like poison into the ears of the man's own brothers. I . . . I . . . Hear me, O Zeus, and curse the liar's bones!

—No, about eight weeks before we sacked the city, the brave Antilochus was in a valley east of Thymbra, fighting for his life. I know because I commanded the company that went up to relieve him; I saw him in action, and I saw him dead.

—By the spring of the tenth year, we controlled all ways into Ilium save one—Scamander. Winter snows in the eastern mountains had been heavy that year; the spring runoff was equally heavy, and in the main, the great river, son of Zeus, Lord of the Plain, was strong enough, wide enough, deep enough, and swift enough to carry men and supplies. The Mysians, discovering this amidst their mountain fastness to the east, took immediate advantage of the opportunity and managed, under cover of darkness, to slip as many as twenty barges down the river, some loaded with men, some with grain. We discovered them in the morning, empty, beached along the river's eastern bank less than a mile below the Scaean Gate. At the time, Scamander was still on the rise, and, judging from the depth of the snow on the mountains, we thought the river showed signs of remaining high for several more days, for long enough, you see, to prolong the siege—assuming that the Mysians were able to bring down more food and assuming, too, that our ruse of the horse, which we were already preparing beside our ships, failed to work.

—We knew, you see, that hunger was becoming a serious problem behind the walls. Traces of barley and other signs showed that the barges had carried far more grain than men, and not a few captives reported that Trojan dead were being buried at night to hide their number. Had the horse failed to achieve its purpose, I think we could have starved them into submission in a matter of weeks, by summer at the latest, but not, of course, if the Mysians managed to funnel enough food through our lines and into the city while Scamander played their accomplice. The Atreides, then, called a council of war. In the end it was decided to send an expedition upriver.

—As you know, the great Achilles was dead by that time. Patroclus was dead. Tlepolemus was dead, and Medon, and many were wounded, and Odysseus, Diomedes, Teucer, and Menelaus were preparing the horse. In short, Antilochus volunteered and was sent, with six hundred men.

—Consider the place, my friend. Beyond Troy some five, perhaps six miles to the east, perched on the head of a bluff like the sharp, red beak of a vulture sits a Trojan stronghold called Thymbra, and directly below it, through a narrow valley, run the cold white waters of Scamander, born of Zeus, issuing from his loins high in the mountain fastness of Mysia. On the floor of the valley, running east for nearly a mile from the foot of the citadel, lies a single long island, encircled by Scamander's equally long arms. The river's arms are very broad there, and consequently shallow, and far slower than above or below the island; and along the banks footprints showed that the Mysian henchmen had had to disembark and manhandle their barges over the shallows in order to reach the swift, deep water beyond. And there, on the island, which is so very narrow, is where Antilochus chose to stop them.

—Almost immediately, he found himself in trouble. To cut off the Mysians, he had to hold the island. Elsewhere, in deeper water, it would have been impossible to stop them, impossible to get to them; but knowing the ground, the enemy knew this before he did, and knowing it, they had remanned Thymbra—a fortress Achilles had reduced early in the war. The Mysians placed an even larger force in concealment at the head of the island, and then they waited.

—It was an ambush, you see, as clear and simple an ambush as any
ever laid, and no one expected it. They let Antilochus and his six
hundred Pylians thread past Thymbra with perfect ease, ford the river,
and slip onto the island; then, when he was well into their midst, they
hit him from both ends, hard, with more than double his number. He
did, there, the only thing he could do: he deployed his force in two
lines, placed them back to back, and stood his ground. And then, I can
tell you, was much killing.

—From the moment he saw Mysian henchmen begin to appear
beneath Thymbra and wade the river behind him, Antilochus knew
what was happening to him, and immediately he dispatched his swiftest
runner across the southern shallows, away from Thymbra, and off
down the south bank to carry word to the Atreides, and this man, wing-
footed Epeus of Aepy, I intercepted on the Plain, less than a league
above the Scaean Gate. I had about me no more than three hundred of
my islanders, but we set off at once, running hard, and reached the foot
of the island by mid-afternoon, attacking the rear of the Mysians who
had poured down out of Thymbra. Friend, I still remember wading that
river. Everything foamed red: blood and bodies were everywhere, and
already kites had descended and were feeding along the river's banks,
where bodies and parts of bodies washed down by the currents had
become tangled in tree roots and projecting rocks.

—We were too late to do much good. Over the heads of the Mysians
to our front, we could see our comrades fighting on, their shields
before them, but their numbers were pitifully small: no more than fifty,
I think, remained alive. —In the end, we brought out nineteen who
could still stand. I could not see Antilochus, but he was alive, I know,
because I heard his war cry urging on his men, refusing to give ground,
bolstering their spirits against impossible odds, and then I heard it no
more, and we ourselves entered the press of battle, hacking with axe
and sword, pushing and thrusting, trying to break our way through to
our friends. In a matter of moments, we slaughtered the surprised force
between us, but Mysian warriors at the head of the island did much
damage before we cut our way through and only went into final retreat
when my Lord Nestor, who had followed me at some distance after
hearing from Epeus, came onto the island with three hundred more

brave Pylian spearmen and helped me drive the ambushers into the river.

—We finally found Antilochus, standing—dead—propped against his spear, five bronze-tipped arrows in his back, each of them bearing a mark that looked like the mark on the arrow that sent the great Achilles down to Hades. No one, you see, who dared to face him had survived. Loyal Archomenus, his squire, reported that a taunting, fair-haired archer had stood high above them on the walls of Thymbra, shooting arrow after arrow into his lord's back, until the brave Antilochus, dying and knowing he was dying, planted his strong ash spear in the earth, locked his mighty hands around its shaft, and died—still standing, still firm, refusing to fall, contemptuously ignoring the archer who had neither the courage nor the heart to face him.

—My Lord Nestor removed the arrows from his son's back, and carefully, slowly, we pried his hands away from his spear, and when we did, we laid him on his shield and carried him back across the river, and down along the banks of Scamander, and across the Plain to our black-hulled ships, and there we held his funeral and buried his bones beside the great Achilles. —His spear, I know, still stands, rooted like a mighty ash, in the soil below Thymbra.

—More wine, my friend? Please, help yourself: this skin has not so much left, but in the storerooms beside my terrace in Dulichium, we will find a plentiful supply, and bread and meat besides. Perhaps now, after seeing the afternoon sea, we should go down.

Yes, you are quite correct. The liar has defrauded our culture. Thersites, to enrich his own reputation, has ignored the excellence of others. Some of us, I know, have little enough to give, little enough to offer: still, the man did harm here, gave pain to my people and lingering sorrow, and to three, near fatal wounds. Had I caught him, for what he did to my people, I would have punished him with the lash and sold him into Illyria. But for what he did to Antilochus, I think Thersites deserved to die.

—Why, I ask you, did we go out to Troy? By asking you, of course, I ask myself the question, and the answer is ever clear: the doer must suffer, the price must be paid—so much for Paris and Priam. But what was Thersites' crime? Did he not rob Antilochus of his life? Not in the flesh, so much, but consider, Friend, if you will, this simple idea. When the chambers of decay close over us, when we finally go down to the halls of Hades, what remains? Bones? They are, I think, of use to no one. But to our children, and to our children's children—and this, I think, must be taken metaphorically—thus, to our people, we leave our lives, our deeds; and he who steals my deeds steals my life, deprives my children of my triumphs and my mistakes, takes from the people their rightful inheritance—my example, good or bad, one of many, no doubt, but my own individual example nevertheless. That is the crime of a *thing* like Thersites: he leaves the world with a weak illusion—in the case of my brave Antilochus, with something far inferior to the reality and the truth.

—There, look. The lamps of Dulichium begin to flicker beneath us. We have not far to go now before my vines appear, and from there we are no more than a few steps away from my gate. This walk, if I may say so, has made me feel young again, and your company has been most gracious.

Thrasymedes at Pylos

I think, now, that I have taught you almost all that I know, but, my grandson, you would be in error to think, having learned your lessons here, that you have mastered the subject or even looked carefully into all of its compartments, the obvious as well as the unseen. I would, of course, that you had learned from my father, your great-grandparent, that you would have had the opportunity to know and learn from your great-uncle, the brave Antilochus, that now, while the years linger, I myself might rise from my couch and teach you more. But that is not to be. Things are what they are, and you, son of my son, descendant of lordly Nestor, kinsman of brave Antilochus—you, my grandson, must journey east for a time, away from sandy Pylos. Cross Arcadia and the windswept plain of Argos, march up through the pass beside the great stone gates of Mycenae, walk on over the Corinthian isthmus into Attica, and enter Athens. There, my boy, present yourself to my Lord Menestheus and give him my greeting.

—In the Troad, know you, my Lord Menestheus had no living rival in the art of handling infantry, save my own father. Now that my lordly father and brave Antilochus are both long gone into the chambers of decay, you, my grandson, must take your training where you can, make yourself into a master of infantry, and return home to Pylos firm in your knowledge and firm, too, in the strength of your bronze right arm. Had your father lived . . . well, my boy, had your father lived, you might have been allowed a period of leisure, as was I—a period of time in which to watch and experience without having to risk all, without having to carry the burdens of our people fully on your own shoul-

ders. I had that, for ten years after the Troad, before your grandfather
died, but the sisterly ladies of fate measured your father's string very
short, and in his thirtieth year the hand of the Archer came upon him
and slew him, and now, in my grey old age, I must continue to rule,
blind in one eye, tired, and infirm.

—By the time you return, my boy, I will have gone already to join my
father and brothers in the chambers of Hades. When that is so, your
great-uncle Pesistratus will mount the throne, and then you must
instantly return and serve as his commander of infantry. But be aware
that he, too, complains of the hand of Smintheus, that he, too, moves
slowly now, crippled in strength and limb. Aurora has few blushes left
for the sons of Nestor, I think; your time, then, may come much sooner
than you expect. When it comes, my grandson, you must be ready to
spring fully formed into kingship.

—But something more obtains, and now, I think, before you depart,
elements of the issue should be laid before you. Know you, my grandson, that lordly Pesistratus is, by his own admission, more of an administrator than a warrior; he was too young to go with us to the Troad,
and in that respect he resembles others of his generation: lordly Telemachus, past king of Ithaca, and his living son, Laertes, and the sons
of Thoas at Chalcis, and the present descendants, too, of the House of
Atreus. Each, certainly, has had experience in war, but the experience
of each has been limited largely to raiding and small unit combat.
Today in Achaia, very few who fought in the Troad remain, and the
kind of experience they had, the kind that is needed to command large
numbers of men in the field, is swiftly disappearing. Here at home, I
have instructed you already regarding everything I know or remember
about large-scale command, but my well is dry now; together we have
drawn its depths to the last drop. And that is why I am sending you
away, to the Athenian, to a far more able commander than me.

—Know you, my grandson, that I have heard reports from northern
Achaia, and lately they have given me much concern. A new people
have appeared along the borders of Achaia, far to the north, calling
themselves the Encheleans. Where they came from, we do not know,
but they are many, my grandson—many, strong, and barbarous. These
barbarians herd and gather wherever they go but plant few crops, and
they live in tents or crude huts, not unlike the war camps we built

before Troy. As I tell you this, they are camped in masses around the shores of Lake Lychnitis, far beyond swift-running Haliacmon, but they have raided already into the lands of Epirus; and from the Aethices, the people who live beyond Dolopia, we hear that the barbarians have sent horsemen to probe for weak spots in the Achaian rim. They carry spears, these barbarians, that are tipped with iron, and painted shields that are smaller than ours, and their swords, I am told, look grey when drawn, like silver or iron. The outland herald who came to us with this information said that the barbarians are capable of moving very swiftly across open ground; he said that they are fierce in the field but exhibit no apparent knowledge of tactics. That is as much as I have been able to learn about them, but it is enough to make me apprehensive. Oh, may the Lord of Thunder prevent it, my grandson, but I think it likely that in your lifetime Achaia will have to revive the alliance and defend herself from invasion. If the time ever comes, see that our hard men of Pylos are well trained and ready to take their place in the forefront as we did in my youth, once, far away in the Troad.

—Pardon? About my Lord Menetheus? —Indeed, I know much about him. But sit you down, my grandson; sit here, beside me. On the night before your departure, I think it correct and fitting that the son of my son should sit beside me, here, by the throne of his forebearer, and drink deeply from a skin of bright Pylian wine. Long months will pass before you taste this wine again, I think. When you do, perhaps you will pour out libations to me, too, as I do now to the gods and the brave spirits of our ancestors.

Certainly, if the Argives must fight again en masse, my Lord Menestheus is the right man to teach you about tactics. As I said before, excepting your great-grandfather, who was the most skillful general among us, my Lord Menestheus had no rival as an infantry commander: his Athenian spearmen were admired everywhere for the skill and daring with which they accomplished their operations. When I tell you this, I imply nothing about the Athenian's personal ability as a warrior: be sure, my grandson, that you are more diplomatic than to say as much in Athens, but as a warrior, lordly Menestheus was merely one among many. The great Achilles, master of us all, outstripped him as a fighter by many lengths, and so, I think, did the Aiantes, the great

Diomedes, your great-uncle Antilochus, the Ithacan, lordly Idomeneus and his squire, and others . . . Pardon?

—No, but thank you, my grandson; your respect for your elders is admirable. But no, I was only one among many, myself, and make no claims to have been a bulwark to the army. But we are speaking of the Athenian, so do not distract me to stories about myself which you have already heard many, many times before.

—No, as a warrior, my Lord Menestheus was an average man amongst us; brave, able, ready, he was a noble warrior on a noble field but hardly as godlike as the men I have mentioned. Still, as a commander of infantry, he was brilliant, and to me that makes him one of the greatest Achaians on the Plain.

—Know you, my grandson, that the ways of war have changed. In the old days, when first we landed in the Troad, the well-greaved Achaians fought always hand-to-hand. I speak about the kind of battle in which each man was virtually alone on the Plain, fighting as an individual, relying only on his own pure courage and the strength of his hard bronze arms. That was the kind of fighting, certainly, that was bound to make the strongest men preeminent. And it *did;* without question, men like Achilles and great-hearted Aias were men without peers. But the thing I want you to understand is something your great-grandparent understood from the start: war waged on the chance of a melee is both costly and dangerous. My lordly father knew that even before we attacked in the Troad. For years he put forth his ideas, argued their merits, and urged their acceptance; but it was not until the ninth year of the war, when most of our great field warriors were slain or wounded in Hector's offensive, that the whole Achaian army finally began to see his point. Then the Achaians began to evolve a whole new way of fighting in which strategy and tactics began to replace mere strength and courage. Prior to that, my Lord Menestheus had done his duty on the Plain and fought well, but in the ninth year his virtues as a field commander, as a master of infantry, elevated him to a new position in the heart of the army, and his Athenians achieved better results with the loss of fewer men than any other contingent fighting.

—Ah, Capaneus, my servant. Where have you been? Pinching the maidens in the kitchen, perhaps? Call you for the slave who keeps my wine jars and have him bring before us cups and a skin of that bright

Pylian wine that comes from the foothills beneath Mount Minthe. And order, too, that one of the house-maidens brings us a tray of figs and honeyed apricots.

Of course, I know of many, but let me recall a single example which will be both fitting and clear.

—Know you, my grandson, that by our ninth year in the Troad, Achaian manpower was seriously depleted. Trojan manpower, you understand, was far more depleted than ours—*far more depleted;* nevertheless, our reduction in numbers measured somewhere between a third and a half of the warriors who had stormed ashore nine long years before, and much of our loss we suffered during the time when illustrious Hector struck us so ferociously across the Plain in the offensive that ended with his death. Lordly Patroclus was killed then, and swift Medon, the brother of Aias, and Schedios, Lord of the Phocis, and Otos of Cyllene, and many others. And most of our mightier sons of Achaia were either wounded or lamed while they fought at the forefront. After the battle, the Trojans simply retired behind the high walls of Ilium, so we of Achaia resumed our siege. But we were badly hurt by the attack, and, with an eye toward reducing the number of casualties we were taking, the Atreides stopped in council with your great-grandparent and the Ithacan where, between them, they devised a new strategy for conducting the war. Then, my grandson, in an attempt to seal off Troy's landward supply routes as tightly as we had closed her sea approaches, we began some serious campaigning upcountry. That is when my Lord Menestheus came into his own—not at the forefront of our massed army but upcountry, where carefully, skillfully, he reduced or captured stronghold after stronghold, garrison after garrison, supply column after supply column through sound tactics and calculated strategems. It is true, of course, that he did consult with my lords Nestor and Odysseus before and after each foray, and it is also true that he received his orders directly from the Atreides, but once his Athenians took the field, he made his own decisions, and I was amazed to see the skill with which he conducted his operations and the results he invariably achieved.

—My Lord the Ithacan had men of his own upcountry—isolated, independent men who wore the garb of shepherds, or Trojan couriers, or smiths thought to be passing to or from Ilium—and in the winter, in the beginning of the tenth year, he received from one of them an information reporting that upwards of fifteen hundred Phrygians were working their way down the valley of the Simoeis, preparing to reinforce Ilium. The Ithacan carried this word to your great-grandparent, and he, in turn, called up my Lord Menestheus with more than twelve hundred Athenians. Then my father turned to me and said, "You will go as lieutenant, Thrasymedes. Take four hundred of our bronze-armed Pylians and follow Menestheus's instructions exactly as if they were my own."

—I called up my men then from the warm hollows of their huts beside our ships and assembled them in the Athenian camp, and there my Lord Menestheus met us and took us into the Athenian huts, where his men were busy cutting field cloaks from sailcloth. He was not a large man, as I remember; probably he was not much taller than Teucer, Lord of the Bow, but his chest and shoulders were broad, his legs thick, and the fire in his eyes burned sharp and clear. When he spoke, his voice was low, powerful, and his words were delivered with authority. "We will not move," he said, "until after nightfall. Tell your men to cut cloaks like those my own men are cutting. Then I want them to eat and sleep. When Helios drops below the horizon, we will begin to move: I intend to be in position long before Aurora thinks to blush across the snowbound valley of the Simoeis."

—Each of us cut his cloak then, and ate heartily of barley bread and steaming mutton, and then we slept long in the close warmth of the huts. But in the hour when Night finally swallowed the Plain, we rose swiftly, wrapped ourselves in our sailcloth cloaks, and marched rapidly out of camp, carrying only our spears, swords, and smaller ox-hide shields, wearing only our lightweight leather armor, in a long serpentine file led by my Lord Menestheus, myself, and the Ithacan's man, who, wrapped in a shepherd's fleece, acted as our guide.

—Outside the camp the snow was deep, the air bitterly cold. Ahead, the Plain was silent, still, covered by snow so white that the face of the earth seemed blanketed by a smooth, wide sail. At first our route lay due south, and as we marched we moved directly toward the white-capped city of Ilium, which, far away in the distance under the glistening moonlight, looked to the eye like a towered pinnacle of ice. No man spoke as we plodded across the Plain. The order for silence had been passed even before we left our camp, and as I looked back over my shoulder I saw my Pylians and the Athenian spearmen hugging the earth, filing out into the distance, man after man, like a long, thin string of hooded ghosts.

—We had moved a mile upcountry, perhaps more, when suddenly I heard a roar at my back and realized that the wind had come up. Each man hugged himself tightly in his cloak then, and, as a spitting snow began to swirl around our heads, we quickened the pace of our march. Behind us, Thracian Boreas blew up a rage, roaring down across the whitecaps of the Hellespont and up onto the Plain in sharp, freezing gusts that gnawed at our backs and sliced around our helmets into our eyes. Against the raw edges of our legs, snow, and sleet, and slivers of cutting ice drove hard, stiffening the sailcloth and flattening it against our skin until we felt frozen between moulded sheets of tin. Each man drove himself harder then, not seeing because the biting snow had blinded sight, not feeling because the stinging ice had deadened feeling, but knowing—knowing that up ahead, somewhere in the howling darkness, we would turn east, cross over the frozen face of Simoeis, and enter the lee of the long, low range of hills that rose above the river's northern banks, separating the watercourse from the cold open reaches of the sea.

—We continued in silence, my grandson, each man's breathing drowned by the blast of the wind, each man's footsteps falling cold on the track of the man before. Finally, when our numbness had turned to pain and our pain had frozen into a penetrating misery, lancing our flesh to the very bone—finally we turned east, and crossed the ice-bound face of Simoeis, and started to climb that first low range of hills that shielded the river. The snow deepened there, but the men seemed not to mind because the wind began to die. Without dropping our pace or lingering, we made straight for the crest of the ridge but then turned again and began working our way east, through a forest just beneath the rim line. "If Artemis returns," said my Lord Menestheus, "we will not be seen here, below the crest, for we will cast no silhouette against the broad night sky. Up ahead, a narrow supply road forks down from

Phrygia and crosses Simoeis to enter Ilium from the east. We are going into ambush there, and I want no risk of exposure until we are set and ready to take the enemy."

—Those were the only words my Lord the Athenian spoke to me along the entire line of our march, and after that we seemed to march on for hours, half blind in the dim moonlight that somehow penetrated the clouds. We felt our way over rocks and fallen trees, through deep drifts that sometimes swallowed us to our waists, and in between the frozen tree trunks that glistened dimly with encrusted ice and snow. And all the while my Lord Menestheus remained silent, concentrating on the guide, listening, watching.

—Finally—and it must have been near morning—we swung south again, entered a narrow defile, and, wading through snow that reached to our hips, began our descent into the valley of the Simoeis. We dropped down, I remember, very quickly, moving far more rapidly, even through the deep snow, than when we had first climbed onto the ridge. The men, I think, sensed that their ordeal was about to end, and it lifted their spirits, filling them with energy. Warm in his fleece, our guide nearly left us behind, so my Lord and I plunged forward at a break-neck pace, trying hard to keep him in sight until suddenly we nearly overturned the man where he crouched on his knees at the mouth of the defile. Ahead, I could see the face of Simoeis, no wider than the throw of a stone, cutting across the floor of a deep-shadowed gorge. In the half-dead light, I could still see that the river was frozen hard. "Do we attack from here?" I asked. "No," said my Lord, "come with me; we need to reconnoiter."

—We moved out into the gorge then, just the two of us, hugging the shadows of boulders and trees. Soon we found ourselves athwart a narrow track that proceeded beside the river. "This is where they must come," said the Athenian. "Below here, perhaps half a league, the road forks. One branch continues on toward the Plain, beside the river, but the other turns south into the hills and then turns slowly again to enter Troy from the east. Bring your Pylians out now, my Lord Thrasymedes; take them across the river and cause each man to lie down in the snow, pulling his sail cloak over him until he looks as white as the floor of the gorge. On this side, I will cause my Athenian spearmen to come out of the defile and lay themselves down in the snow along the gorge's northern face. Each man is to remain silent, still, quiet beneath his cloak with his arms buried in the snow beside him. Then, we will wait. The Ithacan's man informs me that the Phrygians are camped no more than a mile or two above us; in this cold, they will rise and move early, hungry for the warmth of Troy. We will attack them as they pass between us. A ram's horn will be the signal: when you hear it blow once, cause your men to leap to their feet and shout their war cry. The enemy will be much shocked by your sudden appearance, as though sprung like so many ghosts from the ground. Gripped by terror, he may give you time for an unimpeded volley: cast your spears, then, and rush forward as though in assault, but halt your men along the bank of the river. The Phrygians, I think, will quickly recover and rush you across the ice; in that instant, I will blow the ram's horn again, and my twelve hundred Athenians will rise and go over to the attack. The shock of our numbers should unnerve them completely. Then, if the ice beneath them does not collapse under all their weight and leave them freezing in their armor, the fury of our combined attack will bear them down and break them."

—The ambush took place, my grandson, just as my Lord anticipated. I took my men across the river then, one at a time, in single file where the ice was firm and hard, and laid them side by side on top of their shields in the deep snow, covering each man with the whiteness of his sail cloak, burying each man's sharp bronze arms beside him. Eighty, perhaps ninety paces away, along the gorge's northern face, just beyond the narrow track that ran beside Simoeis, my Lord Menestheus put the Athenians into hiding beneath their own sailcloth cloaks. And then we waited, each man flat on his back beneath his cloak, each man numbed, shivering, waiting for the cold light of dawn and Phrygian henchmen.

—The dawn came first, clean and bright, an Auroran pink spreading across the whiteness of the gorge, and then, not long after, the Phrygians, wearing thick blue cloaks and bronze armor, talking and laughing, making no attempt to conceal their movement, secure in the illusion of their own security. When their column bunched full between us, my Lord Menestheus sounded a single clear note on the ram's horn, and like a mass of spirits rising from the dead, my Pylians were up, shouting their war cry, charging across the snow, hurling their javelins as they ran. The effect was grim: seized by terror, the Phrygians froze, and in that instant, we dropped two, perhaps three hundred of them with our long ash spears. Surrounded by the hiss of death, jarred by the groans of their comrades, the enemy recovered, and with piercing screams of rage, they hurled themselves over the banks of the river and out onto the ice, bent upon bloody destruction. In that moment the second ram's horn sounded, and across the river at the Phrygians' backs, my Lord Menestheus's twelve hundred Athenians rose to their feet, rent the air with their own high war cries, and hurled their spears. Surprised again, shocked, the Phrygians whirled in terror and received the full weight of the blow on their front. More than six hundred went down then, crashing against the ice, and, unable to support the weight of so many massed men, the ice itself began to collapse beneath them. Some, mostly the wounded, drowned; others, enraged even more by the disaster that was befalling them, managed to make their way ashore and, crawling up one bank or the other, went over to the attack, but they were few in number and quickly went down under our swords. Most, caught in the frigid waters of the river, unable to fight, or swim, or escape, allowed themselves to be helped ashore, where they gave themselves up as captives.

—All in all, the battle lasted less than the amount of time it takes for a man to run a single league. We killed nearly nine hundred Phrygians that morning, took four or five hundred prisoner, and in our own combined force lost only six dead and fourteen wounded. That, my grandson, is what tactics can do when the doer knows what he is about, and that is why I am sending you to my Lord Menestheus.

—Would you like some more figs? Here, if you don't mind, pour me another cup of our bright Pylian wine. I, too, feel slightly parched, and the sweetness of the fruit has wetted my taste.

You are quite correct, of course: we didn't linger. As soon as we had disarmed and bound our captives, we began to move out swiftly, the Athenians down the river's north bank, my Pylians down the southern side. This was a time of considerable danger to both of us because our forces were momentarily split, and, owing to the failure of the ice, neither body of troops could support the other in the event of a Trojan attack. We moved then at a rapid pace, almost at a jog trot until finally, a mile, perhaps two, below the point where we had set our ambush, my men and I found strong ice, crossed the river, and rejoined our forces with the Athenians. I can't say that our pace slacked off then, but it must have, a little, because we were herding our prisoners before us like so many cattle, and they were none too anxious to reach our slave ships. Nevertheless, about noon, I think, we issued from the valley onto the Plain, and, covering our withdrawal with a sizeable rear guard, we made haste toward the sea and our camp. We were back among our huts by mid-afternoon, tired, cold, and hungry but greatly victorious and much honored by our fellows.

—Pardon, my grandson? Remember, my ears are not what they used to be, so you will have to speak louder.

—Oh. Yes. Yes indeed, that *is* my point: we took just enough men to do the job, just enough to achieve the victory, but no more. We exposed them to the enemy as little as possible, and when we had done what we went in to do we marched swiftly away. Under another man, under men like Aias or the great Achilles, the Argives might have lingered after the battle, and lighted fires, and warmed themselves; but my Lord Menestheus was adamant in command, and as soon as the battle was won, we left the dead to kites and vultures of the winter forests.

—You see, son of my son, the matter is simply a question of objectives: we did not go up Simoeis to take or hold ground; we went for no other reason than to see that Priam was not reinforced. To do that, we had to destroy the Phrygian column, and we did. The moment the task was completed, we turned around and marched away; and by reducing our exposure to the enemy, the elements, and the fates, we conserved our force. Always remember that, my boy: fight when you must, but in going to or from a battle, never forget the unseen enemy; expose yourself as little as possible.

—Yes . . . to my regret, your brave great-uncle was caught in an ambush and died fighting, but I assure you, my grandson, the brave Antilochus sold himself far more dearly than the Phrygians we captured. He, too, went up a river, went up to Thymbra and the Isle of the Ash, and died where he stood. There wasn't time for reconnaissance, and the certainty of his fate was to be caught in a web of the unknown. Still, my grandson, he faced what he had to face, what we all have to face in that final unknown, and did his duty.

—You, too, my boy, must learn to allow for that: calculate the unknown. Know in advance that you can never fathom it, but know, too, that you must test the probabilities. Know the enemy, my grandson, because the enemy is a part of the unknown: make him your study—his language, his religion, his culture, his ideas, the things which motivate his race. Try to know how he thinks, and then, like my father and lordly Menestheus, you, too, may be able to anticipate his moves. But always add caution to your plans, my grandson, and good reconnaissance, and respect for the element of chance. Like a stalking lion, watch and wait; then, when you pounce, be sure of your kill.

—That is precisely what I mean. We do not know these barbarians as we did the men of Troy. These men of the North are a new unknown. Perhaps, my grandson, if the gods smile on Achaia, you will never have to fight these barbarians, but if you do, be certain that they will not fight like Trojans: they will either be something more or something less, but they will not be the same. No two armies are ever alike, so what we learned in the Troad will be useful to you but only if you adapt it, allowing for a different people, in a different place, at a different time. Learn whatever you can about the barbarians—now, as you travel north and later, after you return—store what you learn in your memory, shape it in your mind. A day may come when you will need all that you have been able to learn about them; if that day does come, remember the things I have taught you and adapt.

—The hour, I think, is late, and tomorrow you must go. Say your goodbyes tonight, my boy: give your mother a parting embrace, and your maidenly sisters, and old Tripclea, who nursed you as an infant and still weeps over your bruises, and then, in the morning, rise and go before Dawn so that her blush may greet you on the road with a long Pylian spear in your hand. May the light of the gods go with you, my grandson, all your long days.

—But wait. There is one more thing I must tell you: beware Thersites. Beware of a man named Thersites. He is a spiteful man, hunchbacked and ugly, and he is very, very dangerous. If you find him or meet him on the road, kill him, my grandson. Kill him. Your grandparent passes the sentence of death over him.

—Yes, my grandson, but there is not now time to explain to you details of the man's history. I only reapply my father's sentence:

remember, the doer must suffer; that is the law. The man Thersites has done a great crime in his time, and he must suffer for it.

—Go you, now, and when the time comes, return to the lands of your forefathers and be a king to your people. Fare you well, my boy, and remember: you are the hope of Pylos.

Meriones at Gortyn

No, that is not the case with me. Actually, I remember things quite well: you see, the Lady of the Flashing Eyes has blessed me in the matter of my faculties, so my recollections remain acute. I must add, of course, that I can no longer walk, that my left hand is stiffly frozen by the winters of my years, and that here, in my chest, I now feel the arrows of Apollo, twisting and cutting near my heart, but my mind is sound, my thoughts clear, and still I remember your grandsire with warmth and admiration.

—No, no, no! Do not apologize, young sir. You had no intention to offend, I'm sure. And you *did not* offend me with your question.

—Of course, I vividly remember my Lord Polypoetes; your grandsire, I assure you, was a close and valued friend, and I deeply regret to hear reports of his lasting sad infirmity. I much admired him in the Troad: I remember clearly the day that he and brave Leonteus held the gate before our high-beaked ships and stood, preventing the Hectorian onslaught that threatened our destruction. They were like two mountain oaks, then, beset by wind and fire, but they held firm, rooted in their glory. On that far-away day, good sir, many Argives—myself included—owed their very lives to the two brave Lapithae, and now that lordly Leonteus is dead, your sad report about bronze-hearted Polypoetes' loss of mind is hard, indeed.

—My Lord Machaon, I have been given to understand, is much like me, much frozen in the winter of his life, unable to travel or practice the healing arts as he once did in the Troad. But in Euboea, I'm told, wise Akastos knows many efficacious cures, and at Elis, ancient Dexamenos continues to study recovery of the mind. His methods, I know, are assiduous; he healed Bias. One of them, perhaps, may be of help, and tomorrow I will send our heralds to each, with sums of silver, to hasten them toward your grandsire. I regret that I am unable to go into Egypt and bring back surgeons for your aid, but unfortunately I can no longer travel. I will do what I can do, however, and offer prayers to the gods.

—Stay, young friend, the night enfolds us, and soon Artemis will unveil her lustre. You must not sail tonight, regardless of your longing heart, but when Aurora blushes, I will send you down to the sea and give you a fast ship. Then you may carry my heralds north, into Achaia, with a following wind. For the moment, though, let us rest ourselves here. Man's fate, I think, is always to be mortal, so here, high above the wine-dark sea, let us eat, and talk, and rest, and then, tomorrow, you may hasten, refreshed, to the aid of your grandfather.

Indeed, I can't say; I saw her only once. At Ilium. During the autumn before the war ended. We were fighting hard, then, on the Plain below the Scaean Gate but close, very close to the walls. Treacherous Pyraechmes, a Paeonian and Priam's ally, sneaked in behind me and struck me with a great rock, and, spitting blood, I was forced to retire from the forefront. My comrades sent swiftly for Lord Machaon and his healing herbs, then helped me away from the battle line, setting me down, finally, beside the trunk of a massive oak that towered above the Plain. I was dazed, you see, uncertain of my life, vomiting in thin red streams; stars leapt before my eyes like angry fireflies. I tried hard to calm myself and did, and as my breathing returned, I began to recover my sight. Then I saw her. What brought her to the walls, I cannot say, but when my eyes cleared I saw her high atop the wall of Ilium, wrapped in a snow-white cloak, her beautiful hair billowing in the wind.

—I would not even attempt to describe her to you; mere words could never do her justice. But I will tell you what effect she had upon me, and then, perhaps, you may judge for yourself. As I told you, my friends at the forefront had summoned my Lord Machaon to heal me, even before they carried me from the battle and propped me beside that oak. The moment he heard what had happened to me, my Lord

Machaon ran to my aid, fearing I might pass into Hades even before he could reach me. And he found me, too, but when he found me, I was no longer stunned beside the oak but back in the forefront, fighting and killing Trojans as though nothing had happened.

—No, excuse me, I have misspoken myself. Something had happened. I had experienced my own personal vision of Helen, and by itself that was enough to restore me. —Believe me: it was enough. For the remainder of the day, I fought like a lion, like ten lions, always at the forefront, always the first to kill my man. I killed many Trojans that day—many. I spat no more blood, felt no more pain, and when night fell, bringing an end to battle, I returned to my hut beside our high-beaked ships feeling sound and whole. My Lord Machaon pronounced me "blessed by the gods," and I—I did not dispute him.

—I never saw her again, after that. I didn't see her when we sacked the city, and I did not see her beside our black-hulled ships when, after ten long years, we sailed for home. Had events gone forward as I expected, I might have met her at Sparta, but now, in the winter of my life, I know that nothing goes forward as we expect. Here, tonight, where the high walls of Gortyn surround us, as we eat and drink, you and I, in peace, I know that the moment has passed, that I must live out the remainder of my days relying on memory, hoping for no greater prize than a clear recollection of my own vision.

—Ah, our meal arrives. Belius, my herald, place venison before us and appoint my steward to fill our cups, and then you, too, must sit down with us. In the morning, you must leave me, my Belius, and, taking Andraxus with you, sail north with the young lord who sits to my right. But for now, seat yourself. Later, I will explain your mission.

You are right, young sir; her power to influence went beyond measure. My Lord Idomeneus was a case in point. —Mmmm. Belius, my compliments to the house women; this venison is excellent. I do not know, young friend, whether the food is pleasing to you, but this is an Egyptian preparation which our ambassadors brought back to us no more than a year ago. As soon as the meat is bled, it is sprinkled with garlic and soaked for three days in wine. The wine, you see, prevents decay. On the third day, we pluck it from the sauce, skewer it, and with onions and figs, broil it over a slow fire.

—Ah, yes, as I was saying, I think her influence over my king was immeasurable. You do not know, I assume, much about the history of my house, and so that you will not think me a fond old man, I will try to bore you with as little as possible; still, I must tell you something for clarity. Let it suffice to say that my Lord and King, Idomeneus of Crete, was the peerless son of Deucalion, offspring of Minos, who was made ruler of Cnossus by the Cloud Gatherer himself. My own origins are far more humble and later: I am the son of Molos, younger brother to Deucalion by a palace concubine, and I did not go north to Cnossus until my twelfth year. I was born here, you see, at Gortyn, in a broad room just beyond those red columns, there, where the myrtle grows. My youth was happy here. I was well educated for the times and ranged the mountains hereabouts with bow and lance, hunting under the watchful eye of my tutor. But in my twelfth year, my father was killed during a raid into Egypt, and my mother, who was determined that I should retain the family's blessing, sent me high over the pass beside Ida and north, down the long trail to Cnossus in company with my tutor.

—Bearded Minos died long before my birth, and fierce Deucalion, too. By the time I reached the palace, my Lord Idomeneus had already been king of Crete for twenty years. He was unmarried, then, and without sons. Because I was the youngest male in the line, I think—legitimate or not—he took a liking to me, placing me at his right hand, and vowed to bring me up as a member of his house. He was a generous man, you see, sure and firm, astute like Minos in judgement, a king to his people.

—I remember vividly the first time I saw him—not in the palace, which he seldom entered other than to sleep or eat, but in the field. He was training troops there—men of the spear—and in the afternoon sun their muscled bodies shone with sweat like wet bronze. His men wore corselets and helms, and carried long ox-hide shields before them for the practice, but my Lord Idomeneus went bare to the waist, his broad chest awash with dusty sweat. He took his spearmen three at a time, making them attack him and then showing them how to thrust and parry with their long ash shafts. I thought I had never seen anyone so bravely strong: as he thrust spearpoint after spearpoint aside, it never occurred to me that he was no longer youthful. I did not notice, then, that his hair was greying, but it was. I saw only the pride of his bearing, the courage of his eyes, the intensity of his concentration. The facts that he had been often wounded, that he exhibited many scars, that half of his ear had been hacked away—such facts escaped me in the moment of our meeting, and I was filled with an admiration that never left me.

—When he spotted me, he stopped the practice, asked my tutor's name, then mine, and, after hearing me identify myself to explain my presence, tossed me a small spear and ordered me to attack him. That was long ago, you understand; then, in the morning of my youth, I was very quick. "Come," he said, "attack me, Meriones. If you want to be my squire and spearman, you will have to show spirit." I charged him instantly, thrusting my spearpoint straight toward his face, but he easily parried my thrust and struck me lightly with the butt of his spear as my lunge carried me beyond him. "Nimbly," he said. "Be nimble, lad; agility is the surest weapon of youth." I charged him again then, more carefully, and sidestepped, but missed again and reddened with shame. I continued charging him again and again for the better part of an hour but never came close to him. He, on his part, spoke to me encouragingly, pointed out imperfections in my style, and kept up the game. Finally, he wore me down. When I knew that I could no longer maintain my play, I resolved on a feint and threw myself into a wild charge, but instead of following through, I stopped short, rolled suddenly on my back, and, coming up between his legs, pinked him on the calf as I thrust myself under his torso and onto the earth behind him. I somersaulted quickly onto my feet then, and prepared to defend myself, but when I faced my King, I found him laughing and, indeed, the whole company, including my tutor. "Well done," said my Lord Idomeneus. "Well done, my boy. Henceforth, we will address you as *my Lord* Meriones, and you will sit at my right-hand and be my squire."

—Later, much later, I learned that no one, ever before, had pinked him in practice. Had he been younger, with a temperament like some others I have known—Neoptolemus of Phthia, to mention a name, or the great Achilles—he might have reacted with pride or anger, but he was older, you see, mature in his wisdom and clear about the nature of things. As I grew to know him and respect him, both as my kinsman and as my wise and lordly king, I came to believe that nothing could shake him. But I was wrong about that. The lady Helen shook him to his roots. I speak figuratively, of course, because even later, even after we had already sailed for the Troad, I still found myself unable to gauge accurately the effect she had had upon him. Speaking truthfully, I don't suppose that anyone could: we are islands, each of us, I think. In my experience, no one person ever participates fully in the feelings of another, no matter how sympathetic the attempt. Even so, I think that I did, eventually, *begin* to understand him—after my own vision, after I, too, had seen her high above the Plain on the walls of windy Ilium. After that, you understand, but only after that, I think I began to glimpse the measure of his pain.

—You would not have thought as much, would you? No, nor did I. When first we sailed for Aulis and then, finally, for the Troad, I harbored no such feelings; in fact, I think I'm safe in saying that I could never even have understood such feelings. To me—and to everyone else, I thought—the necessity for going to Troy involved a simple question of justice. Consider my thinking then, if you will: Paris was guilty of wife rape. My Lords the Atreidae had two choices: to punish or not to punish. In order to punish, we had to go to war, and we did. But what if we had not chosen to punish? What consequences would Achaia, then, have faced. First, *dike*—our most ancient law, the foundation of our people—*dike* would have been broken, not secretly but publicly on a universal scale: *the doer would not have suffered* but, instead, would have enjoyed the fruits of his crime with perfect impunity. And consider what a pack of evils that would have unleashed: wife rape ignored, the sanctity of the family befouled, the law debased, *aidôs* disregarded, the gods insulted, and all the flowering manhood of Achaia blackened with dishonor, the Atreidae most of all—why, the world would have gone to chaos. By the hand of Alexandros, foppish little Alexandros of Troy, even the Cloud Gatherer's own sacred law of hospitality would have cracked. Can you imagine, young sir, the stain on our people if we had allowed such crimes to go unpunished? Clearly, had we not gone to Ilium, we would have lost our *selves;* our identity as a people would have collapsed like dry, harvest straw in an autumn fire. We would have wandered the earth, young sir, faceless and nameless in our shame, unable to call ourselves men.

—So much was clear to me long before Aulis, long before we sailed. In my youth, you see, I thought the question of justice was the whole of

our reason for going. Well, it *might* have been: by any standard, I
think, justice *was* enough, and tomorrow it would still be enough of a
reason to fight again. But justice wasn't the whole of it, only at the
time I didn't know that. I didn't know the whole of it until much later,
until long after Aulis, long after we landed beside Scamander and
began to fight across the dusty Plain. I didn't know the whole of it until
I saw Helen.

—Belius, help our friend to a portion of apricots and honey. Tell me,
young sir, do the Lapithae grow apricots? These are from an orchard
near Phaestus where the summers are long and Boreas rarely shakes his
beard. And try some of the wine; it has only recently arrived from
Cyprus, where the grapes grow large and red.

Yes, he met her at Sparta. I was not there, you understand. I was far
too young to go, too untried, and, in the nature of things, unworthy,
neither a lord nor a king. My Lord Idomeneus went, reluctantly. You
see, Helen's stepfather, Tyndareus—not wishing to offend any unmarried Achaian monarch—invited them all, and my Lord of Cnossus—not
wishing to offend the Spartan—went reluctantly. He was certain in his
own mind, I think, that Helen would choose a younger man. He was
nearly forty-five when he sailed, forty-six when he finally returned
home, and he had never been married. He kept concubines, of course,
but he had never taken a wife or thought to take one—or so he told me
later in the Troad—because so much of his time was spent at sea, either
raiding abroad or guarding our own broad-beamed fleets as they carried goods between Egypt and Achaia. "Mark me," he said on the
morning he departed, "the daughter of Leda will choose Odysseus
because he is the wisest among us or lordly Menelaus, who is rich, and
royal, and the brother of her sister's husband. But I will go for the sake
of diplomacy." And with a cargo of suitable gifts, he sailed, leaving me
with the fleet that guarded our sea lanes and a party of picked elders to
administer the land.

—When he came back to us over the wine-dark sea, some six or
seven moons later, my Lord was much changed. "She is more than
woman," he said, "more than I foresaw, more than I could have fore-
seen. She is the dream itself, Meriones, the idea." I found his words
amorphous, then, his thoughts vague, and even today, sitting here with

you some sixty years after the event, years after my own glimpsed vision, I am still uncertain whether she was beauty, or passion, or both—or neither but something much more important. As I told you earlier, she eludes language: words cannot hold her.

—Once the suitors assembled in Sparta, Tyndareus, I think, faced more of a problem than he had anticipated because the flower of Achaia was on hand, high spirited and hot blooded, and, in their public competitions for the match, each enthusiastic suitor put himself forward as superior to his neighbor. To be sure, a massive quarrel threatened, but, according to my Lord of Cnossus, the Man of Many Turns found a way out when he advised Tyndareus to extract from each suitor an oath: the oath—and all of them swore it in common before the others—the oath required each suitor to defend with his life whatever man Helen chose as her husband. Politically, it was a brilliant idea. With a single stroke, the oath so sworn, the alliance was calmed, strengthened, lent gravity and weight, and bound forever like wasps frozen in amber: in a manner of speaking, you see, any attack upon Helen's husband was to be interpreted as an attack upon everyone. Because the response from an alliance so bound might well prove devastating, no reasonable Argive would ever have dared to risk it. With the oath sworn, peace in Achaia was assured.

—As you know, she chose Menelaus. My Lord Idomeneus thought her looks tended toward Odysseus but that was only an opinion, and, as far as I recall, he only voiced it once, late on the night before we sailed for Aulis with eighty of our long black ships. At Sparta, apparently, he had once said as much to my Lord Odysseus, but the Ithacan, he said, only smiled, clapped him on the back with a broad hand, and replied, "She will go, my Lord of Cnossus, wheresoever she will, but in my opinion, she will either choose you or the brother of Agamemnon." That she especially favored my Lord of Cnossus—of that, I am sure. He would never speak at length on that subject, but during the years that I served him, he did speak often of her, and by the power of my eye, I know what I know. He was close to winning her, you see, very close; and, when she finally chose red-haired Menelaus, my king felt a great weight and came home to us, much changed.

—I would not know, precisely, how to describe that alteration. There was something intangible about it, something fleeting and unresolved.

Time and age may have had much to do with it, but I can't be sure. His hair, I know, was greyer, his movements more pronounced, but by themselves those things were normal, natural, signifying little. His habits, as I recall, became gradually more austere; he ate less, slept less, and, on the field, trained harder, demanding of himself far more than he ever demanded from younger men, including me. Many things in his behavior changed only slightly; each alone seemed barely consequential, but taken together, the composite bespoke a significant shift in his life. Where before, his eyes had often shone with genial animation, after Sparta, they deepened and their twinkle disappeared. When I watched him, then, as we sat in the great hall, talking long into the evenings, I remember thinking that the twinkle had been replaced by fire and smoke. It was not that he was old, you understand; he did not think of himself as old, and later, on the Plain, he could hold his own anywhere, even for hours on end in the press of a pitched battle. No, he was not old, not by many years yet. But the fact is he was no longer young, and after Sparta I think *he* knew it and knew, too, what he had lost. That may also have been a part of what Helen meant to him—I don't know. One is never privy to another's *dreams* or *ideas,* but for him, as he said, "she was more than woman," and somehow her youth may have been a part of it. Who knows? Perhaps I am only speaking for myself and the years that have flown behind me like the darting of eagles.

—Within a year after he returned from Sparta, he married. The marriage was political, an alliance between Cnossus and the Ancient of Rhodes, who sent his granddaughter, my Lady Meda, across the wine-dark sea with gifts of silver and tin. My Lady was intelligent, I thought, but neither young nor lovely. Still, she was able, and anxious to please, and after her arrival Cnossus functioned less like a barracks and more like a royal palace. I would not say that my Lord loved her, exactly, but he respected her, I know, and assiduously saw to her comfort. She bore him a child, a daughter named Cleisithyra, before the end of the winter, and this made him very happy. That they would have had many more children, I'm sure, but the child's cries were barely an hour old when the heralds arrived from my Lords the Atreidae and then, as you know, the world burst into flame.

—Foppish Alexandros had done the unthinkable: he had abducted Helen, and in consequence the alliance armed, preparing for war. Our own preparations here were swift. Word reached us late, of course, as it always does at this distance, but the fleet of a sea people like ourselves must always be in readiness, and even our construction of additional ships took us less than sixty days. When the time was ripe, we put to sea and sailed north toward Aulis with five thousand men. We were not the last to arrive, and the Atreidae greeted us warmly with kingly respect.

—I remember thinking as we sailed into Aulis that never in the memory of men had so many high-prowed ships, so many bronze-armed warriors gathered together under a single command. Everywhere, even unto the horizon, Achaian hulls, black and somber, rode taut against their anchor stones, anxious to be gone. "We will be irresistible," I cried to my Lord of Cnossus. "Priam will quail before our might like a frightened dove!" My Lord Idomeneus looked at me then, through those smoke-grey eyes, and here, now, at this distance in time, I still remember their sadness, their dark, impenetrable depth. "No," he said quietly, standing firm beside his steering oar, "it will not be so. We are going to a hard war, my Lord, and long. The Trojans will never give her up, and we must ever have her back. She is more than woman, Meriones; a war for her sake, a war to recover her, will be a fight to the death."

—Belius, old retainer and friend, the evening air turns cool. Now that we have finished our supper, ask a housemaid to bring me a cloak or a warm fleece to put about my shoulders. And tell her, too, to draw us a bowl of Pramian wine. Are you tired, young sir? —Good, let us sit and talk. The hours of Artemis move slowly in this phase of the month, and many, I think, remain before Dawn takes her place.

The answer to your question is both *yes* and *no.* In order to protect our fleet, the spearmen of Crete were often forced to fight at sea, and, owing to this fact more than any other, we were highly trained for quick assault. Regardless of whether we were destroying an enemy fleet or attacking its base, the men of Crete excelled in delivering the quick, sharp thrust. Thoroughly familiar with our reputation for this kind of action, my Lord Agamemnon placed us in the van when, finally, the Achaian fleet sailed, and then, after we had passed Lemnos, he dispatched us, sending us on ahead, skimming over the white-flecked sea. On the following morning as Aurora blushed, we Cretans stormed ashore across the beaches of Tenedos and reduced the island in a day of hard fighting. The Atreides' intention, I believe, was to secure our flank and the mouth of the Hellespont before attempting a major landing on the Plain, and in this we succeeded completely. My Lord Idomeneus led the assault: he was the first man ashore on the island, the first man to kill an enemy, and, throughout that long, hot day, the first man at the forefront, always. The Trojans had about three thousand men on Tenedos, and we overcame them through pure hard fighting. Although of short duration, the engagement was fought with intense ferocity, and it was costly: we lost no more than one hundred dead in the attack, but our numbers of wounded ran high—five hundred, perhaps six. When the battle was over, our men were exhausted. We came away, I think, with more than four hundred prisoners, ten of Priam's ships, and vast numbers of Trojan cattle. On the following morning, our main force led by the Atreides assaulted Troy, and so it began.

—So you see, young sir, while we were the first to fight, we were not the first to fight on the Plain: we did not go in with the main assault. At the time, I was still too junior in command to be privy to our battle orders, and, resting on Tenedos after our first brush with the enemy, I assumed that we would be thrown immediately into action again, within hours, or days at the most. But that was not the case.

—"We will go in tomorrow, with the main force?" I asked my Lord as the two of us rested from the first day of war. "No," he said. "Look about you; we're spent. And besides, that is not the Atreides' intention." He fell silent then, but my impatience prodded him. "You will have to admit," he went on, "that we are better at sea than many of the others: we are far more experienced over long distances, and furthermore, we know how to move large cargoes swiftly and efficiently. The morsel may be bitter for you to swallow, but for now our job is to garrison Tenedos, guard the approaches to the Hellespont, regulate the flow of supplies, and, when conditions permit, mount raids along the coast." At the time, I remember feeling an intense disappointment in the assignment; it seemed so inglorious that my youth revolted against it, and in the heat of the moment I voiced my anger. "Not so," admonished my Lord. "You are young, yet, and do not see it clearly. As I told you, it will be a long war, long and hard: never before has there been an undertaking like it, and we must fight it in ways that were heretofore unknown. Consider wisely: if we cannot keep the Hellespont open and resupply our men on the Plain, the war is lost. I assure you, we will have all of the fighting that we can handle here, guarding our convoys and holding back the enemy ships that will sail against us from Lesbos, Smyrna, Cyme, Imbros, and Chrysa, so accept your fate, Meriones, and do your duty. Our life strings, whatever they may be, have already been spun, measured, and cut, and who are we to rail against the Sisters?"

—For eight years, then, we garrisoned Tenedos. *Garrisoned* is the word, certainly, that one is forced to use, but the word does not even begin to describe the grinding severity of those years. Fighting beside my Lord, we thrice engaged the fleets of Mytilene, twice raided and sacked Cyme, reduced Imbros, assaulted Smyrna, and took part in more than fifty lesser raids along the coasts of Dardania, Mysia, and Caria. Twice we went out in company with the great Achilles; often we sailed, too, with wise Odysseus or, after he arrived, with stalwart Antilochus, lordly Nestor's son. Across these years, I find it difficult to remember everything, but what I do remember clearly is that we engaged the enemy almost every day. That activity lasted for eight years. Then, during the ninth spring, when angry Achilles withdrew to his huts and man-killing Hector, smelling a victory, mounted his last great offensive, we were called in and fought for the first time on the Plain.

—Let me tell you, my young friend, on the Plain the fighting was awful, vicious, endless. Nevertheless, my Lord of Cnossus was a bulwark to the army, a terror among men. He was well past fifty by that time, completely grey, and physically worn down by the war's long strain, but nothing could hold him back. He *had* to fight, and, for his own sense of identity or self, he *had* to be at the forefront. He was driven to it, you see, urged on by a force that I could not then understand but which, before I came to know it myself, I feared. Nothing that I could say or do had the slightest effect on him, and he plunged himself always into the centers of the greatest danger. Once in he had to stand his ground, holding his own death at bay. Then, I think, is when I, too, began to age owing to my fear for his life. He was too old to run, you see, too old to avoid the greatest hazards when they came his way: he had to stand, fighting where he stood, no matter how great the odds, because youthful agility had abandoned him. Great general that he was, my Lord Nestor, whose years also exceeded the norm, fought his war from his chariot, and in my opinion he was right to do so. I encouraged my own Lord to use a chariot, but he only laughed a little, then, and shook his head. "My Lord," he said, "you speak in absurdities. What do I know of fleet-winged chariots? Am I not a rider of the sea? Are you not the same? No, my Meriones, let us have no chariots: we should hang ourselves in the reins." And so, mostly, he fought on foot, standing before the tide like a great rock as the Trojan waves broke and shattered about him.

—We came ashore again, later in the year, to repel the warrior women of Scythia. They were fierce, unnatural women and savage fighters but hardly as numerous as had been supposed, and actually we saw very little action against them. Along our front, we killed, I think, no more than forty and captured ten, but, rather than submit to the touch of men, the captives hanged themselves at the first opportunity.

—After the defeat of the Amazons, we should have returned to sea. In council, I know, my Lord of Cnossus, the Ithacan, and Pylian Nestor argued endlessly for the resumption of our blockade, but the Atreides, thinking perhaps that seaborne threats had ended, made his decision, and the spearmen of Crete remained ashore, filling the same gap in the Achaian line—between Aias and the lesser son of Atreus— that we had filled during Hector's offensive. The Trojans very quickly showed us the error in this decision; in the middle of the night, the lordly son of Aurora, King Memnon of Ethiopia, slipped more than one hundred and fifty ships up the channel between Tenedos and the mainland, beached them in Besika Bay, and attacked us at dawn with such force that the right side of our line nearly collapsed. Had that same attack come during Hector's offensive, the Trojans would have thrown us off the beach, but coming when it did, it was too little, too late, and by evening we triumphed.

—That was the day that I saw her, standing high above me, radiant atop the walls of Troy. That was late, late in the war, in the last autumn after the leaves had already started to fall. I don't really think that I knew what the war was about until that moment. Even now, I'm not sure I can put it into words; somehow, it defies the limitations of thought and flows with a force of its own, something felt but only partially understood. When I finally saw her, I knew at last why the war had been so long, so very hard—why the Trojans could never give her up, why we forever had to have her back. I knew it, I know it now, but not, you see, in any perceptible, conscious way: I perceived her and I didn't perceive her. My Lord of Cnossus was right, of course; she was more than woman, far more, but she was more, too, than a simple dream or idea. —Was she the center of our people? The source of Achaia? Our soul? How am I to put it? I have struggled mentally with that question for more than fifty years now, but as you see, my conscious conceptions, my endless efforts to fix her formally in my own mind, remain as nebulous as fire and smoke. Sitting here, tonight, I give over the question, knowing what I know, knowing that my heart, or soul, or self will always know and perceive about her what my conscious mind will never be able to define, what my conscious speech will never be able to utter.

—When the battle ended with the destruction of the Ethiopians, my Lord Agamemnon ordered the Cretans back to sea, and that was the last time we ever saw Helen or Ilium. For the remainder of the war, we never went ashore again but maintained our blockade to guard the Hellespont, Tenedos, and the western approaches to the Troad. Once, from a distance, I saw the horse that was building on the beach, and then, during the sea feint, I saw the remains of the great Argive fleet reassemble offshore, although by that time its numbers were greatly diminished. And then it was over. We sailed for home almost immediately, our own share of the spoils transferred to us at sea by all the great lords of the alliance.

—Your cup, young friend, is dry. Belius, summon my cup-bearer to attend our guest; let it never be said that our hospitality neglected the grandson of lordly Polypoetes, guardian of the gate, lion of the Plain.

Most certainly! Those were all lies, all of them! And they were all bred by that same father of vomit, Thersites. He was a vile man, young sir, vile, and ugly, and crude. After my Lord's death, I took ship and sailed north to the land of the Locroi, to Cynos, where Thersites had been seen; I picked up his trail quickly enough, journeyed south, and caught up with him, finally, near Delphi, at the base of Parnassus. I whipped him publicly for his crimes and sent him into exile.

—Oh, he was the greatest liar Achaia ever bred, I assure you, and a braggart, a cowardly deserter who got away from the Plain in the hold of a Lemnian merchantman, even before the sack of the city. No one in Achaia knew a thing about him when he arrived home, so they took him at his word and accepted him as the Atreides' herald, the darling of the army. Then, like a malicious storyteller, he travelled widely across the face of the land, spewing out his venom and leaving in his wake such a trail of filthy lies that it looked and smelled like the residue of the running sickness. Achaia, believe me, is well rid of him, and here, tonight, I think that perhaps I should have killed him as an example to our people.

—Nothing he said about my Lord of Cnossus was true—nothing, not a single word. We did *not* travel to Euboea with the remainder of the fleet but parted from the Argives east of Scyros and sailed directly home; consequently, you understand, we avoided entirely the great storm that drowned so many of our friends. We arrived in Crete with each and every one of our ships intact: every noble Cretan who survived the fighting sailed safely home. And *no* rebellion existed in Crete when we landed, and *none* has taken place since our return. And far from being faithless and usurping the throne, my Lady Meda died in childbirth eight months after we left for the Troad. If that is not my Lord's own son on the throne at Cnossus, I will ask Belius to serve me a boar's tooth helmet for my breakfast, and I promise to swallow it whole. —And who this Leucus is or was who was supposed to have been my Lady's lover, none of us have ever been able to learn; in Crete, we call him "Thersites' lie," and Argos, my present Lord of Cnossus, makes jokes about him for the amusement of company. Lies—those were all lies. And that exile story was a lie, too.

—Now as far as that tale about my Lord's exile . . . well, at least that one had enough to it so that we were fully able to understand how Thersites manipulated the facts. To begin with, I assure you that my Lord Idomeneus was not the Cretan who emigrated to Calabria; that much is perfectly clear, and the facts are far more mundane. Four years after we returned, my Lady Cleisithyra came of age, entertained suit from a Sallentine noble, and, with her father's complete blessing, married and sailed away to Calabria, thereby sealing a sturdy alliance between our peoples that still obtains. Today, I think, my Lord's grandsons rule the land in perfect tranquility. So you see, no one went into exile.

—Had Thersites' lies done us no harm, they might have left us laughing. But in fact they did do us harm—much harm indeed: at least one attack from the south and another from the sea peoples to the east were pressed against us by kings who believed those lies, who thought us weakened by rebellion, and while defending our people we lost both men and ships. We did not know this at the time I hunted Thersites for the lies he was telling about my Lord, and in fact we have only recently made a connection between those attacks and the nature of his malicious misinformation, and, if I could get my hands on the man now, I would hang him high by his heels as live food for vultures. —But I digress; no, my young friend, as I am happy to tell you, my Lord Idomeneus's homecoming was far different than the stories that Thersites loosed in Achaia.

—As I recall—and the image remains quite clear in my mind—we were joyously greeted upon our return and hailed from the beach with songs and laughter. My Lord's children were brought down and met their father with garlands, and little Argos, I remember—much to the irritation of his sister—would not be still until my Lord had handed over his spear and placed his own bright helmet over the boy's head. As you can imagine, I'm sure, this made quite a sight. As he wobbled forward under the weight of the helm, Argos had also to contend with the weight of that spear: it was too big for him by many times, so instead of carrying it, he dragged it, all the way up from the beach, dulling its point considerably as it bounced from rock to rock. Along the way, the road was lined with our warriors' wives and children, who fed us olives, and figs, and barley cakes, and salted fish, and large sweet bunches of summer grapes, and who also encouraged Argos at every step until by the time we reached the citadel he was so youthfully pumped up by the experience that he expected to take part in the purification rites and was only restrained by his father's gentle command. Afterward, we had wine to drink from every household cup, and pray-

ers of thanksgiving, and then we were home, perched on the terrace of
Cnossus like glossy bronze eagles warmed by the sun.

—In the following year, my Lord passed his sixtieth anniversary. He
remained acutely firm in mind, but in body he was tired, exhausted,
too often wounded, worn down by the battles he had fought and the
hard strain of command. And he was crippled, too, in the hips, from a
spearthrust. He gave up fighting then, turned tactical command of the
fleet over to me, and, like Pylian Nestor, contented himself with being
a father to his children, a king to his people. He advised me, of course,
and owing to his wise advice I twice defeated the attacks that came
against us from the kings I have mentioned, taking many captives in
each of my victories, but he would not come down to go to sea with
me, complaining openly that his eye was too slow, his arm too unsure
to lead in battle himself.

—I saw him often, of course, and lived in his apartments as a member of the family whenever I came ashore. And the two of us saw eye to
eye. "When I am gone," he said, "train Argos, and then return to
Gortyn and wall the citadel. For your lifetime, I think, we are secure to
the north; unless I miscalculate, Argos will be able to take his throne in
peace. But I am worried about the peoples to the south and east: by
your report, their ships are much improved since the days when I
fought them in my youth, long, long before you came down through the
passes of Ida and made your home here. Soon, I think, the sea people
may try us again, so be a wall at my son's back, my Meriones, the way
you have always been at mine. Hold Gortyn for yourself and, when you
have them, for your sons, and then for their sons, too. If you can hold
Gortyn, the House of Minos will thrive." I thanked him for his trust
and gave my oath, and within a week sent stone carvers up, over Ida's
pass, to begin the broad, high walls you see around us.

—Less than a month later, my Lord was struck down by the hand of
Smintheus and took to his bed. Unable to walk, he had himself carried
each evening to the terrace outside his white-pillared hall. There, I
would sit beside him, talking, reflecting while Argos practiced with his
spear on the grounds below.

—One evening, as the stars began to come out, he pulled himself up
into a sitting position, looked out across the broad night sky, and said,
"The stars. They remind me of the campfires before Troy." He paused,

and then went on. "My squire," he said, "Lord of the Manly Spear, the hand of the Courier is on me; soon, I think, he will guide me into the chambers of decay. Since you came to me, long ago over the pass, I have tried to teach you all that I know about kingship and generalship; pray you, pass the torch to my son." He shook a little, then, as though a chill had run through him. "If the Courier is going to allow us a final word," he said, "let us have it now, in case Aurora prevents me and I am swallowed at last by deadly Night." I was speechless, then; I couldn't say a thing. "Come, come," he said. "Remember what I told you? The string has already been spun, and measured, and cut: that is mortality, and there is no denying it." "And is that all," I said, "is that all a man can have—to eat and sleep and drink and fight and die?" He laughed, then, the peal of his laughter echoing through the night. "You and I have already been granted far more than that," he said, a twinkle in his eye then mingling with its fire and smoke; "don't be absurd. On the Plain before Ilium, we lived and fought for something far greater than our mere existence, and it elevated our lives. There, for a while at least, we rose above the trough and became more than feeding animals. Such intangibles—the pursuit of them—will always make us rise above ourselves, exceed our limits. Even now, in the winter of my life, as I sit here remembering, as I recall the magnitude of the dream, the idea . . . how larger than life, I feel compelled to reach out and extend my grasp . . ." His hand shot straight out, then, like a bolting arrow, reaching into the night, extending his outstretched fingers . . . and then he died.

—My lords Nestor and Thrasymedes attended his funeral, and the great Diomedes, and your own lion-hearted grandsire, and others as well: Meges, Machaon, Thoas, and lordly Eurypylus. But many were missing, dead by the hand of Poseidon or war-loving Ares, and some, like the lesser Atreides and the Man of Many Turns, were still lost, their whereabouts unknown. I had hoped, you see, to have one final glimpse of the Lady of Sparta come to mourn my Lord, but I never saw her again. After twenty days of respect, we fired his pyre, buried him, and conducted a festival of games in his honor. Then the guests departed, each returning to Achaia in safety.

—Five years after my Lord's death, I gave Cnossus over into his son's hands, and a fine son he is—a gracious man and kind, strong, wise, mindful of his people, a little smaller, perhaps, than his father, a little less sturdy, but a good man indeed. I gave Cnossus into my Lord Argos's hands and climbed back up the north face of Ida and through the pass to Gortyn to be a wall behind my new king. That was more than forty years ago, and now that the hand of Smintheus is on me, in my own frozen infirmity, I know that soon my own grandson, who is presently training in Cnossus, will climb back through that same pass to relieve me and become a wall behind his own new king.

—Belius, at long last Artemis veils her lustre and stars take over the night. It is late now, and our cups are dry, and in the morning when Aurora blushes, you and Andraxus must go north into the heart of Achaia with our young friend and perform a service for the last of the brave Lapithae. But for now, Belius, take our friend inside and place him in my chamber. And give him warm fleeces with which to cover himself while sleep restores his strength.

—No, my Belius, I will remain. This fleece and my cloak are warm enough, and tonight I think I want to lie here where I can still see the stars, where my vision is still within my grasp . . . only a little beyond my fingertips . . .

Eurypylus at Dodona

Indeed, their campfires light up in darkness like swarms of fireflies, but once, long ago—across the broad, windswept Plain of the Troad, when Night blanketed the earth like a smothering cloud and the Argives stood beside their ships in silence, waiting for the blood-red rose of dawn—once, I saw a thousand campfires burning in the night, and around each fire sat fifty men with their spears, shields, and shining helmets. Behind those men stood war chariots, and behind those, munching rye and white barley, the swift-footed horses of Ilium waited for the coming of Hyperion. This, then, is not so bad. Consider our position: we have water; we have enough food to last for a year; my people and yours are healthy; and the walls of Dodona are thickly strong: the barbarians, I think, are not likely to breach them, now or in future. If your decision is to wait, you may confidently withstand their siege until the shafts of Smintheus strike them low—an event, I'm sure, which is bound to take place sooner or later if they continue to remain encamped before us, defecating and swarming like so many locusts.

—Of course, my Lord, other alternatives exist. At Pylene, if you are able to fight your way through to him, sea-raiding Thoas offers you shelter, and to the east kingly Machaon promises you sanctuary at Tricca. If you wish to journey farther to the east, I myself offer you my own hospitality behind the broad, white walls of Asterios, beneath the snowcapped heights of Titanos. Surely, an element of risk obtains in each migration, but no more, I think, than we must face here, in or out of the city.

—Yes, as you say, you have contracted me to defeat these barbarians, to devise the plan and direct the fighting. I am aware of that, of course. Do not doubt my determination to aid you, my Lord; my own Ormeniones number more than a thousand strong-willed warriors. My own company wedded to yours will permit us to field more than four thousand men. Still, if my aging eyes do not deceive me, the bearded barbarians camp before us with a larger force than ours, and I would be remiss in my duty if I did not warn you of the dangers: the risk of doing battle here is immense. You should know that, consider it, and make your decision accordingly. I am aware that you are a young king, pressed to fight, but you yourself would be remiss if you failed to study each alternative and weigh each possible consequence.

—If you wish, my officers and I will withdraw. Then, in the tranquility of your chambers, you and your council may debate the issue, unimpeded by our presence or any influence we might exert upon your diplomatic sense of courtesy. According to our duty in this matter, we will abide by whatever decision you reach: if you choose to go, we will cover your withdrawal; if you choose to withstand a siege, we will conduct offensive operations outside your walls, harassing the barbarians at every opportunity; if you choose to attack, my Ormeniones will lead at the forefront. You have contracted with us in hard coin; we intend to settle our account.

Yes, my Lord, the doer must suffer. It is the law. It is a good rule, but hard; still, it is just. For ten long years in the Troad, we Argives labored to fulfill it, and when we did, we came home. That was long ago—longer, almost, than I care to remember; nevertheless, the law abides, and you have chosen rightly, although beforehand I did not wish to declare myself so openly, in order to give you time to consider your choice. Clearly, the barbarian attack is unprovoked: you have not raided their cattle; you have not burned their homes; and you have not enslaved their children, taken their wives as concubines, or murdered their old people. They have no reason to come swarming out of the north like wolf packs, killing everything in their path. Judging rightly, the just thing to do is crush them. Should we fail to act now, we should only open the remainder of Thesprotia to invasion, or Acarnania, or Aetolia, or even Thessalia. If we withdraw, no one will thank us because we will have opened the gates of Achaia to savages, but if we win, Achaians in days to come may remember us in the same breath as the brawny Lapithae, my Lords Polypoetes and Leonteus, when, like cornered lions, they mauled the army of Asius before our ships in the Troad or mighty Aias when, like a tower of stone, he stood, and fought, and refused to yield before the Trojans when they attacked our ships with fire. If we fight and win, we will stretch the limits of our race and buy them time by upholding a rule of justice that is native to our soil. Each man must fight as though victory depended upon him alone, and, if we do, in days to come the children of your children, and the children of my son's children will honor us like the gods with whom, once on the windy Plain of Troy, I, in my youth, contended. We *must* fight; we cannot yield and still, in the memory of our race, be called men.

My intention, my Lord of Dodona, is to model our battle on the Head of the Bull.

—Yes, you are correct: Pylian Nestor devised the plan late in the ninth year of the war, in order to defeat the Amazons. They came at us across the Plain in considerable numbers, and for a while they were a ferociously deadly threat.

—Pardon, my Lord? What —No, my Lord, and, please, disregard whatever that man said. The man . . . the cur, Thersites, was a dog, and that falsity about my Lord Nestor is merely one among many of his noxious droppings. Know you, my Lord, that that dog berated everyone and everything; if what I hear is true, the Squire of Crete finally whipped him into slavery. In the Troad, Thersites was an offensive braggart; eventually, even before we sacked the city, he deserted, returned home, and slandered us all. But let us not lose our thoughts over an animal of such low degree.

—Decidedly, my Lord Nestor was the most knowledgeable and experienced general among us. The great Achilles, as I'm sure you know, was the army's best, most terrifying warrior: whenever, wherever he took the field, he stormed against the enemy like icy Boreas when, from his Thracian caves, he rages down across a field of wheat, chilling, then freezing, then killing each tender shoot and stem of green, life-giving grain. In battle Achilles was an uncontrollable force, a successful tactician, certainly, because nothing could withstand him. But even in a moment of heat, swift-footed Achilles would give way to my Lord Nestor because, in his heart of hearts, he knew what we all came to know—that Gerenian Nestor understood the craft of war better than any of us. Most of us, you see, knew the fundamentals of fighting long before we reached the Troad, but war is not quite the same thing as mere fighting. During the long years that we warred against Priam, we learned that—most of us, those of us who survived—but my Lord Nestor and, possibly, the Man of Many Turns knew it before we beached our first ship, even before we sailed from Aulis. The point I'm trying to make is that the Gerenian Charioteer was a general—a strategist as well as a fighter—and it will always be to the credit of the Atreidae that they recognized him as such and listened to his advice. It was my Lord Nestor, you understand, and the Ithacan who first taught us the value of intelligence and reconnaissance: that is why, tonight, my officers and I already know the dispositions of the barbarians while they know nothing about ours. And it was Nestor, too, who taught us about concentration and economy of force and, finally, how to combine those ideas to create an effective fighting formation. As you will observe, that is how our smaller force is going to defeat the barbarians, who still mass for battle like a rabble, without purpose or direction, giving themselves over to chaotic passions like so many wasp-stung cattle.

Yes, you see clearly, Aurora blushes. Soon now Hyperion will mount his car, warming our backs and our shoulders prior to setting the ground before us ablaze. In less than an hour, I think, the sun will be full at our backs, and out there—beyond the stream, where the Head of the Bull is concealed—as the barbarians arise and peer up here toward the gates of Dodona, Hyperion's beams will sear their eyes more painfully, even, than the smoking flames of their campfires.

—My Lord, let us move closer to the edge of your watchtower, but carefully, my Lord, carefully: barbarian arrows are bronze-tipped and barbed, and poison, too, enflames their edges. Now, bid your sentry to raise his torch—once, twice, thrice. Thus it begins.

—Do you see, my Lord, there, just above the lip of that twisted, tree-lined defile? Do you see? Good; now watch, watch the bank of the gully.

—There, observe; the left horn of our Bull is rising from concealment, forming along the bank, and beginning its advance. More than a
thousand brave Dodonians are formed in that horn, now sweeping
silently forward toward the barbarian flank. So it was, my Lord, nearly
fifty years ago when lordly Diomedes, Antilochus, and the great Achilles thrust the left horn of the Achaian Bull against fire-eyed Penthesilea
and panicked the Amazons in their shock.

—Listen, my Lord; now you can hear the rattle of our spears; it is
our sign that the attack begins. —Now. Now! Do you see it? The
shock, the surprise in the barbarian camp!

—Quickly, my Lord, whirl your war shield above your head: it is the
signal for our right horn to break cover and go over to the attack.
Quickly, my Lord! We have only a thousand men on the left; if the
barbarians recover swiftly enough, our left cannot withstand the full
force of their rush.

—There! Good! Now our right horn is forming, curving down from
that high line of rocks that flanks the road. We will roll off that hill
and over the barbarian rear like a mountain avalanche—hard, cold,
and deadly.

—This, too, my Lord, I remember well. Here, today, in my grey old
age, as my spear wounds twitch in this morning chill, I remember that
once, far away on the windy Plain of Troy, I, too, raced over the ground
with the right horn of the Bull, crashing my spear against my shield,
sending terror into the ice-bound hearts of the Amazons. The Man of
Many Turns was with us there, and lordly Meges, and Menestheus of
Athens, and the Son of Oileus, and there, just as the vicious war-
maidens were about to crash their full fury against the horn of
Diomedes, Antilochus, and Achilles, we shattered them with our
war cries, striking them unexpectedly from behind and filling them
with terror.

—*Now!* Do you see, my Lord? Do you perceive how our right horn
has confused them? It is their weakness, my Lord! A disordered melee
is no defense; each barbarian out there fights only for himself, only
where his instincts tell him. Notice that he fights beside his fellows, but
he is essentially alone in the battle, unable to rely on anything other
than his own right arm.

—Quickly, my Lord, we must put the Bull's head in motion; without the head the horns will collapse. Raise your purple cloak, O my King of Dodona. It will signal the barbarians' doom.

—They see it, my Lord. They see it! There, beneath us, athwart the riverbed—see how our Bull's Head rises from the ground. My bronze-armed Ormeniones are in the van, as I promised, and one thousand more Dodonians are backing them.

—Wave your cloak, my Lord; the head must run, *they must run!* They *must* provide the main shock, the crushing blow. When my Ormeniones meet the enemy, the Bull's Head and horns will be joined, and the barbarians will be surrounded. Now they're running. Good! Listen to the rattle of their spears!

—Now, my Lord, I think we will see much killing and hear the cries of many dying barbarians. Long ago on the Plain, when my Lord Nestor gave the final signal that sent the Argive head crashing against the Amazons, we in the horns were already contending with more than we could handle. But when the head of the Bull broke cover, pouring across the Plain behind the Atreidae, Idomeneus, and Aias, roaring, shouting, and rattling their spears, then the Amazons panicked as though the Earthshaker himself had unleashed the power of the sea. They whirled, and sprang, and screamed with rage, and drove themselves in a frenzy against us, slashing the air with their high, piercing cries. But they were so seized by wrath, so blinded by terror, that madness swallowed them, leading some to run on their swords while others, even more crazed, unwittingly hacked each other. Against Hector's great counteroffensive, we fought for more than three long days, and the battle was hard, and hot, and exhausting, but against Penthesilea's Amazons, though the engagement was brief, the fighting was far more intense, spurred on by a ferocity born of panic and a desperation mated with terror. I . . .

—Look, my Lord, the head joins the horns! The encirclement is complete! Let us offer libations, my Lord of Dodona, and sacrifice, and call down the spirit of Ares to inspire our men as they crush these barbarians.

As you say, my Lord, today's victory is a splendid vindication of Pylian Nestor: let our celebrations remember him and give him honor.

I myself will give a handsome gold cup to the singer who praises him best.

—No, my Lord, no, we did not always realize his excellence. In the opening months, among those of us who were untried when first we arrived in the Troad, my Lord Nestor seemed . . . well, rather old, a greybeard—long-winded, sententious, even a bit obtuse. We required time, you see, to learn to appreciate him. As I think back, knowing now how little he cared to suffer fools in his presence, I sometimes think his patience was the most admirable thing about him. You see, in the opening years of the war, when most of us still believed that war was a mere matter of individual strength and courage, he gave us quiet, patient instruction, tolerating our foolishness just long enough to teach us our craft. I don't believe we could have learned our lessons any faster than we did, but I do know that we—those of us who were young—squandered many lives, lost many fellows while we learned, and there, on the windy Plain of Ilium where I buried more than half of the men I first took out to Troy, I resolved never to squander lives again. Battles like the one we've won today have to be fought; justice must be preserved or life defended, but not, I think, through mere dash: war is no sport. Thus, if I consider rightly, the Achaians will do well to study what we learned at Ilium, remember it, and use it when no better way unfolds.

—Did I see Penthesilea? —I did, my Lord. The reports are true: she had a beautiful face and a long, lithe body, but there is something savage, unnatural, about a woman who burns off her breast in order to be able to draw her bow. I cannot think her the child of Artemis at all; she made my blood run cold.

—The great Achilles and Penthesilea? —No, my Lord, decidedly not! I know of such a story, but it is one of Thersites' slanders, thought romantic by slaves and serving women. Achilles killed the Amazon, but he didn't mourn her because she came within a hair's breath of killing him, driving her spear all the way through his great shield and deep into his corselet. Had he not struck her with his sword, she might have decapitated him with her axe: the blow was already falling when he struck off her arm, interrupting its force. You see, my Lord, the intensity of the fight did not allow time for reflection but continued to press us with its fury until the very end. I walked from the field in his company that afternoon, and he never looked back, never even mentioned her.

—If we may turn to other matters, my Lord, with your agreement, I would like to rest my men with yours for three days. We need that time, I think, to recover our strength, and to collect and bury the dead: should we not do so swiftly, the shafts of Smintheus may strike Dodona, sending a plague amongst us. We must also honor our dead. Although we did not lose many, the men we lost were our friends; proper burial will ensure their swift entrance into the chambers of Hades. When I leave here with all my men, I want to leave no ghosts to disturb our dreams; when we have done, I want to go home and sleep the sleep of the just. Tomorrow, my Lord, permit us to bury our friends beside your own brave dead, and I will leave sums with your priests to defray the expenses of their annual rites.

—You are very kind, my Lord of Dodona, but costs for sacrifices to the dead were included in our contract, and, possibly, if your people are taxed hereafter to provide libations for Ormenionian graves, they will be less likely to remember us for our victory and far more likely to proclaim us a burden. It is in the nature of things, is it not?

—For myself, do you mean? —My Lord, the shadows are lengthening for me. My twilight is here. Our defense of Dodona, I think, has been my last campaign. As you can see, I grow old. Once black as the wings of a raven, my beard now is grey and thin, and aside from old wounds, which continue to ache whenever Boreas takes wing, I have a lingering pain, deep in my side, that makes me think Apollo's arrow has already entered my body. No, my Lord, I will go home now, but in the chambers of my memory, which are filled with echoes from the Troad, I will now hear, too, a last lingering call from Dodona, where, on a winter morning, the Head of the Bull brought grief to the treacherous barbarians and justice to a city of the gods.

Machaon at Tricca

Yes. Yes, we did learn the art from Asclepius, both Podaleirius and myself. Asclepius was our father, you see, son of Apollo Paieon and unhappy Coronis, and in his youth he learned the secrets of herbs and surgery from Chiron, the horse-man. He became a great healer—as great, some say, as his own immortal father, but he was only with us during our youth: by the time we had grown to manhood, he had gone into the South, and there, I have heard, at Athens, where he went to restore the fair Hippolytus, the Cloud Gatherer blasted him for rivalling the skill of the gods. I cannot attest to that, of course: I was no more than sixteen when he went away, leaving my brother and me here, in Tricca, beside the swift-flowing waters of Peneus, but the great Achilles knew something of the matter, from his teacher, and we had the story from him and also from venerable Phoenix, my Lord Achilles' mentor and guide.

—So Asclepius went into the South, but before he left us, he taught us many things, and much of what we practiced in the Troad we learned from him: how to clean and bind man-flesh hacked by a sword, how to stanch the bleeding from a spear thrust, how to apply spider webs over an arrow wound and, thereby, draw its poison. That and much more, and for ten long years before Ilium, many Argives owed their lives and their continued well-being to the teachings that our father, Asclepius, gave us in our youth. Of ourselves, I think, we had little skill; we lost many men—many, because our skill was not great enough, our knowledge not broad enough to restore their lives, or limbs, or minds, and here, on the porch of my palace as the sun prepares to set over the Pindus—just as it is preparing to set for me, just as it set nine years ago for Podaleirius—I regret my mistakes, my lack of skill, my many failures to keep so many friends of my youth alive, there, on the wide, dusty Plain of Troy.

—No, young man, I think I am too old now to take another pupil. My hands, as you can see, are frozen in the winter of my life, and in the mornings, when Aurora blushes like a gold-red rose, my eyes, infirm with time, and clouded, no longer see her as they did before when I was young and hearty, and stood each morning on the edge of my life, looking forward toward the dawn, and the sun, and the day. —No, now when I wake I'm blind, my eyelashes clotted with a thick yellow rheum, and before I can look again, out across my fields and vines, out toward the Pindus, before I can see, my slaves must heat water and bathe my face to soak away the yellowing, crusted signs of time. The hand of Smintheus is on me, young friend; somewhere, I'm sure, his arrow has already penetrated, seeking my vitals.

—But so it is, young man, in time, with all men. Like stalks of grain, we grow, mature, and yield . . . and fall away into the sear, yellow and infirm. Of itself, each stalk is fated, but not the grain which rises again each spring with the coming of the rains, whether seeded wild or thrown by the farmer's hand, and there, I think, we see some justice of the gods surpassing man's, and for myself, I find it good.

—Stay. Remain a while. Summer nights are cool here, and your visit pleases me. Allow me to call Amphius, my steward, and he will see that we are served with food and wine. The barley meal is good this year, and so, the firstling kids, and today, we have honey fresh from the hive that is brown, and sweet, and filled with the energy of life.

Indeed, the barbarians are a threat to all of us; as you say, they are many and fierce in the field. Here at Tricca, within the space of twenty years, we have already repulsed them twice, and recently our northern outposts reported them on the move again, and we—my men, that is—girded for battle one more time. But their penetration in our direction was a feint; the main force of their thrust went against Dodona. As you may be aware, my Lord of Dodona is young, the son of the son of Gouneus, who fought beside me in the Troad, and, knowing nothing of war or siege, he was wise to call the lordly Eurypylus to command his army. Last year, before the grain was harvested, while, still, the stalks stood high in the fields, lordly Eurypylus marched this way from Asterios, taking more than one thousand of his own bronze-armed Ormeniones west with him into the heartland of Dodona, and there, I understand, he won a great victory over the barbarians, driving them backward, north over shining Haliacmon into the mountain fastness of their strongholds around Lake Lychnitis. But we have not seen the last of them, by any means; according to Eurypylus, their numbers are great—as great, perhaps, as the number of the Achaians at Aulis, *before* we sailed for Troy, and if that report is true—and knowing the great Eurypylus to be the general he is, it *is* true—Achaia faces a dangerous threat, and the citadels to the south must, as they have not, arm and prepare for invasion. I will not be here, myself, when it comes. Of that, I am sure. Lordly Eurypylus has bought us time, I think, and we are safe for this year and for two, possibly three more, but the barbarian assaults here were raids, probes, nothing more; the attack on Dodona was much greater, and still only a small number of the enemy attempted it. Sooner or later, the barbarians will invade in force, and, when that attack comes, their hand will lay heavy on the lands of Achaia, and the Argives will have to fight for their lives. I will be dead by then, I suppose. I would like to think that I might recover my youth, and march, but I am a realist in matters like this, and in my youth my father taught us to be realistic about health, too; I know what I know. When the blow falls, my grandsons will lead the men of Tricca, and may the gods inspire them as once, when I was young, they inspired me, far away in the Troad.

—Of course, as you suggest, we will need many surgeons then, and healers, and men to bind up the wounds of our warriors; but still, I think, you might do better to go to a younger teacher, a man like Akastos of Euboea or even the wise Dexamenos of Elis, who is known far and wide for the efficacy of his cures.

—You flatter me, young friend; I was never, even in my youth, as skilled as you suggest, and if I weaken in my resolve and acquiesce, agreeing to take you as my pupil, you, too, must become a realist and put away such foolish admiration. Considering the times, your decision to train yourself as a surgeon for the field is a good one, and if you have talent and skill and can save men's lives—the gods willing—along the mournful edges of battle and in dreary darkness, amidst the blood-soaked pain of the encampment, you will render a service to the Achaians that will rival the heroes on the field because, simply, healed men may fight another day, and in a moment of crisis even a wounded man on the mend may have value as a warrior or a leader. —Do you know who taught me that? Great lordly Nestor, in the ninth year of the war.

—I was wounded, you see, fighting. Failing to understand my own worth, my own value to the army, I personally took the field for nine years, sharing command with my brother, and led the men from Tricca, from Ithome, and from Oechalia into the press of war. I never had difficulty holding my own in battle: twice I commanded independent raids into the heart of Phrygia, where, from remote Ascania, my men returned as victors with many captured slaves, and cattle, and quantities of silver. But in the ninth year, during Hector's bold counter-attack, when the Myrmidons withdrew and sat disconsolate beside their huts, I fought on the Plain beside the Atreidae, and the Aiantes, and the Man of Many Turns, and lordly Idomeneus of Crete, and the brave Diomedes, and was wounded by that blondly foppish Alexandros, son of Priam, who shot me laughingly and treacherously, from a very great distance, putting a three-barbed arrow deep into my right shoulder. The gods smiled on me, in my pain, because my Lord Idomeneus saw me fall and stood by me, calling my Lord Nestor to my aid; hauling me into his chariot with a strong, firm hand, the great Charioteer extracted me from the forefront—not, I should add, without sharp risk to himself—and sped me to safety beside the high-beaked ships.

—I have never forgotten that ride back to the ships, and never in the days that are left to me *will* I forget it. Once he had pulled me into his chariot where—with a presence of mind that still amazes me—he threw a rope about my corselet and lashed me to the railing . . . once aboard, as I say, that old but mighty horseman snapped the lash over his horses, and then, like hawks in flight, we bolted toward the hollow ships. Among our forces, the Achaians parted before him like waves of grain blown back by a summer wind, but at one point, where a finger of Trojan spearmen jutted out among our own strong-willed men, cutting off our path and preventing our clear escape to the ships, the great Pylian raised his whip high above his horses' heads and cracked it, and the crack sounded like the stroke of a thunderbolt when, from snow-capped towers of Olympus, the Cloud Gatherer roars with anger and unleashes his power across the sky. Then the manes of our horses stood on end, and from their nostrils, which flared back against the wind, a smoking steam seemed to shoot against the sky looking like a sharp hail of stones from Locrian slings or a close volley of black-tipped arrows. And then, like a chariot of fire or a blazing, new-seen comet, we crashed against the Trojan line, broke it, and blackened the trail in our wake. Before us, beneath us, on either side of us, Trojans went down like sunflowers withered in a noonday fire. I could hear their screams, and, beneath our wheels and the hooves of our charging horses as we rode down man after man, I could hear the sounds of bones breaking and the dying groans in the throats of men, and then, suddenly, we were through them, through a corridor of our own bronze-armed warriors, and clear, alone in the midst of the Plain, leaving the dust and din of battle behind us as we raced on toward the ships. And then my Lord Nestor turned to me and spoke what I *had* to learn—and what you will have to learn, too, if you intend to persevere in your course: "My Lord Machaon," he said, "fight no more: let this be your last battle. To us, your ability to cut out an arrow or heal a wound with ointments is worth many, many men, worth far more to us as an army than your leadership in the field, strong though that may be."

—My young friend, *if* I acquiesce and accept you as my pupil, I will only do so after I have heard you swear before Apollo and before me that you will fight no more, that you will absent yourself from the forefront of whatever battle you attend, from whatever army you march beside, in order to remain at the rear and care for the sick, and the wounded, and the dying: you must swear to ease pain and cure, to the best of your skill. If you can do that, if you can consciously disregard the code by which Achaian warriors have always lived—must always live—disregard it, and step outside of it, and swear that you will remain outside, then, my friend, I will set about teaching you what I know. But be aware that my days are as numbered as the last leaves on the trees; considering that, your lessons may be short. Think on that, too, and let us have supper and watch the sun go down over the Pindus.

—Amphius, bring plates and sharp knives, and set beside us those strong, light tables we traded for in Halus. And inform the serving women that we will take our supper here in the clear light of evening.

Your oath, my young friend, has been well given: may Apollo be pleased, and the Cloud Gatherer, whose bounds and proper spheres you must never enter. The gods deserve our respect, our fear, our worship, but never, *never,* my young friend, *never* think to equal them with your skill, or you, like my father, are sure to be thrown down: no one, I think, can alter the length of the string; when the three have spun it, measured it, and cut it, there's an end. Of that, I'm certain, and you must also learn to recognize the moment and let be what *is.*

—I feel well this evening: the kid was to my taste, and together, the barley cakes and the honey have given me strength. Amphius, pour out three cups of Locrian wine and place them on our tables, and you, young pupil, prepare your memory: tonight, while the stars shine like so many campfires, I am going to begin your lessons; give me all of your attention.

—Here, this evening, we have taken food together, and, when Aurora blushes, we will rise and take strength from our nourishment. And so it must be with troops going into battle: always see that they are fed before fighting because their spirit, strength, and courage depend upon their manhood, and their manhood is mortal, and mortality must eat. Too often, young commanders are apt to forget that: in times of passion they hunger only for a quick victory, and the moment Aurora has colored her cheeks, they will want to charge headlong against the heart of the enemy. Fine, they only wish to do their duty; but first, physician, your duty is to see that the men rise and cook their meal early, before dawn, before they fight. On this point, never give ground, never stint your counsel; otherwise, hunger and exhaustion will weaken your force by mid-morning, so much so that by the time Helios reaches his zenith, your army will dissolve, too hungry to fight longer, too weak to retreat. And see that the meat is freshly killed or dried and salted, but if it smells unclean or crawls with maggots, as once it did on the Plain, bury it or leave it for the dogs of the camp, but let none of it pass among the men because, already, it is consumed by the arrows of Smintheus, and he who consumes the arrows consumes their pain.

—Although it is an unpleasant subject to mention while we take our supper, I caution you, too, not to allow your men to evacuate their bodies within their camps. Before Ilium, this was a great problem for us, and early in the war, shortly after our arrival, when we were careless in our arrangements, Smintheus punished the army with a killing plague; again, in the ninth year, we disregarded precautions, and this—added to the fact that my Lord Agamemnon showed disrespect to a priest of Apollo—caused destruction among our warriors, and many died. Never let that happen to your army. Away from camp, as far as an arrow's flight, order the men to dig holes in the earth; let them evacuate themselves there, and no closer, and, in order to prevent unpleasant vapors, make each man throw dirt over his feces, once he has done. If a man or men contract the running sickness, give them no wine, but feed them liberally on cheese, and during their sickness make them sleep outside the camp. But see that they are tended and, in so far as you can, ease their pain. In the opposite case, increase a man's intake of wine and olives, but in the field, I fear, you will have little of that and much of the running disease; so it was on the Plain.

—Tomorrow I will begin showing you how to draw an arrow, but some things, tonight, I may tell you about the procedure, and then you will begin to understand it. Bronze-tipped arrows are often barbed; if you pull them, the extraction will be painful to the warrior and cause much damage below the skin. Unless the arrow can be broken and drawn on through the wound, as in the case of a complete penetration, you are better off to cut the arrow out with a sharp knife, making a clear incision that is preferable to the kind of ragged, rip-edge tear that a forceful extraction will produce. As you make your cuts, let the warrior bite on a stick: this keeps him from cutting his lips, or biting his tongue, or being offensive to the gods, which is something most common among wounded men who come under the knife. A part of your practice, you see, is to heal the whole man, and, if you permit him the indiscipline of curses, you prolong his agitation, increase his fear, and send him to heal with the stain of *hubris* on his mind; In some cases that prideful stain is enough to kill the man when he comes to his *self* again and finds that *self* defiled by its own curses. Then, a man may be in much danger; your job as surgeon is to have a priest purify him and cleanse him of his stain as soon as practicable. If that is not done, the warrior may recover physically and then, considering his offense, make his own way to Hades. There is great danger here, my young pupil, to the men and to the army, and in not knowing that I made one of my greatest mistakes as a healer.

—In the tenth year, when the great Achilles was struck in the heel by Paris's arrow and killed in the very hollow of the Scaean Gate, my lords Aias and Odysseus, bitter in their tears, waded in amongst the blood-thirsty Trojans who were trying to defile Achilles' body, and, after dealing much death amongst them, succeeded in retrieving his corpse and brought it out of battle, returning it to our camp. The task they set themselves was terribly difficult and dangerous: Telemonian Aias, because he was so large and strong, bore the body over his shoulders while behind him my Lord Odysseus covered their withdrawal, dealing bloody death among the Trojans until our own angry men could move up to support them and give them cover. Diomedes went out to them, and Teucer, and my Lord Menestheus, and, just as Aias was stepping behind Teucer's ox-hide shield, a Trojan bowman struck him in the thigh, and the arrow cut clear to the bone. Aias gave over the body, then, to my Lord Odysseus, and Odysseus, in turn, bore it to immortal Thetis. Contrary to popular report—a report, I might add, that was bred by a father of lies named Thersites—my Lord Agamemnon had nothing at all to do with giving Achilles' arms to Odysseus; neither did Pylian Nestor share in the responsibility. Thetis, it seems, in her grief—assuming that the Man of Many Turns was solely responsible for retrieving her son's body—awarded him the armor in the same moment that he brought her the lifeless corpse of her son. Aias learned of this only moments before I began to cut the arrow from his thigh, but he said nothing, and in my haste, in my fear for his life, I made a mistake: I failed to place the biting-stick between his teeth. He remained perfectly silent while I cut into his flesh, sweating, shaking, not saying a word, but then, as I released the barbs and pulled, as gently as I could, the bronze-tipped arrow from his bone, his composure broke, and from the depths of his lungs he uttered a single mighty curse against Athene before passing from consciousness. I cauterized the wound then, with the heated blade of a knife, applied healing ointments in its recesses, spread cobwebs over it, and conveyed great Aias to his hut. On the following morning he woke, but his eyes were feverish, and on the next day his fever was gone, but his eyes still carried its fire, and on the third day he rose and bound his wound with a length of white linen, and then, with his sword in his hand, he waded in amongst a herd of sheep and began killing them, one by one, sometimes calling them by the names of our commanders and brothers: "Odysseus, Agamemnon, Diomedes, Antilochus, Eurypylus," and sometimes calling them by Trojan names: "Hector, and Aeneas, and Alexandros," and then, as he butchered more and more with the long bronze sword he had exchanged on the Plain with illustrious Hector, he began calling upon the Lady of the Flashing Eyes to absolve him, and this went on for some time before our soldiers, who were afraid to approach him, could bear to report the matter to us. When we, his friends, finally found him, he was standing upright, raving, amidst a field of dead and bloody sheep, and it was only with the greatest care that we were able to calm him, and quiet him, and return him to his hut, where we laid him across his bed, covering him with the skins of lions.

—I tended him throughout the night, and once he woke and looked at me, and in his eyes I could see an unspeakable horror. "My Lord Machaon," he groaned, "I have offended everywhere: I have lost *aidôs:* none will respect me." He said nothing more that night, and, as the curls of Hyperion unfurled, I left him sleeping, and sought Calchas, and found my Lord Odysseus already returning with him, hurriedly bringing the instruments of sacrifice and purification. The three of us made haste toward Aias's hut, but we were too late: when we were no farther away than the length of a black-hulled ship, a raging roar broke from the hut, and my Lord Aias, son of Telemon, the steadiest man among us in battle, staggered through the door and, placing the hilt firmly upon the ground, threw himself against the great sword of Hector. The shining blade penetrated his side a little below his armpit, and, when it did, it released his unhappy *self* into the chambers of decay. He was dead before the length of his body touched the ground.

—So stunned by the sight that he could neither speak nor breathe, my Lord Odysseus sank to the ground, and Calchas likewise, and I—I neither spoke nor moved, and then beside me I heard my Lords, and turned, and saw the tears that were streaming down both faces fall against the earth like my own.

—When last I saw him many years ago, as he passed here on his way
north carrying a long pine oar over his shoulder, my Lord Odysseus
still faulted himself, and Achilles' armor, for Aias's death. Possibly an
element of truth obtains there, but at best the armor was a secondary
cause, and when I, too, finally descend into the chambers of decay, I
shall go, I know, knowing that my mistake sent a noble man toward the
terrors of despair. You may heal the body, young friend, but without the
spirit, flesh is nothing. In my haste, you see, to heal his wound, I
neglected the one thing that might have preserved Aias's mind, that
might have protected his *self.* *Aidôs* was everything to Aias: it *was*
Aias—it was the man himself, the thing he stood for, the root and trunk
of his soul—and when, in my unthinking haste to heal a branch, a leaf,
a bud, I failed to protect the root and trunk, the great oak fell, still
physically strong and tall, unbending before the wind.

—Amphius, our cups are empty; now, in the night, as the bright stars
twinkle and shine and my memories pass before me like fireflies flick-
ering on the wind, a thirst comes over me, and I long to drink deep.
Fill our cups again, my steward, and let us sit, and talk, and consider
how—as we watch bright starlight reflected on our wine—*consider how*
our mistakes may haunt us toward the grave. You see, young surgeon,
Aias is ever with me, even unto death.

You remain silent, my young friend. Amphius, of course, is silent as
well, but he has heard my heart speak before, and sometimes, late at
night, he, too, divulges a mistake. But tonight we are not in our cups,
and you who would heal must know the truth, the worst and the best.
You—so full of hope, and commitment, and good intention—you, too,
will make mistakes; because of your mistakes, men are going to die,
and you will have to bury them, if you can. That is a fact; before you
begin in earnest, you had better accept it and begin trying to learn to
live with it. Aias, you must know, was not my only mistake; he was
only my greatest because as a friend I loved him greatly; in his absence
and in my fault, I have had much, *much* pain. But I killed others, too—
by accident, you say? By mistake, say I: there is a difference, you
know, and the difference bears thinking about. Lordly Gouneus went
down by my hand: while extracting an arrow, I flinched and severed a

main blood vessel; before I could cauterize, he was dead, his blood dripping from my hands. And the younger Agasthenes, too, died by my hand: I smeared his wound with a new herb, and he was dead in the instant, without a single pain or tremor, his eyes still fixed on me, still full of hope, his last words, spoken only moments before— *"My friend"*—still ringing in my ears. And there were others, and, as time passed, I learned caution and procedure, and in the years after Troy I continued, cautiously and with procedure, working always to reduce mistakes—to reduce their number, and their seriousness, and their frequency. I have worked sixty years to eliminate them altogether and failed. But you, my pupil, you must continue in that and advance. In the course of your life, should you also fail, teach others what you know, and caution them to teach others as well, and perhaps, as I said earlier, though we each be stalks of yellowing grain and destined to wither, perhaps the whole of the crop through annual renewal may do what we, as individual stalks, cannot.

—You see, my young friend, you *will* make mistakes; nevertheless you must go on. You cannot expect to succeed everywhere; still, even one success has value, and two successes have more. We lost many men before Ilium, and I myself lost many beside our huts, but I also saved many; in the end, in the balance of life for Achaia, it was better that I tried, although sometimes, trying my hardest, I failed. Lordly Diomedes was able to take the field again after my cure, and the Atreidae, and wise Odysseus, and at one time or another, more than a third of the men who fought at Troy. I see no cause to trumpet that success, particularly when I remember my many and manifest failures, but I am certain about one thing: without surgeons, many more Argives would have died on the Plain, and here, today, in Achaia, when the barbarians invade—as invade they surely will—the Argive armies will be much better off with you than without you, assuming that you prove as quick and skillful as I think you will be. In the morning, we will begin your training in earnest, but now, young pupil, my frozen hands grow painful, and my eyes grow dim; let us follow the example of Hyperion and give way before Night.

—Amphius, make up a bed for our friend here on the porch, and line it with fleeces, and give him a warm cloak with which to cover him-

self. And you, young man, do not think too long on the lustre of
Artemis; Aurora will blush soon enough in the east, and to my thinking, at least, her charms are far more beautiful. Amphius, your arm, if
you please; my legs are cold, now, and my knee joints nearly as frozen
as my hands. We must to bed and sleep, for in the morning, if we are to
train a new surgeon for Achaia, we will have to rise early and be about
our business.

Sinon at Elis

Careful discernment is the key. Each scattered atom of probability, no matter how tiny, no matter how abstruse, must be gathered in the mind and rolled like a pebble in a stream until its weight, density, and form naturally distribute it into its rightful place beside the other pebbles, sand, and rock, ordering it according to a clear pattern—a pattern that is instantly perceptible beneath the water's surface. Nothing must pass unnoticed, not a leaf that floats upon the current, not even a particle of loam that has fallen away from the bank to swirl hopelessly in the eddies; to miss what may seem the most inconsequential detail will obscure the pattern, and such obscurity invites disaster. No, young man, the Master of Reconnaissance must know all: he must test the waters and know the pattern, or many men may die.

—My Lord Helios, I see, unfurls the strands of his fan-like hair. Observe; already the little motes that scatter through his curls are dancing in the doorway. Let us leave this morning fire. It grows to embers now, and the house women must be about it to rebuild its heat, or our breakfast may go uncooked. Elaea and her girls will move faster, I think, and more attentively if we absent ourselves from their presence.

—Thank you, but no. As you see, I am still able to walk by myself, but if you will hand me my stick, I will show you the infirmity of old age: once I was young and quick; now I am a man with three legs.

Let us sit here, beneath these olives. In the mornings I often come here now, to take the sea breeze and watch the waves come in, resting myself athwart this bench while lordly Helios ascends. If I were not already deep into the winter of my life, I might attend to more active matters, but I am what I am—past activity—and more than fire or water, the warmth of the sun eases the numbness of my legs. Are you comfortable? —Good. A warm fleece is very pleasing beneath one's body, even here at Elis, where the climate is traditionally mild.

—No, you are imprecise, or rather your information is. Where did you hear that?

—Forgive me, I smile not at you, young Lord, but at myself. And at the simpleton responsible for that lie. If my recollections are correct, that is but one of many spurious inventions borne hither by simpering Thersites, a very small, deformed toad who thought to ingratiate himself with me by everywhere inflating my fame. I will not weary you with his history; let it suffice to say that he was eventually whipped for his falsehoods and sent into exile, and a more just expulsion Achaia has yet to see.

—No, young Lord, in the Troad, my Lord Odysseus of Ithaca was the Master of Reconnaissance. It is true that I was his lieutenant, but clearly, when measured beside his, my own accomplishments seem small. I would not have you think that you are here to learn from *the* Master. I am aware, of course, that, today, the Achaians call me by that title, but look at me: I am old, young Lord, and the title is an empty one, partially honorary, partially based on the lies of a fool, only existent because the greater man no longer walks among us.

—My Lord Odysseus was a man—how can I put it?—a man of many turns, a man of careful discernment and infinite complexity who spun and fitted his webs so skillfully that he surpassed even the spiders of the fields. As you may know, we were kinsmen, both of us grandsons of foxy Autolycus; possibly, we inherited his wiles. Notice that I say *possibly* because, if the truth were known, I cannot think that it would bear the load of such a supposition: the truth, you see, is more dependent on the gods than men, and in my Lord's case, I know, the Lady of the Flashing Eyes was his constant protectress. Certainly, I, too, owe her the libations of my spirit, and I give them to her, gladly, *always.* Time and again, she came to my aid, saved my life, and for me, at least, she rises above the others like a shooting star, pure in the light of her wisdom, sure in the touch of her hand.

—But I digress; excuse me. As I said, I was merely kinsman to *the* Master, but that, perhaps, influenced his choice of me to be his lieutenant. At the time—and this was well before that business at Aulis—I was on Zacynthos, tending and overseeing some of our grandsire's herds, and there, on a cold, rainy day, my Master landed in a red-prowed ship, sought me, found me, and persuaded me to join him. We laid over a day, putting the herds of our grandfather in order and appointing herdsmen, and then, together, we sailed for sandy Pylos, to the sun-drenched court of the Gerenian charioteer.

—In my opinion, my Lord Nestor was the greatest general among us. The Atreidae obviously thought him so because, when the enterprise went forward, they appointed him to a place with the army theretofore unseen in other expeditions. In military matters, in thoughts both tactical and strategic, he was made their principal advisor, and his venerable grey beard was always firm and wise in council. He did not command the army in so many words—the Atreides always maintained supreme command—but in the Troad, among the staff of officers who commanded the various clans, he was deferred to, and listened to, and respected as the first among us, after my Lord Agamemnon himself. This is not to say that my Lord Nestor's will invariably prevailed in the army: sometimes it did not, but whenever it did not, we invariably experienced difficulties and ended by learning a healthier respect for the old Pylian's judgement.

—Throughout all of it, the whole war, my Master was my Lord Nestor's right-hand man and chief of reconnaissance for the entire alliance. When I say this to you, I do not mean, of course, to imply that the great Odysseus deferred to the Pylian or that lordly Nestor subordinated or commanded my Master: their relationship was much more subtle than that, far more sophisticated, more of an equality based upon genuine respect, admiration, and intuitive understanding. Each used different methods, of course; they were, after all, different men and uniquely individual. My Lord Nestor—strong, tall, and grey—drew his strength from a lifetime's experience as a field marshal and diplomatist and, in consequence, and owing to his position with the army, I think, often pressed his points or approached his goals through tactful, circuitous methods designed to avoid offense. My Master—younger, less experienced, but renowned for his intelligence, and far more active—proved variously to be either more blunt or far less direct than the Peer of Pylos. But, young Lord—and this is my main point—their aims were almost always the same: in every instance they had analyzed the particular problem upon which they were working, thought it through to a logical conclusion, and, based upon hard thinking, formulated a plan for success. One might suppose, I imagine, that such a communion of minds could only develop after years of patient progress, but the facts belie the supposition; their mutual accord was instantly apparent from the moment my Master and I landed at Pylos. Lordly Thrasymedes met us on the beach, showed us up the hill into the palace, and there introduced us to the Gerenian charioteer, who immediately closeted himself with us for an hour's council, even before we sat down to supper.

—My Lord Nestor, I recall, greeted us warmly, poured out libations in our honor, and launched himself quickly into a voluminous exposition. "My Lord Sinon," he said, "your moment is great with promise. Ah, if only I could return to my youth and be as young now, as swift and strong, as I was when my Pylian levies were fighting the Arcadian spearmen in the valley beside the swift River Celadon. Their army had retired for the night up the vast edges drear and grassless shingles of the stream, toward the safety of Pheia of the dark and lonely walls. Ereuthalion was their king. He was like a god in his use of stratagems and cast ambushes in his wake, beside the trail, to cover his withdrawal after each day's battle; and twice in a single night the van of our advance up the valley, pressing even in darkness to engage and annihilate the Arcadian rear guard, was trapped and slaughtered by the ambushing companies who struck hastily on our flanks and then fell back in a body toward their next secure position. Old King Neleus assembled us then, calling for a volunteer to reconnoiter ahead and report back; and, with the spirit of adventure working within me, I stepped forward to take the assignment, though I was the youngest of them all. My Lord Neleus did not want me to go; he thought me too inexperienced, but all the same, the Lady of the Flashing Eyes arranged things so that I should go, and I went, first blackening my body with the charcoal from our fires so as to evade notice. I went out, then, amongst them, and, by climbing a ledge along the roof of the valley, obtained a pinnacle of rock overlooking the next three bends of the river. Then, as Artemis unveiled her lustre, I studied the river banks; at the first bend above our own Pylian positions, I counted reflections from helmets and noted the position of an ambush, and at the next bend, too, I saw spearpoints flash in the moonbeams, but at the third bend, I saw nothing. As soon as my observations were sure, as soon as my count was accurate, I descended and returned to our camp, and then, muffling our arms in wraps of linen and moving forward swiftly with our cloaks drawn up over our helms to prevent the glitter of moonshine, we threaded a trail that I had found, skirted each ambush, and appeared the following morning where least expected. Having split both ambushes away from their main body, we easily destroyed them and destroyed, also, the Arcadians' surprised and unprepared rear guard. On the following day, on the plain below Pheia, I challenged Ereuthalion and killed him, and Athene gave us a victory. In such a manner, I acquitted myself among the peers of my time, as surely as I stand before you. Ah, if only I were still as young with all my strength intact."

—He stopped and smiled at my Lord Odysseus and then at me, and then my Master turned to me and said, "He is right, my kinsman; there is nothing for it: you will have to go amongst them." "Amongst whom?" I said, and then both men looked at me, put back their heads, and roared, with long, thundering laughter that echoed the gods'.

—This is Dardanus who brings us our breakfast. He has limped like that throughout his life, and the years on his back are now sixty and two, or three—I have never been certain. Years ago, on the dark morning after we sacked the city, I found him in a passageway, inside Priam's palace. He was too young then even to speak, and sickly, and his leg was broken just above the knee where someone had dashed him against the wall. Possibly he is the son of a slave, possibly the son of a Trojan prince: he was completely naked when I found him, screaming with pain, dirty, and covered with blood, but my Lord Machaon healed him, and he has followed me like a slave since the day that I carried him away. I named him Dardanus in remembrance of my longest reconnaissance.

—Ah, try these eggs: they come from the sea birds whose nests rise above the ocean, there, beyond the cape. Here at Elis, we like to boil them in water and then break them and sprinkle them with salt. Indeed, the taste is elegant, is it not? It is the salt: it heightens their flavor and sharpens the palate. When the goat's milk arrives, you will notice the result even more. It will not be long now: we keep a spring house in the cisterns below the citadel, and its depths make things pleasingly cool; an entrance is beyond the lip of the stairs, there, so Dardanus will not be long.

Pardon? —No. No, I did not sail with the fleet but left almost immediately. That was months before Aulis, young Lord, almost a year. My Lord Nestor gave us splendid entertainment that night, but in the morning, just as Aurora blushed, he and my Master gave me copious instructions and then sent me on my way in a sleek, low, raiding hull, and I caught the wind for Troy.

—We made Cythera in one day, turned north, sailed two more days until we cleared the straits between Andros and Mount Ocha and went on to Scyros. We laid over in Scyros for a night, eating good food and resting, and then struck straight for the windy Plain. On the fourth night out from Scyros, under cover of darkness, I stripped, bundled my clothes in a packet across my back, and dropped silently over the side, swimming ashore north of Besika Bay beneath that long, low line of hills that Trojans call the Wall of Heracles. The water was cold there, the currents swift, and twice I nearly drowned, but Athene of the Flashing Eyes guided me on that night, urging me to float with the currents rather than resist them, and eventually I found an inlet between rocks and made the beach. I rested briefly then, restoring my strength with a small skin of wine that I had carried with me, but when Aurora began to blush, I quickly dressed and disappeared inland wearing the rags of a shepherd. And that is how it began, inauspiciously enough, quietly, in solitude and isolation. You will have to learn to live with those two, my young Lord—with solitude and isolation; for the man who would make himself a Master of Reconnaissance, they must be his only companions.

—During the two days that followed, I remained in the hills, concealed, snaring rabbits, resting, eating, and preparing my mind, and then, on the third day, as Helios began to guide his car low in the west, but with his beams yet full at my back, I crawled over the summit of

Heracles' Wall, and, sitting only a few paces below the eastern crest where the blinding sunlight behind me also concealed me, I took my first long look at the Plain of Ilium.

—Sitting here today, my young Lord, I cannot tell you how its vastness impressed me. Never, in Achaia, have I seen an open stretch of country to compare with the Plain. As I crouched there, beneath the crooked branch of an oak, listening to the sound of kites as they twirled in the sky, the Plain of Priam stretched away from me like a rushing yellow sea, the wind fluttering like a tide across its long, high waves of grass. On my right and far to the south, swift-flowing Scamander broke from the mountains and came rolling across the Plain in a wide, blue ribbon. Far away to the north, dropping its white water from the eastern heights, Priam's other river, Simoeis, twirled out of its valley like a twisting silver eel, and, turning, darted swiftly across the Plain, paralleling the course of Scamander, glinting and tumbling in the afternoon sun until it, too, emptied into the Hellespont. Months later, athwart that same sandy shore that separated the two rivers, a thousand Argive ships would beach their keels in mighty, high-prowed rows, but, as I looked out, I saw only the sand, clean and white in the afternoon sun, the sea birds diving and pecking along its edges. A little farther upcountry, horses were everywhere in sight, and butterflies, and along the banks of the rivers neat fields of barley, and orchards, and drooping poppies that covered the soil with a blood-red hue. And in the center of the Plain, rising above the crown of a long, wide hill, its towers raked by the wind, its great gates glazed by the dying sunlight, I saw for the first time the high, white walls of Ilium ascending into the sky. —It was a fortress, young Lord, stronger than Pylos, stronger than Thebes, even stronger, perhaps, than Mycenae; and when I saw it, I knew its power and strength, and knew that years would pass before we cracked it.

—When Night finally descended and Lord Helios drove his car into the land of the Ethiopians, I crept down onto the floor of the Plain and began my reconnaissance, and then, for ten long months, I lived like a mole in the fields, diving, hiding, burrowing into the earth, showing myself fully only with the greatest reservation—in most cases, only in darkness, only when my Lady Artemis winked or closed her eye but never when she smiled upon the earth with a full, clear face. I became adept at land navigation by starlight and shadow; I knew the sounds of the night, its depths, recesses, and danger points, and in time my senses became sharpened to it so that I could move and survive in darkness almost as well as an animal.

—Paris and the Woman of Sparta had already returned to Ilium by that time, and twice I saw him driving his car across the long, broad Plain in the direction of Thymbra, a Trojan stronghold in the fastness of the eastern mountains, just above the north fork of Scamander. It was manned by Mysians at that time, and foppish Alexandros enjoyed an honored place among their officers, often going amongst them for sport and feasting. But I digress, so let me return to my point: Paris had returned, by the time I landed, with Helen, and old Priam—aware, no doubt, that the Atreides would retaliate but, like his son, reluctant to give the woman up—old Priam had already started to turn the Plain into an armed camp.

—In matters of trade, you see, Ilium commanded an important position because she controlled the mouth of the Hellespont. The Hellespont itself was extremely difficult to navigate, particularly for the deep, broad, cargo-laden hulls of merchant vessels. Consequently, ships from the great trading centers to the south, from Mytilene and Cyme, and Lydian Smyrna, Priene, and Carian Miletus—ships that wanted to trade with the Thracians and Phrygians who lived along the shores of broad Propontis and beyond—used the Plain as their cross-roads. Rather than risk certain difficulty and uncertain safety in the dangerous currents of the Hellespont, the merchantmen put in at Besika Bay, offloading their cargoes onto the backs of Trojan horses or mules, which, I might add, were owned and supplied for a fee by the House of Dardanos. Next they transported the cargoes overland, under Trojan protection, to cities farther up the Hellespont—cities like Abydus, Percote, and Colonae—and there reshipped their merchandise in Thracian or Phrygian hulls which plied the commerce of Propontis. Priam and his sons collected a moderate tax or fee on every stage of the enterprise, but, owing to the volume of commerce that passed their way, the House of Dardanos prospered richly. The narrow, hard-packed road, then, that wound northeast across Dardania from Besika Bay was commercially important to every city and clan within hundreds of leagues of Priam; when the old king sensed impending trouble with Achaia, regardless of the fact that his own pretty son had incited it, he called up an alliance of his trading clients, and they responded en masse.

—By the time I waded ashore and went out amongst them, gliding across the Plain at night—often on the back of a Trojan horse or mule, sometimes in the light leather armor of a Trojan courier, or on foot, through the shadows, wearing the rags of a herdsman—Priam's own Dardanians had already come together and were camped along the banks of Simoeis north of the city. Treacherous Pandarus, the bowman son of Lycaon, had brought in the Zeleians, a prosperous clan from the southern slopes of Ida, and they, too, camped north of the city beside other forces from Percote, Sestus, Abydus, and holy Arisbe. In autumn after the harvests the Mysians moved down in force from their mountain fastness to the east and went into camp below Thymbra, and King Nastes brought a large army of Carians up from Miletus, landed them at Besika Bay, and took up a defensive position along the Wall of Heracles. Other forces arrived during the winter and early spring, and, as I tallied the number and position of each, I realized that Priam had upwards of sixty thousand men in the field and hopes of drawing more when the need arose, particularly from Thrace, where topknotted spearmen trained and hunted, men who were often described by the warriors of the Plain as fierce and unyielding.

—Before the end of autumn, I had become adept in the matter of survival. I have always had a facility with languages and, barring complications, understood one tongue of Phrygia, the speech of the Mysians, and enough Lydian words to make and acknowledge countersigns. Carian speech was so uncouth as to be indistinguishable from the grunting of animals, so I avoided their camps and the Wall of Heracles. But over the remainder of the Plain, I walked freely, although cautiously and only in darkness and only in disguise, and then here and there I was able to develop this or that scrap of information, obtain a bite of food, or inquire about doings in the city as though I were privy to bits of gossip or idle politics.

—Until the first cold winds blew down from Thrace, my isolation was light, but when Boreas burst over Propontis and blanketed the earth with snow, then times were hard, food scarce, and my survival uncertain. Then, thrice, I was almost caught while trying to steal food from Trojan stores. I had great difficulty moving at night because the deep snows would not hide my trail, unless, of course, I moved under cover of the snowstorms themselves, but that was risky owing to the fact that landmarks became covered, making me often lose my way. Once, when I became lost in a violent snow flurry, morning broke to find me beside a Phrygian encampment, and I was forced to lie all day in a shallow ravine, covered only by my cloak and a thin layer of new snow, so that while attempting to avoid what would have meant certain discovery if I moved, I nearly froze to death in concealment. On several occasions I went without food, sometimes for as long as five days, before I could steal a handful of dry barley or snare a rabbit or waterfowl with which to ease my hunger; even then, with food in hand, a cooking fire was a dangerous thing because the smoke could be seen over long distances, even on a dark night, and dry, clear-burning wood that would not smoke was difficult to find. Only once did I build a fire for warmth; that was deep in winter when Boreas blew a cold, driving rain and sent down ice, and had I gone without heat, I would surely have perished.

—In the end, when the ground froze so hard that my chafed feet bled in the snow, I crossed Simoeis over a solid sheet of ice, and, entering the hills above, fronting on the Hellespont, I found a cave and survived the remainder of the winter on whatever tidbits Artemis the Huntress threw my way. Those were difficult times, young Lord, and when, at last, the thaw finally set in and I saw myself reflected in a pool, I found myself gaunt and thin, and the pains in my body told me that I was very weak. Rabbits moved more plentifully after the snows began to melt, and the number of waterfowl increased, and finally one day I drove my lance into a young boar, and killed it, and dried the meat, and then I knew I was through the worst of it. So with spirits rising and prayers to the gods, I resumed my reconnaissance, discovering the enemy with accuracy and precision.

—Two more moons waxed and waned, and the days lengthened, and across the Plain a new green growth appeared, and tiny flowers blooming yellow and blue that hugged the earth like a cloak. And then, early one morning, as I prepared to go to ground beneath a little red-flowering berry bush, I looked out across the Hellespont and sighted a sail, and then another, and another, and then the long pine oars flashing in the sunlight, and then, as a thousand black-hulled ships hove into view, racing toward the shore, I heard the low, thundering chant of the Achaian sea hymn and knew the moment had come.

—I broke cover then and raced toward the beach, passing unnoticed until after I forded Simoeis, but once across the river I was forced to run for my life. By that time, more than ten thousand Dardanian warriors were already on the move, armed and pouring out of their camps. When I was challenged and failed to stop, and put on speed instead, they instantly caught my scent and came howling after me like a pack of dogs. The mass, of course—indeed, the whole Trojan army—was flying toward the beach to repel the Argive assault, swarming over the Plain like streams of hornets anxious to defend their nests in stinging battle, but one company, at least, came after me.

—Roaring with rage, the Dardanians sent out their swiftest runners armed only with darts, and these, well fed and strong, closed the distance between us with each long stride they took. When the race began, when they first spotted me, I was far out in front by more than an arrow's flight, but, owing to my long winter's privation and my weakness, I lacked endurance, and my long lead dwindled. By the time I reached the beach and turned west to race along the edge of the tide, I could hear the running sounds of footsteps behind me, hard blowing, and the jeering taunts of my pursuers, who, as I strove harder and harder to outrun them, spurred on by duty and fear of failure, thought me only a coward and, laughingly at my back, called me a rabbit, weak in heart and loin.

—That was as close to death as I ever came at Troy. When I first reached the edge of the tide, turning and starting my race down the beach, not a single Argive ship had landed yet, though all were close, hurtling toward shore under the power of their mighty oars. I pumped my arms harder then, and lifted my knees, and filled my lungs to bursting, sucking in great gulps of air and forcing them out again in short, heavy blasts. Behind me, my pursuers came on, while off to my left, no more than a few hundred yards away, the great windy Plain sprang alive with Trojans, all shouting their war cries, all sweeping down toward the shore like streams of angry ants overflowing their mounds after men or beasts have disturbed them. I ran then as I had

never run before, thrusting out my arms and legs with the will of a
sprinter, sweating, straining, reaching out for life until I thought my
heart would burst into flame.

—Suddenly, far down the beach a high-beaked hull scudded ashore,
driving hard onto the sand, and then another, and another, and then, in
a flash, one of our red-prowed hulls slid across the sands directly in
front of me, so close that I collapsed against its hull, while another
scudded up behind me, cutting off my nearest pursuer. Hard against the
hull, I looked up and spied my Lord Eurylochus leaping to earth beside
me. He knew me instantly and, helping me to my feet, handed me a
spear and target; then, thinking to defend myself, I whirled and prepared to receive my attackers. But the Dardanians who had sought my
life were already lying dead on the sands, cut down by Ithacan darts.
My Lord Eurylochus encouraged his men, then, and the Ithacans, still
chanting the Argive sea hymn, moved forward into the press of battle,
while under cover of their line, my spear and shield at the ready, I
hastened off down the beach to find my Master and the commanding
Atreides. I found them not far away, gathered for conference beneath a
high-formed prow, and delivered my report, accurately revealing the
Trojan dispositions, their routes of advance and supply, and all that I
had learned about old Priam's intentions. My Lord Agamemnon com-
plimented me for the thoroughness of my findings; I remember well
that my Master seemed to smile with pleasure as the son of Atreus
clapped me on my back. We went to war, then, and secured the beach,
and during the first days' fighting I accompanied the army inland,
showing our commanders many secret trails and paths by which to
hasten their advance.

—May I offer you some more of the goat's milk, young Lord? Here,
please, try some of this: it is cut squid, dried and salted, and beside
these eggs, it adds a pleasing taste. I had never eaten it before I came to
Elis, but the offshore pools here are deep and clear, and my seamen
like to dive for them and spear them with short gigs, or cast for them
with nets after the tide has gone out. They are chewy, of course, but
that is owing to their strength; the effect is not unpleasant.

Oh, certainly: there is no question in my mind about that: my soli-
tary sojourn in Dardania was the longest, most difficult reconnaissance

I ever conducted. My others pale by comparison. Still, I suppose, each in its way had value, advanced our cause. Prior to the Thracians' attempt to relieve Priam by sea, I spent two long months in Thynia, along the Thracian shore of broad Propontis, counting ships and topknotted warriors, trying to discover their plans. Then, when I thought the moment was ripe, I made my way south to Sestus, stole a small boat, and shot the Hellespont, carrying word to my Master the Pylian and my lords the Atreidae and they, in turn, passed on my findings to lordly Thoas. Later, near the isle of Proconnesos, lordly Thoas fought and won a sea battle over the men of Thrace, silencing their threat forever. And I went in on the reconnaissance of Abydus, too, and Percote, and scouted upcountry into Phrygia, even as far as Colonae of the high brown walls, checking Trojan supply routes and the movements of their warriors, and advising about when and where to conduct the most effective raids against the enemy. But for the most of my days, I remained on the Plain, scouting for the army, guiding Argive warriors, and advising about when and where to set ambushes, and where and how to avoid the enemy's.

—What was that? —Excuse me, young Lord, this ear of mine is not what it used to be.

—Oh. No. No, that was not the case with my Master, and know you, too, that that is why I call him by that name. No, my young Lord, my Master's movements were far more extensive, far more adept, and far more dangerous than mine. He did reconnaissance for the most important of our raids, entering Cyme, and Mytilene, and Smyrna . . . and Miletus in the most accomplished disguises—here as a priest of Apollo, there as a collector of taxes, and yet again, at Smyrna, as a Trojan ambassador; he entered, studied the enemy, and then came out again to guide the swift attacks of Argive raiders like my lords Meriones, Idomeneus, young Antilochus, and the noble Achilles. His accomplishment in the body of his work was immense, and our greatest generals never refrained from praising him for his insight, acumen, and keen, analytical intelligence. He almost had, you might say, a sixth sense for finding the enemy's weaknesses and exploiting them. As you may know, he himself was the man who devised the ruse of the horse after deducing the degree of relief the Trojans might feel if they ever saw us take to our ships and sail away. No one else, I think, could have conceived of such a maneuver, but my Lord Odysseus knew the enemy well. He had gone out amongst them often, into the field, into their camps, and even into holy Ilium itself; and, better than any other Argive, he knew the depths of their fear, the sinew of their resolve, and the immensity of their hope. Their hope for deliverance, he said, was their weakness—the one emotion we might turn most easily against them. He knew that early in the war—knew it, I think, after his first nocturnal infiltration into the city—but for a long time he lacked the means by which to transform his insight into action. And then, one day, we went for a walk.

—As I recall, winter snows had already melted away from the Plain, and new grass was lifting above the ground, short, green, and supple. The air was neither cold nor warm, but the trees were beginning to bud, and in a moment of springtime restlessness, perhaps, he picked up his spear and invited me to walk out beside him along the banks of Scamander. "Soon," he said, "the mountain snows in Mysia are going to melt, and then the river's going to rise." He looked away to the east then, into the snowcapped fastness of Mysia, and for a long time his eyes seemed to rest on the tops of the mountains. "You know, my kinsman," he said without warning, "my boy is going to be ten years old soon: it's time we went home, time we finished it." He dropped to his knees then, finally lowering himself into a sitting position, his eyes still fixed on the summits of Mysia, and with his free hand he casually picked up a turtle shell that was lying beside him in the grass and began to dandle it in his palm. Suddenly and quite unexpectedly, the reptile's head shot out and bit him savagely across the thumb, leaving a deep gash and making his blood flow. He winced with pain, dropping the shell on the instant, and the released turtle immediately disappeared into the river. You see, he had thought the shell was empty, dead, and when the hooked beak had thrust out, lancing him painfully, he had become the victim of a nasty surprise. I produced a strip of linen and thought to bind the wound, but he prevented me, raising his hand and saying, "Let it bleed; it will bleed clean." For a moment, he paused, and then he looked across the Plain toward Troy. "That is how he will do it," he said. "We must devise an act of deception. Like the turtle, we must hide ourselves and strike when least expected." He was up then, striding across the Plain toward our high-prowed ships, heading directly toward the Pylian's camp, his broad spear grasped firmly in his hand, and I, too, rose and followed him.

—How was that? —Absolutely not! My Lord Odysseus never murdered anyone. That story was merely a part of our ruse, don't you see—a part of our plan, the key to my success when I carried out my own part of the deception. Throughout the whole, you understand, I merely acted a part. My Master and lordly Nestor designed the entire enterprise, and I take credit for nothing more than following their instructions. The Trojans, you see, had to have reasonable motive for releasing me, or I would never have been able to explain the existence of the horse or signal our fleet to return. So the Ithacan devised a turn about a murder he was supposed to have committed in my sight, and then I told the Trojans that he had left me behind so that I would never be able to return to Achaia and reveal the truth about his crime. Still, today, I am amazed that they believed me. Frankly, I quaked with fear before them, thinking to myself that no one would be taken in by such an obvious, superficial web, but you see, young Lord, they *were* taken in: they were because they wanted to be, they *wanted* to believe. My Master was right: their relief was so great, their hope so immense that when the moment arrived, when they actually saw our fleet sail away into the setting sun, they believed exactly what we wanted them to believe because that was the thing they most wanted to believe. If you ask me what brought them down, what caused them to open their gates to the horse, I would have to say an overhopeful credulity sired, I might add, by their impending starvation. Like the turtle, our last sure thrust was nasty and unforeseen, but just.

—Helios grows stronger, does he not? For you, I think, a little more shade may be desirable. —For me? No. Thank you, my Lord, but I will remain here where my legs are exposed and my joints may be soothed by his warming beams. But you must move closer to the tree trunk, there, where the air will be more pleasant for you.

—Dardanos, perhaps our friend would like a cup of that clear, cold water that is stored in the cisterns, and bring me a cup, too, if you will.

Indeed, the waters of Elis are sweet and gladsomely quench one's thirst. Would you join me in another cup? —Good. —Dardanos, if you will do us the service, I think that we will drink deep.

—Your grandfather, young Lord—may the Cloud Gatherer preserve him—was a respected friend to me, and I am honored that he has sent you to me for instruction. My Lord Peneleos commanded a great army before Ilium, and there I often fought beside him, guiding the young Boeotians into battle. They were splendid fighters in strong bronze ranks, simply splendid; when they went out together to meet the enemy in close armed combat, neither Trojan nor Pelasgian could withstand them. For me, it is an pleasurable honor to think that again in some way I may serve them, aiding Achaia while I do so.

—Know you, then, my young Lord, that the reports I have received are sketchy, none too thorough, and slightly out of date. Nevertheless, I have carefully analyzed the information, and, after having weighed, in my own mind, the various atoms of probability, I have prepared an estimate. Now, I want to communicate it to you.

—The barbarians, young Lord, constitute the most dangerous threat that Achaia has faced since the close of our campaign in the Troad. Even our most conservative appreciations place the number of warriors that they are capable of putting into the field at well above one hundred thousand men. If Achaia expects to survive, the great alliance must be revived and a unified plan developed.

—As you know, I'm sure, before his death my Lord Machaon repulsed two barbarian thrusts toward Tricca. More recently, lordly Eurypylus aided the Dodonians in soundly defeating a barbarian force of more than six thousand men which crossed the swift-running Haliacmon to invade Epirus. At the time both encounters were widely heralded in Achaia as decisive victories, but such reports show a will to ignorance on the part of our people, shame us by their lack of understanding, and demonstrate the same kind of hopeful credulity that the Trojans exhibited when they allowed my Master to manipulate them and bring down their city. As far as I am concerned, the barbarians' attacks have been no more than probes, feints designed to test our resolve, study our tactics, and reveal our weaknesses. Even now, in my opinion, their major thrust is only beginning.

—Three years have passed since my Lord Machaon defeated those small raiding parties that came against him in the passes above Tricca and two since the brave Eurypylus enveloped that larger barbarian horde before Dodona. In the interim Achaian frontiers have remained silent, but now, I understand, the barbarians are on the move, pouring down into the lands of the Dolopians, their flanks guarded by the snow-capped Pindus to the east and the high-flowing flood of Achelous to the west. The Dolopians have not been strongly led since greying Phoenix left them to follow the great Achilles to Troy: they suffer famine and much disease, I hear, and I tell you, my young Lord, they will not stand; they were already on their knees before the barbarian swarm ever thought to strike them. Mark my words, young Lord, if their retreat has not already begun, you will soon see Dolopians streaming out of their homeland into the safer valleys of Aetolia, Phthia, and Thessalia.

—Indeed, if a Dolopian rout is not already an accomplished fact, it *will* be, I assure you; I stake my reputation on it. And then, young Lord, where will Achaia be? The answer to that, I fear, is clear enough and sobering: like the sharp blade of a bronze-tipped spear, a legion of barbarians will be pressed against our northern heart; one sharp thrust and they must cleave us in two.

—So, you see, the moment *is* critical; there can be no question about it. But reflect. Barbarians though they may be, untutored though they may be, these Encheleans are by no means foolhardy. Heretofore, they have shown a cautious cunning in the timing of their attacks; notice that I say nothing about their tactics, which, in so far as we have seen, rely only on mass and savage exhibitions of courage. No, I do not speak of their tactics; instead, I'm thinking of their preparation, their apparent hesitation to attack until they have first stopped to probe, and probe, and find a weak spot. You see, they have given themselves away by that procedure, just a little, just enough, and we must use it against them. In my opinion, having measured Dolopia's weakness, they will overrun the region with ease, but then, I believe, they will halt along the white-watered banks of Achelous, consolidate their gains, and hesitate. They will not go over to the attack again, I suggest, until they have probed our strength in Aetolia, Phthia, and western Thessalia, looking for our softest spot. In that moment, while the barbarians hesitate, Achaia must strike and win.

—You are aware, I'm sure, that Achaian kings have not been idle: diplomatic preparations to revive the alliance are already going forward, and in many places—Euboea, Aetolia, Thesprotia, Phthia,

Locris, Thessalia, Athens, and your own Boeotia—armies have already taken the field to train and harden themselves for war. But we have much to learn, *much,* young Lord: none of the old generals survive now; all of them are sick, or dying, or dead, and their wealth of experience is lost to us. To the best of my knowledge, I am one of only a handful who remain alive, and you can see for yourself that I am fallen into the sear. But I am thankful that my mind remains clear, and that is why you are here, to talk with me and learn whatever I can teach you about the crafts of war and reconnaissance. Then, my young Lord, when we have finished, you and I, you must become the Master of Reconnaissance for all Achaia; you yourself must choose lieutenants and travel north into Dolopia to become the eyes and ears of Achaia. We are too few, I think, to probe with an army as the barbarians do, and in truth the practice is wasteful of lives. Furthermore, as I said earlier, it gives away the game. No, Achaia must be smarter than that, more clever, and probe inconspicuously with trained individuals. Go north, my young Lord, observe, collect, and roll together all the tiny scattered atoms of probability, and then, judging from the information you send back, Achaia will know when and where to strike.

—Something, young friend, a little thing that I said to you a moment ago was misleading, inaccurate. Do you know what it was? — Consider? This is important, now, because *now* we begin your training. What was my inaccuracy? Once, you see, I misspoke myself intentionally, sending before you like a tiny hummingbird a little imprecision that hovered, fluttering before you for the golden length of a second, before disappearing quietly on the transparent wings of the wind.

—That's it! Certainly, young friend, proud Neoptolemus not only survives but continues to lead in Phthia, old but strong and healthy, the lord of his land, the king of the Myrmidons. Tell me, why did you not correct me when I cunningly glossed over such an important general?

—Exactly as I thought: courtesy, young Lord, *is,* indeed, a great virtue, particularly among men who claim to be civilized, diplomatic, and noble. But put courtesy aside in your mind for those parts of your life—and many I hope they will be—that *will be* civilized, diplomatic, and noble. Your life in reconnaissance will not be one of those parts, and the virtues you must now develop are qualities altogether more suited to the tasks you face, and the dangers: intellect, the ability to observe and analyze, a passion for detailed accuracy, something like the intuitive foresight of the Daughter of Zeus, and last, young sir, the strength of the fox, cunning. In the future, when speaking with your superiors, be precisely accurate even to the edge of discourtesy. Let your brother officers be politic and diplomatic; leave such things for the sea commanders, or the ambush leaders, or the guards officers. Your job is fact, cold accuracy, and objective analysis. Tend properly to your job and you will never mislead a commanding superior because you will have presented him with the truth. Now, having unveiled my intentional misrepresentation and swept away your courteous reservations, what do we both know to be true?

—That is correct. Everywhere in Achaia, the Argive alliance revives, comes together, and grows more united—everywhere but in Phthia, where the headstrong son of Achilles refuses to join us. Phthia, my Lord, is a wide crack in our front, and sooner or later the barbarians will discover it.

—No, my young Lord, the problem is far more complex than that. Swift-footed Achilles was a noble man, indeed. In that man, I tell you, one saw civilization, one saw diplomacy and courtesy, one saw nobility. He was a giant among men: physically, he rose above us like a tall tower, and in reality, I think, he was our wall, our bulwark against the Trojans. When we went into battle, the man was everywhere at once, pressing our attacks forward, fending off enemy assaults, protecting and nurturing the Argive army—our heart's core, our brightest star. Beside our high-prowed ships, in the huts of our camp, he was the gentlest man among us, a lover of music, and song, and gifted, refined conversation. Young though he was, he was a paragon of dignity, and then one day in the ninth year, for reasons that still, to me, seem strangely obscure, his temper was touched, and, in a burst of pride that nearly destroyed us, his character became unhinged. He recovered, of course, but he was never the same man after that; he was either more or less than the rest of us, and he fought darkly, and he died pathetically, at the hand of a fop who unexpectedly struck him down by shooting an arrow into his weakest spot, his heel. For me, he will always remain something of a symbol, an enigmatic one, if you like, of Achaia's potential, of what Achaians might be. On the other hand, in the hours of his wrath, he showed us, I think, some of our lowest limits—the dangers of pride and the bloody stench of destruction that always trails in its wake. One would think, remembering him, that his rise and fall would serve as examples to Achaia, that his life would stand like a beacon before us, and perhaps it does, or will, but to my personal regret his son has largely ignored, or completely misunderstood, that example, and today in Phthia his leadership exhibits only the most dangerously maddened aspects of his father's character.

—Truly, as I sit here before you, young Lord, I cannot say that proud Neoptolemus has changed much since the days when I knew him, long ago in his youth, far away in the Troad. He joined us at war only after his father's death, and almost from the moment he set foot on the Plain we began to call him the Butcher. You see, we had been at war for ten long years by that time; Achaian manpower was much depleted; and for the good of the alliance the Atreides, the Pylian, my Master, and all of the other surviving generals had resolved to conserve lives, reducing Troy with as little additional death as possible. Thus the ruse of the horse was well into preparation. When the son of Achilles, young and proud, arrived from Scyros, he exhibited nothing but hot contempt for the generals of the army, laughed at them, called them antiquated, and took his Myrmidons over to the attack in ways so reckless, fierce, and inhuman that he destroyed more than a third of his own company in less than a month: "Attack. ATTACK. ATTACK!" That was all we ever heard from him, and it is a credit to the loyalty of the Myrmidons that they continued to follow him. Finally, in order to put an end to his useless bloodletting, we advanced our timetable for the ruse by more than a week, gave him his father's place in the horse, and only then, by indirection, coaxed him from the field and his endless, pointless killing on the Plain.

—Inside the horse, on the night that the Trojans pulled it into Ilium, my Master had the greatest difficulty quieting and controlling Neoptolemus. He was only able to do so by shaming the boy with the memory of how much Achilles had admired the ruse; thus they avoided premature detection by the Trojans, but even his respect for his father, for what he thought his father was like, could not constrain Neoptolemus for long. When the trap was finally sprung, the ropes let down, and the Argives let loose on the city, wrathful Pyrrhus became instantly crazed and raged through Ilium like a fire, overpowering life with death, killing old men, women, children, and Trojan warriors with such rabid savagery that nothing could stop him.

—That was a horrible night in Troy, for friend and enemy alike. Following Pyrrhus's lead, the men went absolutely mad, launched a Herculean fit of butchery, and ignited a bloodlust that ran through the army like a burning fever. Blood ran everywhere: everywhere the floors, the walls, the streets were drenched with it, sticky with it, begrimed, smeared, and smoking; the smell of death rose like a dark cloud, overpowering life, and hope, and sanity until the men ranged like beasts, killing anything that moved, even the dogs. In the palace, they say, the son of Achilles became so enraged that his mouth foamed red: he struck off Priam's head, there, with a single blow and tossed it spurting into Hecuba's lap. Then, with his own bloody hands, he snapped her neck like a twig. It all happened very quickly, I'm told, and our men were horrified, and then, before Diomedes or my Master could move to stop him, he also snatched up Hector's son from his mother's breast and, dashing the boy's head against the throne, shattering it like a ripe melon, cast the body high over the palace wall and onto the rocks below. —It went on for hours, my Lord, the killing, until it sickened the whole army and the recoil brought them vomiting from the gates of the city.

—And this is my point, young Lord: I think there has been no change in Pyrrhus of Scyros. Today in Phthia, where he is called Neoptolemus by the Myrmidons, I hear the same wrathful butcher's cry, "Attack. ATTACK. ATTACK!" The Myrmidons have a mighty army, my Lord, more than twenty thousand strong, and they are ready and well trained to take the field. If they could be brought agreeably into the alliance and used as shock troops in the van, they would give us great strength and aid mightily in repelling the invaders, but, unfortunately, I do not foresee that happening. By the hand of Ares, no, my young Lord: Pyrrhus is too wild, too filled with pride, too mad to join a concerted action; he will fight alone, thinking in his madness that the Myrmidons will prevail. But this time, you see, the Atreides, the Pylian, and my Master will not be there to restrain him; outnumbered so greatly, the Myrmidons cannot survive. So watch, my young Master of Reconnaissance, and listen; when the barbarians move to attack Phthia, or when Neoptolemus moves up into Dolopia, seeking to attack the barbarians, *then*, Lord, the time will be ripe. Pyrrhus will never bother to tell us what he is doing, so you, young friend, must sense it, report it, and, for the remainder of the alliance, coordinate the times of our attacks so that we all may strike the barbarians at once, so that the Argives may *seem* to present a united front. Allow the barbarians to absorb the initial Myrmidon blow; then, when their warriors are distracted, the remainder of the alliance must fall upon their flanks, one army marching up from Aetolia while the other strikes from the heights of the Pindus. In this way, whether Pyrrhus wants it or not, whether he allies with us or not—and if we have the will of the gods—we may crush the barbarians between two massive horns on the Head of a Bull. If you succeed, young Lord, Achaia may still have a chance to survive: if you fail, I expect to see the barbarians on the Gulf of Corinth within the year, and shortly after that they will come amongst us here in the Peloponnese.

—My young Lord, Helios rides high now, approaching the zenith of his course. Perhaps you would care to walk out for a while with Dardanos and allow him to show you the citadel, the arms and treasure rooms, and our intricate system of cisterns for catching and storing rainwater. For myself, I think I must sleep for an hour, here in the sun, and then we will take our lunch. When our tables are cleared away, I want you to show me some of the disguises you intend to wear during your long journey into the North. If you are to pass in Dolopia, even at night, as a shepherd, or a slave, or a singer, we want to be sure that not even assiduous barbarian discernment, or a chance rolling of the atoms of probability, will unlock your identity.

Menestheus at Athens

No, my Lords, little Peteos is my *great*-grandson, the son of my son's son. You see, I *am* much older than you thought: the years on my back are now eighty and four, so perhaps you may want to reconsider the request that you have so graciously made. I am honored, certainly, that the kings of Achaia think me worthy of such a trust, and, when you return to your various homes, please convey my salute to each of your monarchs, too, for his choice of an ambassador: each of you has urged his case with tact and courtesy, so I bask in the warmth of your words.

—My Peteos, cast thy ball in the court below—there, near thy brothers and sisters, by the pool. —No, *Gumpa* must speak with these gentlemen of Achaia now, but later, before the sun sets, I will tell you a story, and *then* we will play again with your ball. —Yes, my boy, *Gumpa* promises. Fly along now, and imitate the eagle with your silence, and be kind to your sisters.

—He is not yet four, my Lords, but see how he runs; by the hand of the Cloud Gatherer, he is going to be swift-footed, I think, and a great spearman. —Oops. Well, the negotiation of steps is ever a problem, for the old as well as the young, as my experience lately has shown me. Thank you, my Lord of Salamis, but he is a sturdy boy, and see, his mother already gathers him. Thus, an end to pain.

—Please, noble ambassadors, please seat yourselves. I myself would stand in your honor, but the joints in my legs are no longer as firm as they were when I marched in the Troad, and now, in the afternoon of my life, I find it necessary to sit and take strength from the sun. Thus, you find me here on my porch, my third leg resting beside me.

—Oeneus, my steward, have tables placed beside us, and wine, and a luncheon fit for the ambassadors of Achaia—something not unbefitting the glory of Athens.

I am aware, of course, my Lords, of the threat that we face. As you know, we have a man in Dolopia—in fact, many men—men trained by Lord Sinon himself, and the reports they send back are grievous to my ears. The barbarians are numberless, my Lords, and fearless, and they are overrunning the entire province with a swiftness that curdles my blood. In the Pindus, I understand, Lord Machaon's sons still hold the passes, so for a while Thessalia remains safe. And to the west my Lord of Dodona reports that he continues to hold his line along white-watered Achelous. My appreciation is that the barbarians could overrun either army at any time, but, if I correctly apprehend their intentions, I do not think the barbarians are interested; rather, I think they intend to press south, cutting our alliance in half. Even now, I'm told, their scouts are already being seen along the borders of Aetolia and Phthia. Does this information accord with your own?

—As I thought. The northern heart of Achaia faces a great danger, my Lords. If the Myrmidons, the Phthiotes, could be persuaded to join the Argive alliance, our case would be tremendously strengthened, but perhaps, as you are aware, my Lord of the Myrmidons exercises prideful independence of mind—it was even so in the Troad, I must report— and in my estimation he will elect to follow his own council, maneuvering his own army with little regard for the needs of the alliance, and that will be unfortunate. I think that in the face of this present peril a unified command and a unified plan are both essential to Achaian survival; one army alone has little chance against these barbarians, but, unless I misconstrue, that will be the way the Myrmidons respond to the threat. Neoptolemus has given his army superb training, raising their offensive spirit to a peak, but, much as I might like to, I cannot believe for a moment that either quality will be a match for the enormity of the barbarian numbers.

—Those, my Lords, are the facts as I see them. In my grey old age, my usefulness to Achaia is swiftly coming to an end, but I will do this much: I will go north in person and remonstrate with Neoptolemus. But I must warn you at the outset that I am not likely to prevail; he had a small opinion of my worth at Troy, and I doubt that the years will have altered his attitude toward me. Know you, my Lords, that sixty years ago, on the Plain, your fathers and grandfathers held a high regard for the skill with which I handled my Athenian infantry. Indeed, gentlemen, I am honored by that memory, and I am honored, too, by the confidence you and your masters show in me today, but do not expect Pyrrhus to share your enthusiasm. His attitude toward my ideas about maneuver, economy of force, and concentration was—and, I'm sure, still is—that they were the mouthings of an old woman, too weak to attack, too timid to fight and prevail. He told me as much, more than once, before Ilium, and, judging from what I hear about the new Phthian army, I cannot think his views have changed. His is an army designed to shock, designed to crush the enemy with a single blow, but such a force will not prevail in Dolopia, I think, where the odds will be as great as seven to one: the barbarians will simply ingest him like an owl swallowing a mouse. Still, I will go into Phthia and do what I can.

—Ah, gentlemen, our dinner arrives. The dish that Oeneus places before us is a Mysian delicacy that we learned to prepare in the Troad. The meat is white, you see, and taken from a bull's head that is wrapped first in clay and then buried in coals for the length of a day. We serve it with olives, and barley cakes, and cool skins of Euboean wine from the hills above Eretria. —Please, proceed.

Now, my Lords, concerning this other matter, it is my opinion that you should reconsider, that your masters, the kings of Achaia, might make a much better choice to lead their embassy to the barbarians, might better serve our cause with a younger, more able man.

—Pardon, my Lord? —No, my Lord, you are the victim of a false impression. While it is true that I have some experiences as a diplomatist, some skill as an ambassador and negotiator, the story to which you refer is a misrepresentation of fact. I was never my Lord Agamemnon's chief diplomatist at Troy: I am acquainted with the story to which you refer, but I assure you all, my Lords, it is adamantly untrue. A person named Thersites, a person who . . . well, who tended to metamorphosize fact according to his need, was responsible for that part of my reputation as a diplomatist, and, owing to the falsity of his claims—this one and others—I decline to respect him for the empty honors he so mendaciously heaped on my head. The exaggeration was given birth, I believe, right here in Athens, even before I had returned home from the Troad. From my present vantage point in time, I can assure you that *the person's* primary interest was in flowering his own path; he came among my people early after his return, and, owing to his falsifications, they were misled to honor him as a man of my own right hand. He remained in Athens several weeks, living extremely well, but overshot himself a little near the end of his stay by suggesting to the elders—members, mostly, of my own family—that I had no intention of returning to Athens after the war but planned, instead, to conquer and rule Melos. When *the person* suggested, next, that he might be a suitable replacement on the throne, the elders of the city concluded that an ass had brayed and invited it to depart, and it departed, I'm told, in some haste, disappearing into the Argolid just ahead of a tempest of stones.

—No, my Lords, I assure you that the truth about Menestheus of Athens is something much less than you have been led to believe, and I apologize for any delusion that *the person* may have created. Someone, I heard, punished him for other fabrications he contrived, but the facts of the case have escaped me. —No, gentlemen, in the Troad, I was merely a commander of infantry, a setter of ambuscades, a leader in night assaults, a lieutenant on the Plain, and many were the men whose abilities exceeded my own: my Lords Nestor, the Atreides, the Aiantes, kingly Idomeneus, brave Diomedes, young Antilochus . . .

—Oh, indeed, my Lord, the great Achilles was in a class by himself—noble, cultured, brave beyond words. In my youth, I felt fortunate to count him among my friends, and today I revere his memory.

—Who, my Lord? —Yes. Oh yes, I was coming to that, and that, no doubt, is where *the person* found the source for his misinformation about me, but, again, the facts are far less than his claims. It *is* true, my Lords, that I was sometimes employed on diplomatic missions, but always—and this is my main point of clarification—always as an aide or assistant to the Man of Many Turns. Never once did I conduct an embassy alone, and truthfully, my Lords, I had no such desire, not when I could accompany the Ithacan and observe the skill and care with which he handled the Atreides' interests. No, gentlemen, I assure you that I was perfectly content to observe, listen, and wonder at the craft of the master.

—My Lord Odysseus, as I'm sure you have heard, was not a man who excelled, particularly, in physical features, and in comparison with others on the Plain—Achilles, Aias, Diomedes, young Antilochus—he was . . . well, by no means as powerfully built or able as a fighter. Now as I say that, I want to qualify, of course, because today, measured beside the average Argive spearman, my Lord of Ithaca might exceed him by a full factor of two. But in the Troad, his own physical presence was average, a norm among heroes, and the mere sight of him in the midst of his contemporaries raised no special suggestion of his worth. I mention this because in the beginning, before I learned to appreciate his worth, I considerably underestimated his person and his value; as far as I was concerned, when we went out to the Troad, he was merely one more king. But then something happened that changed my mind; then, my Lords the Atreides sent us swiftly across the Plain on the first and the last of our open embassies into Ilium. We had other meetings with the House of Dardanos, of course, but those were secret, held in whispers at night under the cover of darkness, and I did not attend them, never entering the city again until the dark hour when the city fell, when our men from the horse opened the massive Scaean Gates, and my Athenian infantry poured through. No, my Lords, I went publicly into Ilium only once, for the expressed purpose of seeking peace, and on that occasion I learned the Ithacan's worth.

—Ah, my Lord of Locris, your plate is empty. Oeneus, attend our guest, and now I think, too, that the house women should bring before us the peppers stuffed with cheese, and the tender meat of a boar, and the barley cakes browned with honey, and the fish, dried and salted, that our seamen have brought up from the Saronic Gulf. Please, my Lords, indulge yourselves, and pour generously to the Cloud Gatherer, who watches us from above.

Yes, as I was saying, I went only once into Ilium for purposes peaceful; that was three days after the beginning of the war. You see, we Argives landed at Troy early on a clear spring morning when, scudding through the waves like hunting sharks, we beached our black-hulled ships at the foot of the Plain and leapt to the earth for war. For three days afterwards we fought a pitched battle with the Trojans unequalled in its fury at any time thereafter save in the ninth year of the war when the valiant Hector struck us so hard with his last counteroffensive. On the third day, by the time Helios had reached his zenith, a lull had developed: quite simply, both sides had fought to exhaustion. Behind the Argive lines, which had fought slowly but steadily up from the beach toward the city, hundreds of our Achaian brothers were lying dead or wounded in the dusty, trampled grasses of the Plain and beside them, many more Trojans. In fact, the warriors on both sides were so fatigued, so utterly worn down by the noise, the press, and the toil of battle that not infrequently they dropped to their knees and merely stared at each other across a distance, too spent to rise, stand, or fight. By that time, I think, we had already captured more than two thirds of the Plain; we were less than half a league from the walls themselves, which rose up before us like the massive white-tipped towers of a crown.

—My Lord Agamemnon called a sudden halt there, ordering our warriors to rest on their spears but firmly hold their ground, and within moments the battle ground to a stop, our own flint-eyed Argives standing silent under the midday sun while across an interval on the windy Plain the withdrawing Trojans lapsed equally silent, anticipating our next assault. Swiftly, I remember, the Atreides called for an assembly of the staff behind the center of the Argive forefront, and then each commander made haste to appear. I was out near the right flank of the army, my Athenians formed between the contingents of my lords Meges and Podarkes. Swift-footed Achilles held our extreme right flank, and as he moved over toward the center I fell in beside him, and we hastened toward the council. But when we arrived at the army's midst, directly behind the men of Ithaca, events had already moved beyond us, and we were just in time to see the great Odysseus mount his war chariot. "We will call for their surrender, now," pronounced my Lord Agamemnon. "The Ithacan goes as my ambassador with terms for Priam. Menestheus, my sharp Athenian henchman, accompany Odysseus, and may the scales of the Cloud Gatherer weigh heavily in your favor." I didn't hesitate but leapt quickly onto the chariot beside the Ithacan, my ears tingling with excitement, and then we were away, sweeping across the broad, dusty Plain like eagles on the wing.

—"Will they surrender, do you think?" I said to my Lord Odysseus. "No," he said. "This is a ruse, to rest our troops. The Trojans know it, and we know it, but the amenities will be observed: their warriors are as exhausted as ours. I am going to turn toward them now; raise your shield on the end of your spear so they will know that we come as envoys."

—We turned sharply then, and in the instant my Lord Odysseus raised his whip, cracking it high in the air above his horses' heads. Like flaming thunder the pair bolted forward, charging straight toward the center of the long Trojan line. Raising high my shield, I saw the line draw back, parting before us like a human furrow, and suddenly we were through, having glanced neither right nor left, but looking only straight ahead, clear-eyed, up past Priam's great oak, past the lonely fig which stood before the walls, straight toward the Scaean Gates, which loomed larger and larger as we approached until they seemed like the faces of snowy Helicon folding open before us. My Lord's horses never faltered a step but shot straight through the opening like flint-maned arrows, and the great gates crashed closed behind us with the long echo of thunder.

—Inside the city my Lord Odysseus neither flinched nor flared but stood firmly to his reins, grim-eyed and keen. Our horses continued to bolt forward, snorting hard up the high stone street, turning, pressing forward again past house after house painted blue like the clouds, turning sharply around a tall white temple of stone, catching the wheel ruts of another long, ascending street that narrowed near its end until suddenly we shot through a second great gate capped by sleek marble horses prancing upward toward the sky. "This is the citadel," said my Lord Odysseus, reining in his pair. "Walk beside me now, but say nothing. Look as if the issue is decided: make your eyes shine with victory."

—Dismounting behind our car, we walked across an open court and began to ascend a wide flight of polished stairs toward an immense palace fashioned from hard, white marble that glistened in the sun like mirrored bronze before a forge fire. "Don't gawk," commanded my

Lord, and, indeed, I tried not to do so because we were surrounded by
Trojans, men and women both, who stood at a distance, staring at us
with bitter eyes from the sockets of hard bronze helms topped by horse-
hair plumes or from beneath delicately smooth curls of feminine coif-
fures, staring but saying nothing, eyeing us silently with hate, or fear,
or both. When finally we reached the top, we passed through a glitter-
ing throng of these people, who backed slowly, silently away from us,
and then entered a throne room brilliantly lighted by fires. Against the
far wall, raised on a dais flanked by wall murals of Troy itself, we saw
the Lord of Ilium, grey but strong in his grandeur.

—Without even breaking his stride, my Lord Odysseus walked
directly to the center of the room, faced the throne, and removed his
helmet with slow, stately care. I imitated his every gesture and stood
smartly beside him, casually cradling my helmet in the crook of my
arm.

—The Lord of Ilium looked at us then, neither smiling nor frowning,
alert, sensitive, composed, old—older then than I am now by many
winters—but still sound and firm in mind as well as body. "I am listening," he said at last. And my Lord Odysseus, neither smiling nor
frowning, opened his mind and began to speak: "Prince of the Horse-
Taming Trojans, Lord of the Plain, King of Ilium, I the Ithacan salute
you in the name of the House of Atreus. Hear me, my Lord, in the
name of Achaia, for I come to offer you terms. Through the length of
three terrible days, the Sons of Ilium have fought on the Plain and
defended their homes, acquitting themselves with honor and dignity in
the eyes of Achaia. Warriors of Ilium, we of Achaia salute you with the
bright bronze of our swords and the blood of our bodies: like windy
Ilium itself, the towered crown of your glory is great and shines among
men like gold. And yet, my Lord of Ilium, your crown is incomplete:
three of its towers—the towers of peace, virtue, and justice—are stolen
away by a night thief, stolen away or mislaid. Lord of the Plain, Prince
of the Horse-Taming Trojans, Achaia invites you to recover the towers
of your crown: recover the tower of justice, my Lord, by returning the
woman and her treasure, by making the night thief suffer, by restoring
the heart of Achaia; reerect the tower of virtue, my Lord, by recon-
structing the sanctity of marriage, of home, and of family; reestablish
the tower of peace, my Lord, by ending the war, by stopping the kill-

ing, by preserving your people. Achaia invites you, Lordly Son of Dardanos, to recover the towers of your crown because they will be greater by far as defenses for Troy than that cold stone tower above the Scaean Gate. Rediscover your towers, my Lord, Achaia bids you, for if the night thief goes unpunished or the towers remain mislaid the crown must, of itself, break, shatter, and fall to pieces across the Plain."

—My Lord Odysseus finished his speech then, and stood back, resting his weight gently but with dignity on his right leg. "Well spoken, Ithacan," said the Lord of Ilium, "but we will win, I think, at the odds. Look you to this day, Lord of the Sea, and weep for Achaia that she ever invaded Ilium. Convey my respects to the lordly Sons of Atreus and take them this speech: the towers of my crown are my own brave Trojans, the fighting Mysians, the topknotted lords of Thrace, the bronze-armed warriors from Percote and Practius, from Sestus by the sea, Abydus and holy Arisbe, the death-dealing Phrygians, the noble Carians, the flame-eyed Alizones, and thousands more who will come to defend me; and all of them stand firm, and tall, and hard against Achaia and shall not fall. Return, Ithacan, to the men of Achaia, and tell them we will allow twelve days to bury the dead; then, we will drive you from our shores."

—The throne room remained silent after Priam's speech. Behind me, I heard some shuffling of feet, but no one spoke, and above us the wind whistled through the roof beams. My Lord Odysseus stepped forward a few more paces, and I followed him until we were standing directly before the throne. Then my Lord Odysseus resumed his speech, so quietly, so imperceptibly, that no one in the room save Priam and myself could hear him. "My Lord of Ilium," Odysseus whispered, "you will lose, and Troy will be destroyed. Pray, my Lord, reconsider." "Ithacan," said the King, in a low, almost silent voice, "he is my son, and she is the treasure of Ilium: we will withstand siege far longer than you can give it. Say that to your masters: the Achaians will starve to death on the Plain before the holy city of Ilium ever feels your pinch. Desist, young Ithacan, save the flower of Achaia and go home. I have no wish to see your bones whitening beneath the sun amidst my fields of barley. Desist, young Ithacan, and be gone. Return to your homes, and your wives, and your newborn sons of Achaia."

—My Lord Odysseus and I stepped back then, and drew on our

helmets. "My Lord of Ilium," Odysseus said, "recover the towers of your crown, or at the odds Troy is doomed." Without waiting for a reply, he turned on his heel and strode from the room, and I also turned and hastened after him, leaping up with him behind his horses. And then, like the lions of summer, we bounded down from the citadel, down through the narrow streets between the sky-blue houses, roared through the Scaean Gates, and struck the Plain, running hard, a horizon of Trojans before us.

—Excuse me, gentlemen, I am being a poor host. Oeneus, call for the house slaves. Let them clear away the leavings of our meal and bring us dates, and figs, and honeyed apricots, and lemons from the trees of Crete. Come, my Lords, freshen your cups.

My Lords, let us allow that I recognize the barbarian danger as well as any prince in Achaia. Let us allow that I, too, have already mobilized my infantry and sent them into the field to train. Let us allow that even in the face of enmity I know the value of the Myrmidons to our cause and, therefore, have willingly agreed to go into Phthia to plead that cause with the son of Achilles. And let us allow, too, that I have the spirit, the will, and the desire to travel even farther north in order to treat with the barbarians. But, my noble Lords, look at me: I no longer have the strength, the body, the means; I have never had the eloquence. Consider the kind of speech I have tried to recall for you, the kind of speech that is designed to persuade: beside my Lord of Ithaca, my tongue was always thick and barbarous, my mind heavy and dull. Pray, am I, a decrepit old man, really to be the representative of my people, the symbol of Achaian will and might? —The barbarians will jibe and laugh at us, thinking that all, like me, must be reflections of Tithonus. It is not a brave front for Achaia, my Lords, for at my age, I think, I am unable to frighten even my servants.

—Possibly, my Lord of Euboea, but I cannot be sure that what you have so generously called the wisdom of my age will impress a barbarian king. Still, let me offer a suggestion, a condition under which, your masters agreeing, I could agree to attempt the embassy into Dolopia. We cannot, I think, prevent their attack indefinitely: that it will come, eventually, I am certain. But let me go north, not to threaten or negotiate but to buy time. Let me dangle something before the barbarians, something attractive, the apple of Athenian neutrality. In this way, let me buy as much time for the Argive alliance as possible while in the meantime you arm, train, and fortify Achaia as swiftly as you can. In my turn, I will draw out the seeming negotiations for as many weeks or months as I am able—*this* week saying that my people will not oppose the barbarians if given specific assurances and royal hostages, *that* week suggesting that the men of Athens are of two minds and require more surety, another week offering to intercede with the Lords of Thessalia, or Aetolia, or Locris, and so on, thus holding out the hope of peaceful conquest as a ruse until I have wrung as much time from the barbarians as these dangerous hours will bear. That, my Lords, is what I am prepared to try for Achaia. I have not my Lord of Ithaca's eloquence, skill, or cunning, but I do know a little about tactics. After conferring with the son of Achilles, I will ride on into Dolopia and try, one last time, whether or not I can manipulate my infantry as a *force in being* with which to outmaneuver an enemy.

—Will this, my Lords, meet with the approval of your princes? —Good, I have a free hand then. Please to so inform your masters, but bid them hurry their preparations, my Lords: these barbarians will not be fooled for long.

Oeneus, go to the armory and bring me a spear and my greaves, and my hard bronze helm, and the great ox-hide shield that hangs on the wall. And then go you to the stables: see that my bays are fed, watered, and curried, and assemble my chariot. And put in ropes, my steward, to lash me to its rails, for tomorrow we go north and without the ropes I will not be able to stand.

—Oh, and, Oeneus, send the boy Peteos to me: I have promised him a story and a game with his ball, and I should not like to leave anything undone before we ride once more into uncertainty, once more into the unknown.

Neoptolemus in Phthia

Know that you offend me, Barbarian, and be silent! With little effort old Machaon has already repulsed you twice, and, where another of the doddering greybeards, old Eurypylus of Asterios, supported that springtime, pink-cheeked prince of Dodona, the two of them handed you a stunning defeat that sent you reeling. And none of them—*not one of them,* do you hear?—had talent enough, or skill, to command any more than a company of cooks here, amongst my lordly Myrmidons. And now you have the temerity to offer terms to me, *me,* Neoptolemus of Phthia? You are an ass, Barbarian, bred of a goat and a swine! Your king is a lord of fools! What matters to me that you have conquered the Dolopians? They were a people already weak with disease and famine; since I buried their old Lord, Phoenix, in Molossia as we returned from the Troad, they have drifted aimlessly, tossed hither and yon by fate, like wood chips in a stream. Their conquest, I assure you, merits no praise, and your assertion that you are poised like a bronze-tipped arrow against our heart is pure bravado. Consider your position, herald of a swinish people: you are surrounded on three sides: to your west the grandson of Gounes and prince of Dodona hems you in behind the swift-flowing waters of Achelous; to the south ten thousand Aetolians led by the sons of Thoas are armed and fortified behind their own white-watered branch of Achelous; to the east you are thwarted by the snowcapped towers of the Pindus and flooding Peneus, and old Machaon's sons still hold the passes and the fords; and here, in the southeast, the Myrmidons await you like prides of lions, hungry for the kill. You are not poised like a bronze-tipped arrow, Barbarian; you are extended like a fat joint of mutton waiting to be bitten off and devoured. I invite your king to attack me; I encourage him to come on, for here in Phthia we Myrmidons are lean, and hungry, and anxious to dip our swords in the flesh of your puny bodies. Tell your monarch *that,* Barbarian! Tell him to make haste! Tell him we will await his coming at Alos and that Myrmidon spears are long and sharp!

—Hold, Heathen, and wait! I have not yet dismissed you because I want your goatish king to know, when he attacks me, the power he comes against. Stand! *Stand* in my presence, Barbarian, or I will send you howling for the southern tip of the Pindus with your nose slit and your ears in your hand!

Know you *me,* Barbarian, and hear the words of the mighty, for I am Pyrrhus of Scyros, son of the great Achilles. Here in Phthia among the Myrmidons I am called Neoptolemus; all around me the hard-fighting Achaians revere me as "the Firebrand," and far away in the Troad, across that long, broad, dusty Plain of Skulls, the living still fear me for I am "the Butcher of Men," "the Sacker of Troy."

—Hear me, Barbarian, and attend my words. I do not make war like the rest of our people. The old generals of Achaia are all dead now: the Atreides, the Aiantes, Idomeneus, Menestheus, Meriones, Antilochus, Diomedes, Odysseus, the senile charioteer of Pylos, and my own lordly father, the peerless Achilles—they are all dead, and their antiquated methods of fighting died with them. When I went out to Troy in the tenth year, I initiated the change myself: I did not go into the war until my father had been killed, but when I went, I went with one aim in mind—the total destruction of the enemy.

—When first I reached the Troad, what did I find? I found *old* men, Barbarian, tired men, young men's bodies worn out by strain and time, committed men who were breaking under the tension and the long, drawn-out press of combat. Many were young in years, but the length of the battle had made them old in mind, senile in method, defensive in purpose: they had lost their edge, Barbarian; they had lost their offensive spirit and gone over to siege tactics, the tactics of exhaustion; they had forgotten how to attack. At any time after the ninth year, after the Hectorian offensive had been slaughtered, they might have sacked the city by massing for its destruction and simultaneously firing each gate.

The Trojans could never have withstood such an attack, but they never had to because it never came. It never came because the Achaians had softened and become cautious; they had listened to the counsel of old age, and in the end they sought only to reduce casualties and preserve Achaian lives. Decrepit old Nestor with his watering eyes and grey-headed ideas had finally entered his dotage and advised the Atreides to conserve men, and the Son of Atreus, more worried about Achaia and Achaian manpower than about Priam, listened and vacillated, and quaked over the condition of his kingdom, and behaved like a mother of fields and crops rather than a warrior, and drew back, and then the war dragged on and on.

—Think not to find me like the Atreides, Barbarian, or ancient, cautious Nestor, and tell your goatish king that if his armies move toward Phthia we will attack him beyond our borders. We will attack when he moves forward; we will attack when he retreats; when he stands still, we will attack; we will attack at night, in the morning, in the afternoon; we will attack so hard and so often that your men, and women, and children will not even have time to prepare their meals, sleep, or evacuate their bodies. I have more than sixty years on my beard now, Barbarian, but look at this arm: it is as mighty now as it was on the night I struck old Priam's head from his shoulders and slung it from the top of the walls, and if your king comes this way, I will hunt him to death until I hang his vitals in a tree as food for vultures.

—Bear this word, Barbarian: the Myrmidon method of war is total. We will not even leave your dogs alive. That is the lesson of Troy, Herald, a lesson you would do well to remember to your king. When, finally, I reached the Plain, Odysseus of Ithaca, a man with at least a grain of offensive wit, had devised the ruse of the horse and convinced the Atreides to follow him in its use. It was an inglorious device, to be sure, crude and childish, but its one virtue was that it worked, owing, no doubt, to the stupidity of a people so weakened by siege and hunger that they had lapsed into credulity so as to be cheated out of their city. Had I arrived at Troy earlier, I would have laughed the plan away, but it was set when I came from Scyros, the horse built; and, taking the forefront in the eyes of the horse, I watched the rejoicing fools pull us into Ilium, into their very midst, and then, when they were befuddled with wine and the time was ripe for their slaughter, Odysseus and

Menelaus checked our hand. Once again, the old men were cautious; once again, they hesitated. In those days, when I was young in years, new to the Plain and, to those old men, inexperienced, my advice was set at naught. To my everlasting shame, we waited like vipers hidden beneath a tree root until, finally, the trap door was dropped, and cowardly Epeius, builder of the horse, whose spirit had gone womanish during Hector's only real attack, fell out and broke his spindly neck. We emerged, then, descending on ropes, killed the gate guards, and, opening the gates, allowed the strength of Achaia finally to enter Troy. But even then, Barbarian, the senile absurdities of the old men continued, weak and womanish in intention, pathetic and ineffectual in action; they wanted to spare the suppliants: Agamemnon, Menelaus, Nestor, Diomedes, Menestheus, Teucer, even Odysseus—all of them—they wanted to spare any who gave up resistance. I laughed in their faces, and the army followed *my* example.

—Listen, Barbarian, and tell your king. The Myrmidons ask no quarter, expect none, and give none: we will conquer or die. Tell your goatish king to return to the north; tell him that the virtues of peace are better than war; tell him to go back, to plant fields, to raise herds, to nurture his people as I have nurtured mine; tell him to rejoice in the purity of sport, and music, and song. Tell him to take wives and listen to the laughter of children because if he attacks Phthia I will teach him the meaning of war, and our kind of war is a terrible thing. When the Myrmidons fight, Barbarian, we kill everything: we *are* butchers. The old men of Achaia knew my meaning, and sometimes they berated me for my methods, but they were fools, Barbarian; they wanted to conduct the war as though it were sport—with rules and nobility and honor. Hear me, Barbarian! War is killing: it is not play and recognizes no rules; it is simply killing, and killing, and more killing until the enemy ceases to exist, until no one remains—no one who in a later day might rise to the attack. The old men berated me for killing Astyanax, but they were fools: grown to manhood, that boy would have formed a people and attacked Achaia, but I prevented that. Tell your king, Barbarian: I snatched the boy from his mother's hands, dashed his head against the walls, and flung him high into the air to fall lifeless, crushed on the rocks at the foot of Troy's high wall. We kill everyone, Barbarian, *everyone!* First we will kill your warriors in the field; then we will hunt down your camps and kill your women and your children, and then we will put our dogs on your aged grandsires. We will break your pots, we will burn your tents, we will consume your herds, we will even open the bellies of your dogs so that kites and vultures may eradicate them. When the Myrmidons have done, Barbarian, no trace of your people will remain, and the very name of the Encheleans will disappear into Night.

Behold, Barbarian, see my army massed! When I give the signal, they will pass before you, thousand after thousand, striking spear against shield with a thunder to match the Cloud Gatherer, the Lord of Lightning. They are young, they are strong, they know only attack. They can run twenty leagues in armor and still stand to fight, and win against all odds. They can survive for days on a few grains of barley; they can survive, and fight, and go without drink. And from birth, we train them to do without sleep. Attack the Myrmidons, and we will swarm over you like clouds of summer wasps.

—Go back, Barbarian: tell your king to war no more in the valleys of Achaia, or I, Neoptolemus, Victor of Troy, Butcher of a Race—I and the Myrmidons will throw open the great bowels of the earth and drive you howling into the Chambers of Hades. Go, Barbarian, take my word to your king!

Pheidippus at Cos

News? Look about you, my friend; the harbor is filled with it. Do you see the blue-prowed ship that is anchored just inside the cape? It is from Olizon, from the land of Philoctetes, bringing sixty survivors. The two red-prowed ships beside the rocks—they are from Alope and carry nearly two hundred Phthians. And there, along the beach, where those five trim hulls are drawn up in a row—those are from Boeotia. They arrived last week loaded with more than four hundred men, women, and children. If it is news that you seek, look about you, noble Rhodian, and read the pain of Achaia lined deep in the faces of her people. Clearly, the wars do not go well, and here on the fringes we collect the debris, save it, and wait. And what you see here is merely a trickle, merely a bare indication, a sign. Already I have sent fifteen hundred refugees on, south to Carpathus, and nine hundred more to Casus of the snow-white beaches, and to tiny Nisyrus, where the seafowl nest, we have sent five hundred surviving Lokroi running before the wind. And, my friend, they are only a trickle, only a sign of what is taking place all the way up the Aegaean Sea as far north as Samothrace. Everywhere, the offshore islands are being swelled by our displaced people. As the press has become steadily greater, the overflow has spilled over even onto the mainland, into Cyme and Smyrna, and lovely Chrysa below Ida, and into spacious Colophon in Lydia, and even, my Lord, into Carian Miletus, cities which we raided and sacked no more than sixty years ago during the great war on the Plain of Ilium. Indeed, my friend, sad though it may be to think so, Achaia like the tide has entered her ebb; all that remains is the moaning lament of her long, exhausted withdrawal. Let us be thankful, my friend, that your grandsire, the most lordly Rhodian of them all, did not survive the Plain: had he been forced to see the sights we see today, his heart would have cracked.

—My Lord, forgive me; these gnarled old legs give way beneath me. I must stop to rest. Please to follow me beyond those nets where dwells a freed slave of mine, one Mesthles, once a Trojan infant whom I captured during the sack of Ilium and brought home, here, to Cos to be my cupbearer. Now, with small strong boats of his own, he is a fisherman, but he keeps fine wine and will give us a cup for the asking.

It is worthy of you, Mesthles, to have taken so many into your home, to have given so many shelter. The Boeotians are good people, strong in the justice of their hearts and strong, too, in their own right arms. An act of hospitality never goes unrewarded by the Father of Thunder, and add to his my own small reward in silver, for the upkeep of your guests. And now, my loyal cupbearer, tell me: could you possibly find a cup for an old warrior and his own honored guest? We two have been walking beside the beach this morning, and my Lord Helios has shone strongly upon us. —Ah, my Mesthles, you are a gift from the gods.

—Here, my young friend, let us sit beside the hull of this high-prowed Boeotian ship. The shadows will be cool here, and because Mesthles stores his wine jars in his house, there, beyond the beach, he will require time to go and return.

—Observe, my Lord, a sail—there, beyond the cape. Can you read the color of the prow from this distance? My eyes are no longer as clear as they might be. . . . Green? It is Phocian! By the hand of Hermes, my Rhodian, they have come a long, long way, all the way from the Corinthian Gulf.

—Who? —No, my Lord, stalwart Schedius and spear-eyed Epistrophus commanded the Phocis at Troy; Lord Prothous, the friend of your grandfather, commanded the war-minded Magnesians. They were fierce sea-riders, the Magnesians, but their citadels were upcountry, lying inland above the lands of Philoctetes. Their homes stretched away from the banks of swift-flowing Peneus, south past Mount Ossa, all the way down to Mount Pelion of the trembling leaves.

—Pardon? How was that? —Oh, my Lord, I know the story about which you speak, and I am sorry, heartily sorry, that you have heard it. It is adamantly untrue, my Lord—a slander, a vile lie that knavishly disserves both your grandfather and my Lord Prothous. It is the scum of night soil, my Lord, and nothing more. But let me lift the veil from your sight and show you the truth.

—The man who started that . . . that *perversion* had a mind like the inside of a slop pot—dirty, crude, and foul. Your grandfather and lordly Prothous were revolted by the mere sight of the man and distrusted him deeply. The thing's name was Thersites; where in Achaia he ever came from remains unknown, but that he was completely without nobility, in birth or character, has never been in doubt. I myself saw him for the first time at Aulis, where he was the center of attention amidst a swilling Theban rabble who caroused the streets, parading from one wine shop to another—drinking, fornicating, cursing the gods—running riot nightly in debauchery so wild, so bestial, that Peneleos, Lord of Boeotia, placed the entire waterfront under curfew. Then he rounded up the Thebans and shipped them all to labor gangs in Euboea, where Boeotian bottoms were being lined with pitch prior to our departure for Troy. After that, I did not see the man again until we landed in the Troad. He reappeared there in the guise of a warrior but was notorious for his cowardice, and once, when your lordly grandfather and iron-eyed Prothous fought side by side on the Plain, throwing back an onslaught of fierce and bloody Lydians, they stumbled across him, trembling like a rabbit, cowering beneath an overturned chariot. They whipped him for that, publicly, in the midst of battle, and I don't think he ever forgave them for it; the lie, you see, was his lasting revenge.

—Had Thersites not been so venomous, had he not done Achaia so much harm with his slanders, he might have existed, even today, merely as an object of derision. Know you, my Lord, that he was as ugly as a toad and not unlike in appearance, having round green eyes that bulged beneath his brows like soft, rotting limes. His eyelids, as I recall, could close only halfway, never more, and his mouth stretched grotesquely toward his ears, holding a long, narrow tongue that always reminded me of something for catching flies. Like his character, his body was deformed, his torso thick but squat and disgustingly hunchbacked so that in standing he assumed a perpetual crouch that pointed his nose toward the ground. When he moved, he minced along a pair of spindly legs, so thin and awkward that he reminded me of a field hen, and, with his short, flabby arms jerking at his sides like a pair of broken wings, the whole absurdity was complete. As I say, the mere sight of him was enough to incite our contemptuous laughter for his having escaped exposure at birth. Had that been the whole of him . . . well, he might have provided the army with a clown, with comic amusement amidst the daily pressures of battle. But, in fact, that was not the whole of him, my Lord, not at all: his ridiculous exterior merely acted as a superficial cover for a spirited mind, so malignant that I find it a wonder the man was not consumed by his own poison.

—Know you, my Lord, that beyond his manifest deformities of body, beyond his cowardice, Thersites was a constellation of lies and hypocrisy, a concentrated universe of malignance. That he was responsible for the death of lordly Antilochus, I am almost sure, but . . . .

—Observe, my friend, the Phocis lower their sail. They will come the remainder of the way around the cape under their oars, I think, and it is a wise decision. Somewhere aboard, they must have a seaman who knows the harbor of Cos.

Excuse me, my young friend. I must be careful, musn't I? If I allow my mind to wander thus, you may think me senile and report to Rhodes that I began a second childhood.

—What I was saying is that I am certain Thersites had a hand in the massacre of brave Antilochus and his noble six hundred. In the tenth year of the war, you see, after repeated provocation, the coward finally wore out the patience of the Achaian command, angered them so thoroughly that he nearly earned his death as a consequence. Much time has passed since then, and at this distance I begin to have difficulty separating one week from another, but at least I am sure about the significance of the moment. We had reached a critical time in the war, only months, perhaps weeks before we finally resorted to the ruse of the horse, and the Atreides, the Man of Many Turns, and my Lord Nestor, Marshal of the Plain, were committing every fiber of Achaian strength to tightening the siege around Ilium, hoping to starve Priam into submission. We were, in fact, close to success, close to ending the war without the kind of grisly bloodshed that later developed. And had Thersites not entered the scene, we might well have finished it without ever having had to use the horse. You see, at the Atreides' bidding, my Lord Odysseus was negotiating with the Trojans. At the time, mind you, few people were aware of what was going on, but almost nightly the Man of Many Turns went secretly into Ilium to confer with members of the royal house, returning at dawn to the huts of the Atreides where the terms of surrender were being carefully hammered out. So, as I say, the war might have ended there, then, moderately, without the ghastly carnage that followed, but for Thersites. In the middle of the night, some very few months—weeks—before the night of the horse, when negotiations were nearing success, Thersites' negligence, or treachery, permitted a clandestine Mysian convoy to come all the way down Scamander, beach along the banks, and resupply Ilium through the Scaean Gates.

—Whether Thersites was motivated by a spirit of cowardice or treacherous revenge, I have never absolutely been able to determine. At the time, of course, we assumed his consummate cowardice. You see, my Lord, shortly after the young son of Achilles reached the Plain, Thersites managed to meet him and then, playing the sycophant, ingratiated himself so thoroughly with the young butcher that Pyrrhus gave the wheedler a small command, a company of auxiliaries—cooks, skinners, and pyre-makers. Beside the huts under normal conditions, Thersites might have been relatively harmless in command of such types, but, owing to our blocking operations upcountry, manpower on the Plain was in short supply; as the critical moment neared, as the Atreides drew the siege tighter and tighter around Trojan throats, they called out all available men from our camps and threw them instantly into combat roles. In this way, you see, after a lengthy period of disfavor, Thersites reappeared on the Plain in command of his Phthian auxiliaries, one small contingent in Pyrrhus's Myrmidon host.

—For a while—for as long as Pyrrhus retained his reason— conditions remained stable, and our peace proposals moved closer and closer to realization. Then, without warning, the whole plan ruptured and weeks of patient negotiations crumbled away like dust. Impetuous as always, hotheaded to the point of blundering, Neoptolemus grabbed the initiative and, acting without orders, struck upcountry on his own,

looking for a battle, for any battle. He was angered, you see, by the fact
that my Lord Nestor had assigned the Myrmidons to guard the banks of
Scamander: Neoptolemus considered the mission to be colorless,
pointless, and demeaning to a warrior of his stature; so rather than do
his duty and accept his share of the common toil, he rashly decided to
take his blocking force away from the river. In his place, then, to guard
more than two miles of the river's bank, he left Thersites with his small
command of auxiliaries. On the staff, of course, we thought the river
was well guarded, the approaches to Ilium shut tight, but what we
really had on that chilly night was a small force of about two hundred
bakers, commanded by a coward, watching the river, while Neoptolemus and the remainder of the Myrmidons were floundering around in
darkness, somewhere east of Troy, looking for an enemy that didn't
exist, that was hiding much farther upcountry in the mountain fastness
of Mysia.

—It was a quiet night, as I remember, a clear, cold night in early
spring, and the snow waters of Scamander were still running high. At
sometime, then, under a starry sky, with my Lady Artemis at the full
bright—neither winking in crescent nor veiling her face in a cloud—the
Mysians managed to float all the way down the river, beach their
barges less than a league west of the Scaean Gates, and pass unnoticed
across half the width of the Plain until they entered Troy itself. In the
morning, while running a routine reconnaissance, my lords Odysseus
and Nestor discovered Thersites and his entire command asleep in a
gully not far beyond the point where the Mysians had come ashore.
Whether this was cowardly negligence as was then thought or treachery
as later events hinted, I have no firm way of knowing, but, regardless of
the motives, the results were the same: the Trojans were resupplied and
their hopes soared. The fact that a few Mysians had been able to elude
detection, penetrate our blocking forces, and squeeze even a few day's
supply of food into the city—less, I think, than twenty small barges of
grain—seemed to revive the Trojans, exhilarating their hopes beyond
reason. In a matter of hours, this one small trickle of food, this one ray
of hope, rekindled their fighting spirit to such a pitch that they broke
off all further negotiations by attacking us with small units in the midst
of the Plain. Thus the patient, careful diplomacy of weeks fell into
dust, trampled by the hollowest of empty Trojan hopes.

—My Lords the Atreides favored hanging Thersites as an object lesson to the army, but the moment the point was raised, it became politically complex. It must be owned, I think you will agree, that the impetuous son of Achilles bore much responsibility in the affair, and in an attempt to avoid an open rift in the alliance, a rift which might have struck a damaging blow to the army's morale, the Man of Many Turns and my Lord Nestor, both, advised against Thersites' execution so as to avoid the public confrontation with Neoptolemus that was sure to follow. Instead, they advised Agamemnon to issue Neoptolemus a private reprimand while they, for their part, dealt with Thersites. And so events fell out. In the confines of his hut, my Lord Agamemnon severely rebuked Neoptolemus for the rash arrogance of his behavior, and Thersites was not hanged; rather, my lords Nestor and Odysseus quietly arrested the coward, escorting him to a spoils ship where he was bound in chains and intended for transport to the slave markets of Lemnos. No public disclosure of the negligence was ever made to the army, and very few Argives, even among the officers, ever knew anything about it. I myself only entered into the secret because I was on staff assignment with the Atreides when the infamy was discovered.

—Had this been Thersites' only offense, this single instance of gross misconduct would still have been responsible for leading to the sack of the city, for causing monstrous loss of life among Trojans and Argives alike. So, as I say, had that been the end of Thersites, it would still have been more than enough to glut the dogs of war, but it was not the end of him, and, as events later showed, I think he compounded his crime. You see, my Lord, he escaped—how, we do not know—and, eluding recapture, got clean away. Within days, I hear, weeks before we sacked Ilium, he had already returned to Achaia but not, I should add, before he did us much additional harm and had his revenge on lordly Nestor. Oh, at the time, you understand, we had no knowledge of his further part in events—that is, we all thought him safely in chains on his way to Lemnos. Well, he reached Lemnos, certainly, but not in the way we anticipated, but that . . . well, that is something else again.

—By the hand of Poseidon. Have you ever seen a more majestic sight, my Lord? —No, nor have I. Now, even in the winter of my life, I still thrill to the sight of a well-oared ship, scudding over the waves like an eagle of the seas.

—Ah, here comes my Mesthles. Now, my Lord, you will experience the bright, cool wine of Naxos. Here on Cos, we like to take it with cheese and bits of bread that are baked from mainland grain.

—My Mesthles, may the Lord of Heaven smile upon you for the hours of your splendid hospitality.

Indeed, my Lord, treachery is difficult to detect. I never suspected treachery. On the Plain, in those times, betrayal was foreign, Trojan, too heinous to consider. But for a single chance incident that I met with on the night we sacked the city, my suspicions would have remained dormant.

—Troy was already in flames by the time I led my islanders up through the Scaean Gates and on into the blood-drenched streets. Above us, from the rooftops, sparks shot high into the night, disappearing rapidly into swirling black clouds of smoke. But below, in streets so slick with blood that a man could scarcely hold his footing, eerie shadows clawed at the walls, or ran, or stumbled, or fell, screaming moaning howling with rage, shouting shrieking whirling into the air—such a hopeless sound, my Lord, as the crack of despair—and above it all, the horrific war cries of one race butchering another.

—I rushed on, then, borne ahead by a mindless human wave, so densely packed, so maddened by the smell of blood, so hot in its fury that had I tried to stop I would have been dashed to death where I stood, trampled by thousands. I can't say how far I ran or where—up one street, down another, through gates arches doorways, over walls weapons bodies, always over slippery streams of blood, always overborne by noise heat flames, and always, always, my Lord, the shadows ringed about me, screaming and shrieking in the dead of night. And then, suddenly, I turned up one more street to find myself alone, deserted, divorced from the fury at my back.

—Instantly, my muscles tightened, and I moved ahead cautiously, hunched behind my shield, my long ash spear poised high in my right hand, ready to make its thrust. I was somewhere behind the citadel, I think; I remember glancing up once and seeing its flaming towers against the dark night sky, but the impression lasted only for a second, for the blink of an eye, before my nervous apprehension forced me to reconcentrate all of my attention on the street.

—Without any warning whatsoever, like the bolt of an arrow, a Mysian suddenly ran through a doorway, his sword half-raised, and on instinct I hurled my spear, struck him, and brought him down, my spearpoint piercing deep into the flesh of his thigh, even into the bone. He screamed, then, in short, high shrieks of pain that echoed against the night like howls from a dog that has fallen beneath a chariot wheel or been trampled by a horse. And, as his blood began to spurt, I rushed in to give him a deathblow, to silence his suffering. Only then did I discover that I had dropped a terrified old man, hiding in the armor of a warrior.

—He caught my leg, you see, and, between his agonized screams, begged me to spare his life, told me he was a Mysian counselor, and offered to reveal an Argive traitor to me in exchange for mercy. Tense in that narrow, shadowy street, I held my hand, and, while each successive wave of pain rolled over him, the old man began to gasp forth his convulsed description of a hunchbacked man with bulging eyes who had found entrance into Ilium only a few weeks before. "An information," he jerked, "he sold us an information!" He bawled, then, clawing at my spear. "Get it out! *Get it out!*" he screamed.

—I stood up and pressing my foot against his leg pulled steadily on the long ash shaft. When the spearpoint came away, widening the gash in the old man's thigh and increasing the flow of his blood, he shrieked with pain, jerking spasmodically in the sticky, warm pool that was forming beneath him.

—"What information?" I shouted. "Tell me his name!" In his anguish, he couldn't hear me. "What information?" I shouted. The old Mysian's teeth began to chatter then, and from the pit of his bowels, he emitted a long, low groan. *"Thymbra, Thymbra,"* he grunted. "Mysian ambush!" Suddenly, he pierced the air with a long, blood-curdling shriek, his whole body shaking with the cry. "What?" I shouted at him, "What about Thymbra!" In response, his mouth flew open, his jaw going half-slack until, with an effort of tremendous will, he brought himself momentarily under control and rattled out pieces of a story between his tightly clenched teeth.

—In the main, he offered again to identify an Argive informer if I would stop the flow of his blood and try to save him, and I agreed, thrusting a wad of linen over his wound and binding it tightly. His story was sketchy, of course; his suffering constantly interrupted it, but even today a few of its elements remain vivid.

—According to the Mysian, a squat, frog-eyed man appeared inside the walls of Troy within hours after the Mysian convoy had brought their few fresh food supplies into the city. The man came at night, wrapped in a field cloak, and refused to reveal his point of entrance until the Trojans had agreed to his terms; then he offered to sell both Trojans and Mysians a military information in return for silver and a guaranteed escort to Lemnos. The safe passage to Lemnos was very difficult to arrange, but apparently the Mysians managed it and the terms were fulfilled. The information given by the hunchback revealed that on the following day an Argive general would lead a strong force up Scamander, up beyond the perimeter manned by the sea peoples of Lord Meges, and up past the abandoned fortress of Thymbra. Once there, the general would establish a blocking position above the forks of Scamander to prevent any further Mysian supplies from reaching Priam. Thus forewarned, the Mysians and some Trojans, including members of Priam's own family, slipped from the city and, after linking up with larger Mysian forces upcountry, contrived a deadly ambush for the Argive blocking force. On the following day, they caught our men in the open, on an island below Thymbra, and slaughtered most of them. The Mysian victory was incomplete, and they did not succeed in preventing our blockade, but they did massacre many, many of our noble Pylians and one, the brave Antilochus, who was irreplaceable.

—The old man might have told me more, but at that moment his pain betrayed him, wringing from him all will to continue. "Hunchback," he gasped, "Hunchback!" I tried to pressure him for the hunchback's name, but on the instant a pack of Myrmidons broke into the street through the doors of a burning house, and, shouting the Argive countersign, I hurriedly grabbed the old man's arms and tried to pull him to safety. We never made it. I hadn't dragged him more than a few feet before the butchering son of Achilles, snorting like a wild boar, burst from the Myrmidon pack and sank his axe deep into the old Mysian's chest. "No mercy!" he shouted as he tore away the axe head. "Show them no mercy! *Kill them all!*"

—It was maniacal, that cry, there in the depths of the night with the city burning around us, and then, even before I could stand upright, he was gone, his blood-crazed Myrmidons swarming after him like ants, devouring everything that crossed their path.

—Look, my Lord, is not the ship of the Phoci magnificent in the stroke of its oars? Keen seamen, these. If they came away hearty, we shall keep them here on Cos as additions to our fighting fleet.

Perhaps you will allow me to pour you another cup, my Lord. Is the wine of Naxos not delightful? It is a good thing to free a slave, my Lord, when he is old and wise and as generous in his gratitude as Mesthles.

—As you say, my Lord, the matter is incapable of proof, at least on the evidence I presently possess. But in my own mind I am sure that Thersites was the frog-eyed hunchback who betrayed us to the Mysians. And I'm sure, too, that the ambush he described was the one below Thymbra in which my Lord Nestor lost his bravest son and so many fine countrymen, slaughtered where they stood. They put up a magnificent defense, my Lord—by the gods, they were splendid in their glory—but they died a hard death, there on that island, and very few survived.

—You understand, my Lord, that I don't think Thersites sold specific information about our plans: he was never privy to them. Rather, I think he sold the Trojans an assumption, nothing more—a sound assumption, certainly—and brave Antilochus had the grave misfortune to be caught by it. It was like the bite of a viper, my Lord—small, seemingly unimportant, but deadly: had it not killed my Lord Antilochus, it must surely have murdered someone else—Meges, Teucer, myself. Because I, too, volunteered to lead the blocking force. But the three sisters control our strings, do they not, my Lord? And for brave Antilochus, like your own lordly grandsire, the string was spun, measured, and cut very short, and there's an end. What is finished cannot be undone, and we must learn to live with it, but I assure you, my Lord, the gallant Tlepolemus died through no fault of Prince Prothous; that swill is only more of Thersites' revenge and must never be believed.

—No, my Lord, your grandsire was killed through no act of cowardice, through no act of treachery. In the hour of his death, lordly Prothous had not deserted him but, rather, lay wounded in the huts of the

Magnetes; poison from a bronze-tipped arrow had caused his wound to
fester and swell, enlarging his leg to twice its normal size. That was in
the ninth year, during Hector's hard offensive, when, fighting beside
your grandsire, my Lord Prothous lunged in and took an arrow that
might otherwise have killed Tlepolemus. The act was instinctively selfless, one of the purest demonstrations of friendship that I have ever
seen, on the Plain or anywhere else. Shedding hot salt tears, your
grandfather raised Prothous from the ground, the arrow still imbedded
in his leg, and bore him from the field in his arms, shielding him from
further injury with the thick spread of his Rhodian shoulders. After
leaving Prothous to the care of our surgeons, your grandsire returned to
the field bent on Trojan destruction, and there, supported by his own
flint-eyed Rhodians, fell afoul of his long-time enemy, god-like Sarpedon, son of the Cloud Gatherer, prince and general of Priam's Lycaian
allies. They were old enemies, those two, having fought against each
other often owing to the nearness of their southern domains, so they
recognized each other instantly, and cast their spears, and both spear-
heads went home deep into man-flesh. As you know, young friend,
your Rhodian grandsire was struck instantly dead by the blow he
received, but some god, I believe, turned his own spear aside—just a
little, just enough. Still, when Sarpedon's henchmen dragged him from
the field, your grandsire's long ash spear was sticking so deeply in his
enemy's thigh that Lycaian blood gushed everywhere around it, and
know you, my Lord, Sarpedon clawed the ground in pain.

—And seek not, my young Lord, to find iron-eyed Prothous among
the survivors who daily track our coasts. Know that he was a true
friend to your lordly grandsire, as loyal and selfless as a friend may be.
And know, too, that he is dead, high in a sleet-swept pass on the slopes
of Mount Ossa, where once again in his grey old age he put on his
armor and tried to stem the barbarian tide. He was a true friend to
all Achaia, my Lord, and noble in his death. The tales of Thersites
are lies.

—That is true, my friend: the doer *must* suffer. And, as we sit here
beside this high-beaked ship drinking the bright wine of Naxos, I
pledge you my word that Thersites will not escape. Once, long ago, my
Lord of Gortyn caught up with him near Delphi and flogged him for his
lies. But, knowing only a few of his crimes, my Lord Meriones did not

punish him fully; instead, he sent the man into exile, where his venom grew even more poisonous. So he eluded justice, but I assure you, my Lord, I have ever hunted him for his hair, and if I find him justice will be final. Even today, as we sit here watching the Phocis race toward our shore, I await their arrival, thinking that I may find Thersites cowering somewhere aboard: if not with the Phocis, then in the next ship to take refuge in Cos, or the next. And thus I watch, and wait, and bide my time, knowing that sooner or later I will catch the man and render justice to the long dead heroes of Achaia.

—Pardon, my friend? —Oh, yes. For many years I sent out agents to search for him, both in Achaia and abroad, but when the northern invasions began my men returned here. Several times, I think, they had been close to catching him—once in Egypt, once on Melos, and twice on rocky Lemnos—but each time, you see, the man eluded them. Now his trail is cold.

—Indeed, my Lord, I applaud your suggestion. May Athene of the Flashing Eyes always so guide you.

—Yes, you are right, of course; Thersites is a survivor and it is amongst survivors that we must seek him and hunt him down. I would that I could sail with you, my Lord, but now in my cold, old age, the sinews in my legs will no longer support me at sea: I would only slow your search and delay justice. But I will give whatever aid I can. In the morning I will dispatch my brother's son to Chios and my own strong grandsons to windy Colophon and high Priene. Send you your own bronze-armed heralds, my Lord, to Cyme and Smyrna, but for yourself, go you, my Lord, to Mytilene. It is the lewdest of all the ports I have mentioned—the dirtiest, the foulest, the most debauched—the place he is most likely to be.

—If you will help me to my feet, my Lord, I will thank Mesthles, and then you and I together will go down and greet the Phocis. Who knows? Perhaps they may be able to help us. —Ah, see how their ship slides toward the shore; their steersman is a master.

Thersites at Mytilene

Indubitably, my dears, the wine of Cyme is very fine, and Cyme is very fine in wine. Observe, my dears, I rhyme. Perhaps I shall become a poet and titillate you tomorrow with satires on a gnat. —*Oh? Canst thou rhyme, Amphimachas? Or thou, darling Tataemenus? —Oh, splendid boy!* Thy luscious throat is golden! Thy soul trills in the sunlight like a gossamer fly! Now rhyme thy coins, too, and bid the tapster draw us another vessel of that sweet Dionysian divinity. —What! Why *hush,* you naughty thing: I've *hardly* had a drop! Why, I'm *per*fectly brilliant tonight, I assure you; my hump, as you call it, is *absolutely* the latest fashion in the East. —*Well!* And so was the mother who bore you! I certainly shan't sit here and be insulted by your kind, I'm sure. Ta, darlings, don't exchange a skin rash.

Pardon, my Lords, is this bench taken? —Who? Those two? *My* friends? Indeed, my Lords, I assure you they are *not!* Those two are absolutely no friends of mine. The tapster seated me when I first entered, before my eyes had adjusted to the light in here, and then I only discovered who was beside me after I had waited some moments for a cup to be set before me. Quietly, my Lords, for I do not like gossip, but those two . . . well, my Lords, they are not like us: they are more like the mothers who bore them. That one on the left, Amphimachas by name, is the son of a magistrate and notorious hereabouts for the behavior of his . . . diversions. The other, the boy in the lavender tunic, with the pale eyes, is his . . . ah, consort, one Tataemenus, son of a tax collector. Together, they make a very pretty couple, indeed, if you see what I mean.

—Thank you, my Lords, you are very kind; may the hands of Zeus guide you in your journeys as once, long ago in my youth, they guided me.

—Permit me to introduce myself, my Lords: I am Thersites of Achaia, once Marshal of the Field and Warden of the People on the long, broad, dusty Plain of Troy, but, of course, that was long ago— long, long, ago—and now, as you see me here, I am in the winter of my life and grey like the northern sea. I live not far from here in a small house behind the theater and come in each evening for a single cup of wine and a bite of supper before retiring. Perhaps you will allow me to offer you some refreshment—a cup, perhaps, of Pramian wine, a barley cake with honey, a . . . oh, indeed? *Oh,* yes, my eyes are darker still than I thought. I see your jug now, and your barley cakes too; but certainly, my Lords, I cannot impose upon you like this, I . . . well . . . well, of course. If you insist. You do me great honor with your hospitality. I assure you gentlemen that, when I seated myself, I contemplated no such thing. If only the owner would permit the lamps to burn a little more brightly in here. . . Indeed, let us pour out a libation to the Cloud Gatherer, who protects each of us, you in your generosity, me in my humble gratitude. My Lords, I am your servant.

—*Ah,* Pramian wine is the sweetest in the East, I'm certain of it. The wine of Cyme is sometimes good, of course, but here, in this place, quantities of water are added to it to dilute its strength. Ah, indeed, gentlemen, I thank you; my first sip has refreshed me beyond words.

—Pardon, my Lords, but you are not, I think, of Mytilene? Or, perhaps, my question is imprudent?

—Indeed, I thought as much. I myself am an old citizen of the city and removed here for my health—from Achaia—long before the present influx of my countrymen. I did not think I had seen you before, hereabouts, and consequently the originality of your fashion ignited an old man's curiosity and made his tongue wag: I hope, good Sirs, that I have not offended. —Thank you. Thank you; you are very liberal. —Ah, so you are merchants from Syme? By the beard of the Earthshaker, my Lords, you have had a long journey—a long journey, indeed—fraught, I don't doubt, with great peril to your persons and cargo. Permit me to commend you for the resolution and courage of your undertaking, especially in times like these. At its best, a life of commerce is difficult, but afloat, on the wine-dark seas, it is even more so, and now, when all Achaia is thrown into upheaval by the invasions, your way of life, my Lords, assumes a danger and nobility rivaling even the daring of our warriors. Do you carry grain, perhaps, or cargoes of wine, or bolts of Egyptian cotton, or high amphorae of oil? —Ah, an even more noble cargo: on Imbros the soil, I'm told, is weak and needy; the dried goat's dung you carry will enliven it and make it prime for cultivation. I applaud your undertaking.

—Pardon? —Oh, yes, I did say that, but that was long ago, in my youth. —Yes, I was a Marshal of the Field, the right-hand man of the great Achilles. —Well, those times are long past, are they not? —Nireus? My Lord Nireus of Syme? You know his grandson? —Well, the world is smaller than one thinks, is it not? Why of course I knew him. He was a brilliant commander, simply brilliant! As I recall, my Lords, the Atreides—when they gave me command over the army: that was in the second year of the war, when I was no longer able to hide my talents in the field—well, as I say, the Atreides pointed to my Lord Nireus and told me that I would find him a bulwark to the army, one of the two or three best fighters in our forefront. Tell me, my Lords, were your fathers or grandfathers in his force? —No? A pity: he was a great man, indeed. I wish that you could have known him.

—Well, many years have passed, of course, but it is not well that such a man should so soon be forgotten by his people. Let me see; he took to Troy, as I recall, upwards of thirty ships. He had been, I am told, one of Helen's more important suitors, and when Paris stole her away my Lord Nireus swore a terrible vengeance and denuded Syme of half of its manpower in order to go north with the army. For a while, he was a sea commander and won a great battle over the Cicones, after which my Lord Agamemnon asked me to bring him ashore and put him in charge of the Athenian infantry. The Athenians had sent a fool to command their warriors, a man unwise and completely without talent, and within six weeks after landing I had had to assume temporary command of the contingent until a more skillful general could be found to relieve me for higher duties. My Lord Nireus was the man, and when we brought him ashore and added the men of Syme to the Athenian spearmen both forces gained in strength. Invariably, he used to thank me for the role he came to play, although, as I said, I merely tried him out after the recommendations of the Atreides, and in a short time we became fast friends. I remember that he used to come by my hut before the Myrmidons and bring me little gifts—skins of wine, well-made weapons, tripods captured in his raids—and leave them for me with brief speeches such as "My Lord Thersites, Marshal of the Plain, we would be lost without you" or "May the Cloud Gatherer protect you, my General, and make your life plentiful," or "The men of Syme will never forget you, my Lord," but time, as you know, my Lords of the Sea, pales all things, and when my Lord Nireus died in the great plague that Odious of Ithaca brought upon us by his disrespect for Apollo, my heart sorrowed and my protégé fell into the sear. Hermes, the Guide, who must someday conduct us all, came then and led him deep into the earth, far into the fields of Elysium, where today, I am sure, he takes his rightful place beside the Atreides on the one hand and the great Achilles on the other.

—My pardon, my Lords; I did not think so to move you with a story of your countryman. Perhaps another cup of wine might soothe your pain. —*Oh,* for myself? Well, my Lords, as a rule, a single cup is my limit. But this is a special occasion, is it not? Yes, tonight, I will break my rule: tonight, my Lords, let us drink deeply and celebrate the Master of Syme.

No, my Lords, that story is in error, I assure you. Where, by the ears of Apollo, did you ever hear such a tale? —*Oh,* yes, well, of course, that explains everything. Noble sirs, believe me when I say that it pains me to hear *that* name spoken again in my presence: I had hoped to forget it; I had hoped, my Lords, that time would have erased it from memory like a tide that washes a man's footprints from the silent sands of a beach. You did not meet him, yourselves, did you? —Good, I thought not: count yourselves spared. Of all the men who went to Troy, my Lords, the creature Meriones was the least erected of the lot. Commerce with Crete has brought home to you, no doubt, a variety of tales, and this one has done you great disserve.

—As I said earlier, I am no lover of gossip, gentle sirs. Would that a man's character could be read in his face, but the complexity of life allows for no such simplicity, and in that man's case, particularly, the face may prattle and smile, and still, my Lords, *still* speak the lie. He was no compeer of the man-destroying war-god, I assure you, and, while it pains me to speak ill of any man who fought beside me at Ilium, the truth is the truth, is the truth. Deformed Meriones of Gortyn was an abject coward who served his Lord meanly, both at home and abroad. Time and again, as we marched into battle, he alone hung back, whimpering inside his hut, terrified even by the war shouts of Priam's most uninspired warriors. And time and again, old Idomeneus of Crete, grey and aged as he was, went back with his staff and hauled the creature forth, kicking and screaming, into his chariot. He did it, I'm sure, because the slinking squire was his bastard brother, but the deformity of his body, you see, was as much an image of his character as any man I have yet to meet, and, believe me, he was enormously deformed, both in leg and arm.

—Now pardon me, Lords, because I know that as I say this your eyes will naturally be drawn to the curve in my back. —No, no; it is true and natural that you should look at me and see me bent. I am a hunchback, my Masters of the Sea. My back bends now, like a bow under tension, but, while it forces me to walk with a limp and move like a tortoise, I take no shame in my deformity because I have it as an honorable wound of war. I was fighting on the Plain, you see, in the ninth year of the war, alongside the great Achilles as we pressed back Hector's last counterattack. Somehow, a Phrygian company pushed in between us and separated us, and in the heat of the moment I found myself fighting side by side with Odious of Ithaca and little Diomedes. For a while, we held our ground, but then, with shouts like thunder, the great Hector, noble Aeneas, and man-killing Deiphobus burst upon us with the fury of war-gods backed by Apollo. The fighting was hot and heavy then, and within seconds the courage of my comrades failed: both turned and fled, leaving me to face the enemy alone.

—I gave ground grudgingly then, fighting all the way, but I was isolated on the Plain, far out in front of our lines, exposed, exhausted, and beset by impossible odds. I concentrated on Hector, of course, caused him to fall once by the near cast of my spear and immediately turned on Aeneas with my sword, but, unable to watch everywhere at once, I failed to prevent the wily Deiphobus from getting in behind me, and, at the very moment when I struck Aeneas such a heavy blow as to cleave his ox-hide shield in twain, the treacherous Deiphobus, too frightened to come in close, struck me from behind, from a distance, with a great rock that sent me crashing onto the earth. Then, being down, I had surely perished, but in the last moment the swift-footed Achilles, seeing me somehow from afar, came to my aid and drove back the enemy. I remember that he helped me to my feet and with the respectful humor he always showed with me, gently began to remonstrate with me, "My Master Thersites," he said, "an army has many men and many warriors, but only one General: hang back, my Lord; yours is to command, ours is to do the fighting. *Please,* my Lord, Achaia cannot afford to lose you." And so pleading, he helped me back to our lines.

—At first I thought I had suffered no hurt from the blow, but in the hours and weeks that followed, I became gradually aware that my back had been severely injured by the tap that Deiphobus had dealt me, and then, owing to the gross incompetence of our surgeons, I was denied proper care and returned to the field, thinking that my condition was only a temporary discomfiture. As you can see, of course, the deformity was permanent, but here, today, I cannot think on it with anything other than the quiet pride that rises from having done my duty in spite of the cowardice that my subordinates showed when they abandoned me to my fate.

—But think not long on me, my Lords of Syme, for I was explaining to you about the wretched Meriones, who did not come by his deformities in battle but came by them, rather, far to the rear, far back in our camp when, in a cowardly attempt to avoid battle, he threw himself beneath the wheels of a chariot. At the time, you understand, I was all in favor of returning him to Crete, dishonored, with his ears in his hands, and tonight, as we sit here enjoying these cups of bright Pramian wine, I still think that my judgement was right. But in this I was overruled, for sound political reasons, I suppose, by my Lord Agamemnon, who, as he attempted to hold the Achaian alliance together, wanted to avoid giving pain to old Idomeneus, who seemed to feel a lingering pity for his kinsman and continued to protect him, illegitimate or not. Old Idomeneus, of course—as I'm sure you know—lived to rue the day that he saw me overruled. After the war, as I have been given to understand, the cowardly bastard Meriones no more than returned to Cnossus before he seduced his old master's queen. Then, together with the whore's kinsmen, in an act of consummate treachery, he raised such a rebellion that the dottering old man was overthrown and forced to flee for his life, ending his days in Calabria as a senile pensioner in the court of a minor Sallentine noble, a man known far and wide for the depravity of his behavior.

—Believe me, my Lords, if your sailors returned to Syme with a story unlike the one I have just told you, they have been victims of serious misinformation, although they could hardly be blamed for that, could they? I mean, of all man's faults, hypocrisy must be the most difficult to detect; and honest men, wanting to do right by their fellows, wanting to believe and trust, wanting to see in other men what they see in themselves are, I regret to say, the most easily deceived. Well, thus the world goes, and we as men must learn to live with what we cannot change. —May I pour you another cup of your sparkling wine?

Really? May the hands of the Cloud Gatherer protect us and prevent us from hearing such lies. My Lords, I must tell you as we sit here that what the remains of Achaia need are honest singers—singers who can recall the truth about our people without either inflating it like a pig's bladder or changing it into the thing that was not. I ask you, where are we to find such men?

—A moment ago, I spoke to you, briefly, about the sad condition of old Idomeneus, but be aware, my Lords, that in the early days of the war, for a while at least, he still went out and led his troops in battle. But that so-called Gerenian Charioteer, as you have named him, was never able to lead anything; he could barely stand. My Lord Agamemnon took him to Ilium, hoping, I think, that the old man's experience would count for something, that he would be able to provide sound advice and competent, mature leadership for the army, but in the early days, just after we reached Troy, everyone became quickly aware that whatever talent the old fool might once have possessed had left him. I remember him vividly, of course; he was tall, very grey, and thin like a pole that holds up vines in a field. He had more than thirty years advance even on the old man from Crete, and before the first year was out the pressures of battle wore away any vestige of judgement he might have brought out to Troy. But the important fact, you see, is that he was noble; that alone kept him in his position until conditions in the field became so very confused that he had to be relieved.

—As, perhaps, you have determined for yourselves, I did not derive from noble antecedents: my father, some say, was a passing god who alighted in Achaia just long enough to sire me and then returned to snowcapped Olympus, but such stories, as we know, are legion among our people, and I, personally, credit the tale with very little truth. Still, by the end of the first year's fighting, I had shown such personal prowess in battle, owing, I think, to the efforts of my tutor, and shown such a grasp of tactics and the use of strategems that when the old Pylian finally experienced his nervous collapse, my Lord the Atreides called upon me in my hut and begged me to lead the army. I ask you, Masters of the High-Prowed Hull, faced with such a request, what else could I do? —Exactly, I did my duty and served the alliance. I felt sorry for the old man, naturally; his body was so overcome by his ordeal that his sons even had to feed him, and what a pair of sycophants they were, always pleading and wheedling with red-haired Menelaus to intercede on their behalf and restore their father to command, but clearly that was impossible. I had trouble, too, with Odious of Ithaca, a small, clever man who thought himself a genius and thought, too, that by seeing old Nestor back in command, he—through his friendship with the Pylian—would be able to control the army and the war, but the Atreidae were not devoid of all good sense, kept me in command, and in good time, through the ruse of the horse, I led them to victory. I retired then, naturally, refusing to fall back on mere reputation or live on my laurels, and immigrated here to the Isle of Lesbos and the quick, salty life of Mytilene. But—and I freely admit my error—it was a dark day for Achaia when I did so because, during the years that intervened, the old lords who were once my loyal subordinates on the Plain died away, and Achaia forgot me or—where I was envied, where this or that lord who was jealous of my talents took his revenge upon me—so besmirched my reputation with falsehoods and innuendo that in many quarters I was rendered useless to my people.

—Yes, my Lords, honest singers might have prevented that, might have kept alive the memory of my exploits long enough so that Achaia in her need might have recalled me from retirement, and thus the great disasters might have been prevented. But memory is a short thing, my Lords; with vipers like that cross-eyed Demodocus still casting their slanders, the truth has been lost. So here I am in Mytilene—old, tired, and forced to live as I can, long forgotten by my people. Of course, had my Lady Helen remained alive . . . well, the case would have been much different, *much* different, for she always remembered me as her brave protector.

—Helen? Of Troy? —Why, of course I knew her. On the voyage home to Achaia, she and her husband asked me to command her honor guard. Oh, indeed, my Lords, she was a great beauty, by any account, with hair so golden that the sunrise could not match it, with skin so smooth and soft that words may never describe it. She had to be seen, my Lords, seen in the flesh to be believed.

—No, ironically, that is not entirely true. But soft; word of this secret seldom goes abroad. Helen herself, you see, is dead, but what few men know is that, aside from the daughter she bore to my Lord Menelaus in Sparta, she had another child, by Paris, not long before the end of the war. —No, that child was also a daughter, but she, too, is dead. But let me backtrack and explain. You see, my Lords, after Paris was killed, Deiphobus took over the pleasures of Helen's body, and at her request he had the girl child, a mere infant, spirited out of Troy only hours before we entered and sacked the city. The child was, as I later learned, sent here to Mytilene in company with a nurse, and the nurse raised her, eventually giving her in marriage to another escaped Trojan—one Ennomeus, who at one time commanded a company of Mysians. The pair lived quietly here, in a house just up from the theater, following a peaceful life. But old Ennomeus was struck by the hand of Smintheus, sickened, and died, and very swiftly thereafter the daughter of Helen followed him into the chambers of Hades. But, you see, the old nurse yet lives; she owns a wine shop just up from the seafront, and there, in her apartments, she still watches over Helen's twin granddaughters, who are ripely young and firm, just now entering the full bloom of their womanhood. And this, my Lords, is my point: except in the color of her hair, each girl is the perfect image of the Lady of Sparta.—No, my young Masters of the Sea. I assure you, I speak the truth; I swear it by the gods. But the girls are kept well out of sight, and only on rare occasions is someone allowed to look upon their faces. A surety of silence must be presented, of course, or the secret would be out in an instant, and yet another devastating war might begin to contest their possession.

—Pardon? —Well, yes, I do know the old nurse: after all, I was my Lady Helen's own protector during the long voyage home from Troy when she told me about the woman and described her, and then, too, I was neighbor to the nurse for many years near the theater, over there. Of course, she has never known my true identity, but I have always known hers, and the girls'.

—Well . . . well, *normally,* my Lords, I would have to say no. The secret is in my keeping, as a favor to the Lady of Sparta, so I must show care, but I have told you because you are men of Syme, kinsmen possibly of my Lord and closest subordinate at Troy, peerless Nireus, and if you can give me assurances . . . that is, if you are so much in earnest as to be able to pay the surety required by . . . the nurse, well, I will attempt to arrange for you to see their faces, and, possibly, to speak with the matchless granddaughters of Helen.

Laugh at my back as you like, Hawk of the Sea, but remember, in Smyrna they call you One Eye, and the lords, there, have placed a high price on your head. —*Aghaa,* do not strike me, Seaman! I have hard associates, the same as you, and I am strong in my power: a word to the magistrate, the father of my friend over there, and you and your crew will be sold to the barbarians.

—Soft, now, listen. Is your high-prowed ship nearby? *Sssst*—I did not ask where; I don't even want to know where. I only want to know if you are in the market for an information.

—Little enough. I have had little enough out of you of late, and you and your men have profited mightily by what I have told you, so you can afford to pay well.

—Oh, spare me your threats. I have to live, don't I? I may look old and grey to you, Spoiler of Calm, but young or old, the belly must still eat, and young or old, my information is still sound. Do you want it or not? My time is valuable. —Not enough, that's not enough. —No, five pieces more, and do not think to cheat me with tarnished copper, either. My eyes are not so dim that I can no longer distinguish silver from copper even in this darkness. —One more piece! —All right, give me a jug of wine instead; the tapster will allow you credit, and my information will make you rich. —No, only the wine of Cyme; I want none of that Pramian swill. —Good: done.

—Now, swallow your tongue and listen carefully. A ship of Syme lies now in the harbor, near the cliff face, down by the swine pens. It sails tomorrow for Imbros, and thence to Thynia. I have just spent the better part of an hour with the masters; they are both foolishly young, and after befuddling their wits with wine I passed them on to the red house and the bitches of Antissa. The simpletons tried to tell me that they are carrying a cargo of goat dung, can you imagine? Well, they may be, in part, but their clothes smell more of oil than dung, and my guess is that their real cargo is buried beneath sailcloth and only a thin layer of *goats' breath.* I have reconnoitered the ship; the crew numbers less than ten, and they are all equally young. Do you still pull twenty oars? Regardless of the fact that your steersman isn't worth half a man, still, you should have an easy time of it, if you can catch them early enough. But in the name of Hades don't turn around and sail straight back in here like you did the last time, the moment the job is done. Sell the cargo at Chrysa, or even down at Chios, and lay up somewhere for a few weeks, out of sight.

—I don't know whether they are armed or not. Tell me, my Sea Kite, would *you* go unarmed in these times? —Nay, nor would I. Have you seen, yet, a barbarian hull? I am told that they are very swift.

—And don't forget to tell the tapster about my wine as you depart.

Well, my little dears, still drinking, are we? Still hugging and cooing like turtledoves? —That man? The one with the patch over his eye? My dear, you're not jealous, are you? —Well, my little dainty, he's no one to you, I'm sure. —*Oh,* don't behave like a slut, Tataemenus; he never even noticed you. And look at that succulent young Rhodian over there, the one who just came in, the one in royal robes. —*Ha!* My dear, he isn't even the least bit interested in you. Why, look at him: he can't even take his eyes off me.

Glossary

The ACHAIANS (ACHAEANS, ARGIVES, DANAANS). Homer's terms for describing the people who fought against Troy (Ilium). The word *Greek* is not used by Homer.

ACHILLES. The hero of *The Iliad*. He is the son of Peleus and Thetis, a sea nymph. In battle, where he commands the Myrmidons of Phthia, he is the greatest fighter on the Plain. In *The Iliad*'s climatic moment he kills Hector, son of Priam, field commander of the Trojan forces.

AENEAS. The hero of *The Aeneid*. He is the son of Anchises and the goddess Aphrodite, and he is Hector's cousin. In *The Iliad* he plays an important role as a war leader, and later, having survived the Sack of Troy, he escapes to Italy, where he engages in activities which eventually lead to the founding of Rome.

AGAMEMNON. The king of Mycenae and supreme commander of the expedition against Troy. He is often called ATREIDES, and when mentioned with his younger brother, Menelaus, the two are often referred to as the ATREIDAE. Elder son of the ill-fated House of Atreus, Agamemnon sacrifices his daughter, Iphigenia, at Aulis so that his fleet may obtain favorable winds for the voyage to Troy; for this and other reasons, he is murdered by his wife, Clytemnestra, upon his return home.

AIAS (AJAX). The king of Salamis, Telemonian Aias is a bulwark to the Greek army. A massive man of steadfast courage, he is known in *The Iliad* for a variety of exploits, particularly his dogged defense of the Greek ships as Hector attempts to set them on fire.

AIDÔS. Heroic courtesy and respect. By definition, an epic hero pits himself against the unknown in terms of a code which has been predetermined by his culture, and, in so doing, the hero tests the limits of his culture and defines it for all time. *Aidôs* is one parameter in *the* Argive code: the man who has it recognizes his true position and duty with respect to whomever or whatever he comes in contact (i.e. superiors, inferiors, the enemy, or the gods).

ALEXANDROS (PARIS). The seducer and abductor of Helen. The foppish son of Priam and Hecuba, Alexandros is Hector's younger brother. Although he sometimes engages in hand-to-hand combat, he more often opts for the less heroic bow and a bronze-tipped arrow. Traditionally, he kills Achilles, not in open combat, but by shooting him in the heel from behind, from a secure position on the top of Ilium's wall.

ANTILOCHUS. Second son of Nestor. He is prominent in *The Iliad,* particularly in the funeral games held for Patroclus.

APOLLO. Variously the god of music, poetry, the arts, medicine, and prophesy. At times, he is also associated with the sun and may also be called PHOEBUS or PHOEBUS APOLLO, the Archer-King. Occasionally, he is referred to as SMINTHEUS, a title he assumes when death by disease is attributed to the unyielding penetration of his arrows (see *Iliad,* I). He is the son of Zeus and Leto.

ARTEMIS. Apollo's sister. She is the goddess of the hunt and protectress of wild animals. She is also the goddess of chastity and, therefore, associated with the moon and its cycle.

ASCLEPIUS. Father of Machaon and Podaleirius. He was a renowned healer, but he was cast down by Apollo for an attempt to rival the god in the practice of medicine.

ATHENE (ATHENA). The goddess of wisdom who sprang fully formed from the forehead of her father Zeus. She plays an important role in *The Iliad,* where she backs the Greeks; in *The Odyssey,* where she is Odysseus's patron, her role is even more significant.

ATREIDES. Agamemnon or Menelaus. Together, they are the ATREIDAE. Atreides is a patronymic for a son of Atreus, the House from which both warriors spring.

AURORA. The blushing goddess of the dawn. Wife of the mortal, Tithonus. She is the mother of Memnon, king of the Ethiopians.

AUTOLYCUS. Crafty grandfather of Odysseus. Supposed grandsire of Sinon.

BIAS. "The Great Captain" is a minor Pylian general serving under Nestor.

BOREAS. The north wind.

CALCHAS. The chief prophet-priest of the Greeks. It is Calchas who reads the signs and advises Agamemnon to sacrifice a virgin at Aulis.

CHIRON. A centaur. Wise and gentle, he is supposed to have had skill as a healer.

DEIPHOBUS. One of Priam's sons, a younger brother to Hector. He is sometimes said to have become Helen's husband following the death of Paris.

DEMODOCUS. A blind singer. His role as oral poet is significant, for as such he proclaims and preserves the heroic reputation—the immortality—of the men who fought at Troy.

DEUCALION. Father of King Idomeneus of Crete. Founder of Cnossus (Knossus).

DIKE. The Greek concept of justice: *the doer must suffer.*

DIOMEDES. The king of Argos, Diomedes is also the son of Tydeus, one of the Seven who failed in the attack against Thebes. He is conspicuous in *The Iliad* as a young warrior who "earns his spurs." He is a model of the heroic code.

EPEIUS. Reputed builder of the Trojan Horse.

EPISTROPHUS. Minor Greek commander, leader of the Phocis.

ETHIOPIANS. A mythical people who were thought to live along the edges of the world. They were much visited by the gods.

EURYLOCHUS. A subordinate commander to Odysseus.

EURYPYLUS. A minor Greek general from Thessaly who is eventually wounded by Paris. He commands the Ormeniones, who bring forty black ships to Troy.

THE FATES (THE MOIRAE). Three old women who determine fate by a process of spinning, measuring, and cutting a thread. Clotho spins, Lachesis measures the length, and Atropos cuts the string.

GLAUKOS (GLAUCUS). Sarpedon's second-in-command and his cousin. Glaukos is a prince of Lycia and a general in the Lycian army, which is allied with Troy.

GOUNEUS. A minor Greek general who took twenty-two ships to Troy; he was king of the region around Dodona.

HADES. Brother of Zeus and Poseidon. Lord of the Underworld, the dead, and the Chambers of Decay, Hades gives his name to the place he rules.

HECUBA. Wife of Priam, queen of Troy, mother of Hector, Paris, and many more.

HELIOS (HYPERION). The sun.

HERMES. Messenger of the gods, Hermes also conducts dead souls to Hades.

HERMIONE. Daughter of Menelaus and Helen.

IDOMENEUS. Son of Deucalion and king of Crete. One of the older generals in Agamemnon's army but also one of the most able.

ILIUS. The founder of Ilium (Troy) and Priam's line.

IPHIGENIA. Youngest daughter of Agamemnon and Clytemnestra. She is sacrificed at Aulis by her father in order that the expedition might obtain favorable winds for the voyage to Troy.

LEDA. Mother of Helen and Clytemnestra. According to myth, Zeus assumed the form of a swan in order to seduce Leda without attracting his wife's notice. According to some renditions of the myth, Helen is the offspring of Zeus while Clytemnestra is the daughter of Tyndareus, Leda's natural husband and king of Sparta.

LEONTEUS. Leader, along with Polypoetes, of the Lapithae. Renowned for his stout defense of the gates to the Greek encampment when Hector storms their walls.

LEUCUS. Supposed seducer of Meda, Idomeneus's wife, and usurper of the throne of Crete.

LOCRIANS. Known for their accuracy with slings, these Greeks took forty black ships to Troy.

MACHAON. See ASCLEPIUS. With his brother, Podaleirius, Machaon is the Greeks' chief healer.

MEDA. Wife of King Idomeneus of Crete.

MEGES. The Greek general who commanded forty black hulls from Dulichium and the Enchinean Islands.

MELEAGER. An ancient red-haired king of the Aetolians, an ancestor of Thoas.

MEMNON. Son of Tithonus and Aurora, the Dawn. He is king of the Ethiopians, who join Priam against the Greeks in the tenth year of the war.

MENELAUS. The Atreides, the cuckolded husband of Helen, and king of Sparta. It is on his account that his older brother, Agamemnon, leads the expedition against Troy.

MENESTHEUS. An Athenian general who had no rival in the handling of infantry, excepting Nestor. He commanded fifty ships in the expedition.

MERIONES. Squire to King Idomeneus and second-in-command of the army of Crete. He is the son of Molus.

MINOS. Son of Zeus and Europa, he is also father of Deucalion, grandsire of King Idomeneus.

MOLUS. Father of Meriones.

The MYRMIDONS. See ACHILLES.

The MYSIANS. Warrior allies of Priam who are commanded by

Chromis and Ennomus. Their homeland is located in the mountain fastness east of Troy.

NELEUS. Once king of Pylos, he is Nestor's father.

NEOPTOLEMUS (PYRRUS). Son of Achilles and Deidamia of the Isle of Scyros. He is brought to Troy by Odysseus in the tenth year of the war, not long after his father's death.

NESTOR. King of Pylos, father of Thrasymedes, Antilochus, and Pesistratus. He is the oldest of the Argive generals fighting before Troy, and close study of *The Iliad* shows that among the Greeks he is a master of his craft and wise beyond all others.

NIREUS. Prince of Syme. Homer considered him the handsomest Danaan who went to Ilium but also called him a weakling. In the Greek force, he commands only three trim ships.

ODYSSEUS. The hero of *The Odyssey,* the king of Ithaca, the son of Laertes and Anticlea, the father of Telemachus, Odysseus is also husband to faithful Penelope, who waits twenty years for him to return. He is particularly beloved and protected by Athene, and, owing to his wit, he is called the Man of Many Turns, the wily Odysseus.

OENEUS. Father and ancestor of red-haired Meleager, king of the Aetolians.

PANDARUS. A Trojan bowman. Owing to the manner in which he ambushes Menelaus during a truce, the theme of treachery is often associated with this warrior.

PARIS. See ALEXANDROS.

PATROCLUS. Achilles' best friend, who is killed by Hector when Achilles sends him into battle. Patroclus's death precipitates Hector's death, and then Achilles'.

PENELEOS. A minor Greek general who commands a Boeotian army before Troy.

PENELOPE. Odysseus's faithful wife and mother of Telemachus.

PENTHESILEA. The queen of the Amazons who allied herself with Priam in the final year of the war. According to some accounts, Achilles was moved by her beauty.

PESISTRATUS. Youngest son of Nestor. He did not go to Troy owing to his youth but figures importantly in *The Odyssey,* where he befriends Telemachus.

PHEIDIPPUS. Minor Greek general who, in company with Antiphus, leads thirty hollow ships from the islands of Nisyrus, Carpathus, Casus, and Cos.

PHILOCTETES. Famous Greek bowman. On the voyage to Troy, during a water stop on the isle of Lemnos he was bitten by a snake; the bite refused to heal, and its condition became so odious that the Greeks were forced to leave him behind as they sailed on to Troy. Embittered by ten years of involuntary exile, Philoctetes turned his back on the Greeks only to be lured to Troy in the war's last year, an accomplishment credited to Odysseus. When Philoctetes finally reached the Plain, his wound was healed by Podaleirius. Afterward, Philoctetes shot and killed Paris, helping to bring the war to a close.

PHOENIX. As an outcast, he was befriended by Peleus; later, he became Achilles' tutor. By the time *The Iliad* commences, he is already an old man.

PODARKES. Brother of Protesilaus. Minor Greek general who commands the men of Phylace, Iton, and Antron, he only assumes this command after his brother, the older and better man, is killed by Hector in the opening minute of the war.

POLYPOETES. See LEONTEUS.

POSEIDON. Brother of Zeus and Hades, Poseidon is Lord of the Sea, the Earthshaker.

PRIAM. King of Troy, husband of Hecuba, he is also the father of Hector, Paris, and many others.

PROTHOUS. Minor Greek general who leads the Magnesians to Troy in forty black ships from around the vicinity of Mt. Pelion.

RHESUS. The king of Thrace, who allies himself with Priam. He is killed in his sleep by Odysseus and Diomedes during a night raid behind Trojan lines.

SARPEDON. Son of Zeus. He is king of Lycia and leader of the Lycian army, which allies itself with Priam. He is killed in battle by Patroclus. After Priam's sons, he is Troy's most important friend.

SCHEDIUS. Minor Greek general who leads the warriors from Phocis. With his brother, Epistrophus, he commands forty black hulls.

SINON. The Greek who is supposed to have persuaded the Trojans to pull the Trojan Horse into Ilium. Masquerading as a victim of Odysseus's enmity, Sinon approaches Priam as a suppliant; then he convinces the Trojans that the Greeks have departed forever, leaving the horse as an offering to Athene. The Greek departure is, of course, a ruse designed to lull the Trojans' fears while providing cover under which the Greeks may reenter and destroy Troy.

SMINTHEUS. See APOLLO.

TELEMACHUS. Son of Odysseus and Penelope.

TEUCER. Half-brother to Aias, son of Telemon. Aside from Philoctetes, he is the best bowman in the Greek army.

THETIS. A sea nymph, she is the wife of Peleus and mother of Achilles.

THOAS. Andraemon's son. He is the minor Greek general who commands the Aetolians in battle.

THRASYMEDES. Son of Nestor.

TITHONUS. A mortal who married Aurora, goddess of the dawn, he is also father of Memnon. He is usually a type for pride owing to the fact that at the time of his marriage he asked the gods for (and was granted) immortality. This attempt to go beyond what is a proper limit for man proves costly: although the gods granted his request, Tithonus forgot to ask for immortal youth; as a result, as years passed, his body aged and shrivelled to a point where he begged for death. Eventually, the gods transformed him into a cicada, and he died by nightfall. *Sôphrosynê*, nothing too much, a kind of temperance, suggests that a man must recognize and accept his mortality; this is another element in the heroic code by which each of the heroes must learn to live.

TLEPOLEMUS. Son of Heracles. Minor Greek general who commands nine trim ships of lordly Rhodians.

ZEPHYRUS. The west wind.

ZEUS. King of the gods. Lord of the Thunderbolt, the Cloudgatherer, he is also Hera's husband and brother.

Gazetteer

For ease of notation, the following symbols will be used for map references in the Gazetteer:

Map I—Achaia (Greece)	I
Map II—Troia	II
Map III—Ilium	III

Map references will be included in parentheses following place names.

ABYDUS (II, III). Blue city by the water's edge, Abydus is located in the eye of the "fishhook," on the coast of the Hellespont due south of the Thrynian citadel of Sestus. The Dardanians who inhabit Abydus are Trojan allies.

AETOLIA (I). A region in western Greece bounded, roughly, by the Ionian Sea to the west, the gulfs of Patrai and Corinth to the south, the river Achelous to the north, and Locris to the east. Major citadels include rocky Calydon, Pylene, Chalcis by the sea, Pleuron, and Olenus. The Aetolians are commanded by Lordly Thoas.

ACHELOUS (I). Principal river of western Greece, courses south through Aetolia and empties into the Ionian Sea. The river's west fork originates at the head of the Pindus Mountains; the eastern fork springs from the foot of the Pindus. The forks join about twenty miles east of the Gulf of Amyrakia.

ARGOS (ARGOLID) (I). The base and body of the easternmost peninsula of the Peloponnesus, including the Plain of Argos. Extending from the head of the Gulf of Argos to the south, the Argolid is bounded on the north by the Gulf of Corinth, the Corinthian Isthmus, and the Saronic Gulf. It is the heartland of Achaian Greece, containing the citadels of Argos, Tiryns, and Mycenae.

ARISBE (II). A Dardanian stronghold on the Hellespont which is allied with Priam. The citadel is east and north of Abydus.

ATTICA (I). Directly north of the Saronic Gulf and south of Euboea, Attica is separated from Boeotia by the uplands around Mt. Parnes. The region's chief city is Athens, and the island of Salamis, home of Aias, is immediately offshore, at the head of the Saronic Gulf.

AULIS (I). The bay from which the Greek fleet sails for Troy. Here, on a coastal promontory, Iphigenia is sacrificed. Aulis is located on the northeastern coast of Boeotia, due south from Chalcis, the Euboean city located at the foot of the Euboean Gulf.

BOEOTIA (I). This section of central Greece is located north of Attica and west of Euboea. It sends six thousand men to Troy.

CALABRIA. The area around the toe of the Italian "boot," east of Sicily.

CARIA (II). The area in Asia Minor that is immediately north of the island of Rhodes. The Carians, Trojan allies, are uncouth in speech and manner.

CARPATHUS (II). A small Greek island in the vicinity of Cos.

CASUS. Small Greek island in the vicinity of Cos.

CHALCIS (I). Located on the southern coast of Euboea, at the foot of the Euboean Gulf, Chalcis is well positioned to control north-south traffic that seeks to pass through the narrows between Aulis and the Euboean shore.

CHRYSA (II). Phrygian city located on the southern slopes of Mt. Ida, northeast of Lesbos.

CNOSSUS (KNOSSUS) (I). Located along Crete's northern coast, in the shadow of Mt. Ida, Cnossus is the island's chief city and citadel of King Idomeneus.

COS (II). A small Greek island northwest of Rhodes.

CYME (II). Mysian city located due north of the Hermus River and southeast of the city of Mytilene on the island of Lesbos.

DARDANIA (TROIA, THE TROAD) (II). Troy is the chief city of Dardania, the coastal region north of Mt. Ida and the River Scamander, bordered by the Aegean Sea to the west and the Hellespont to the north. The region also encompasses the Plain, the River Simoeis, and the citadels of Thymbra, Dardanos, Abydus, Arisbe, Percote, and Colonae.

DARDANOS (III). The Trojan citadel at the tip of the "fishhook."

DODONA (I). Chief city and religious center in northwestern Greece.

DOLOPIA (I). This triangular region of Greece is bounded on the west and south by the two forks of the Achelous River. The western slopes of the Pindus Mountains form the rough, northeast border of the area, which is immediately north of Aetolia.

DULICHIUM (I). An island due west of Ithaca in the Ionian Sea.

ELIS (I). This Greek settlement is located not far from the coast in the northwest corner of the Peloponnesus. This is the area to which Sinon retires.

EPIRUS (I). The northwest corner of Greece bordering the Ionian Sea to the west and Illyria to the north. Dodona is its chief city and religious center.

EUBOEA (I). Running northwest and southeast, Euboea is the long island which separates Locris, Boeotia, and Attica—the Greek mainland—from the Aegean Sea. Chalcis, on Euboea's southern coast, is the island's major city. Mt. Ocha caps its southeastern tip.

GORTYN (I). Meriones's citadel located almost due south of Cnossus on the southern slopes of Crete's Mt. Ida.

HADES. The underworld.

HALIACMON (I). The northern river which separates Greece from the barbarian hinterlands. The river drains into the Gulf of Thermais.

IMBROS (II). A large island west of Thynia, northwest of Troy, whose people are allied with Priam.

LEMNOS (II). This island, which is located west of Troy and Tenedos, is held by the Greeks; its chief port, Myrina, is a thriving trade center and slave port where the Greeks exchange their spoils for war material.

LESBOS (II). West of Mysia and south of Dardania, the huge island of Lesbos is allied with Priam. Its chief cities of Antissa and Mytilene are later noted as depraved seaports.

LAKE LYCHNITUS (LAKE PRESPA) (I). North of the Haliacmon River, the shores of this lake form a temporary homeland and base camp for the Enchelean barbarians.

LYDIA (II). Bounded by Caria to the south and Mysia to the north, this region is allied with Troy. Lydia is home to Sarpedon and Glaukos.

MILETUS (II). Carian city on the coast of the Aegean Sea.

MYCENAE (I). Chief Achaian citadel and home of Agamemnon. Situated on a rocky promontory at the head of the Plain of Argos, Mycenae was uniquely positioned to control all of the trade routes in and out of the Peloponnesus. In part, the citadel's importance in Argive politics may have resulted from this fact.

MYTILENE (II). Allied with Priam, Mytilene is the chief city on the island of Lesbos.

NEMEA (I). About six miles northwest of Mycenae, this citadel overlooked one of the Mycenean roads which moved north from the Plain of Argos toward the Isthmus and city of Corinth.

NISYRUS (II). This small island is less than fifteen miles south of the island of Cos; politically, the island is aligned with the Greeks.

OLENUS (I). A citadel in Aetolia.

MT. PARNASSUS (I). Located in central Greece immediately north of the Gulf of Corinth, Mt. Parnassus is sacred to Apollo, the Muses, and the poetic arts. The temple of Delphi and its oracle are located along its slopes.

PERCOTE (II). Dardanian city located on the Hellespont northeast of Abydus.

PHRYGIA (II). The vast hinterland extending from Troy's eastern borders into the heart of Asia Minor. The peoples of this region are Troy's allies.

PHTHIA. (I). Northwest of Boeotia, this region is south of Thessalia.

THE PINDUS (I). Running roughly northwest and southeast, the Pindus Mountains form the backbone of central Greece, separating Thessalia and Phthia from Epirus.

PROCONNESOS (MARMARA ADASI) (II). An island located in the Propontis, midway between the Thracian and Phrygian coasts.

PROPONTIS (SEA OF MARMARA) (II). The broad inland sea which connects the Hellespont with the Bosporous and the Black Sea. Prior to the Trojan War, the area was a Trojan lake, owing to the fact that access was controlled by Priam.

PYLENE (I). Aetolian city on the Gulf of Corinth.

PYLOS (I). The citadel of Pylos guards the western approaches to the Peloponnesus. Located on the edge of a beautiful bay and perfect natural harbor in the southwest corner of the Peloponnesus, Pylos is the seat of Nestor.

SALAMIS (I). Salamis is less than two miles from the Attic coast at the head of the Saronic Gulf. Close to Athens, the island serves as a power base from which Telemonian Aias leads twelve ships to Troy.

SAMOS (II). Aegean island located west of the border between Caria and Lydia and due west of the mouth of the Meander River.

SCAMANDER (XANTHUS) (II, III). The largest river on the Trojan Plain. Running west from the Mysian and Phrygian highlands, Scamander passes Thymbra and then swings north, running all the way across the Plain until it empties into the Hellespont.

SCYROS (I). Birthplace of Neoptolemus, the island of Scyros rises from the Aegean Sea between Euboea and Lesbos.

SCYTHIA. (not shown). Southern Russia. Mythical home of the Amazons, who fight like men in their glory. Recent digs in Scythia have suggested that Scythian women did, indeed, go into battle beside their men.

SESTUS (II, III). Thracian stronghold on the Thynian peninsula. Sestus is allied with Troy.

SIMOEIS (II, III). The second largest river on the Plain. The course of Simoeis roughly parallels the Hellespont until, like Scamander, it turns north and empties across the Plain into the Hellespont.

SMYRNA (II). South of the Hermus River, Smyrna is located at the tip of a finger-shaped gulf that recesses into Lydian territory.

TENEDOS (II, III). This offshore island, which covers the mouth of Besika Bay, also guards the western approaches to the Troad.

THESPRONTIA (I). The coastal region of Epirus.

THESSALIA (I). Thessalia is bounded to the north by the Peneus River, to the west by the Pindus, and to the south by Phthia. Located in the heart of north-central Greece, Thessalia is home to Eurypylos, Podaleirius, and Machaon.

THYMBRA (III). A mountain citadel guarding the eastern approach to the Plain along the banks of Scamander.

THYNIA (III). The peninsula which forms the northern shore of the Hellespont. The Gulf of Saros is north of the peninsula. This rocky, mountainous coast figured importantly in World War I because Galipoli is located near the peninsula's northern root.

TIRYNS (I). Seaport to Argos, Tiryns is located on the Gulf of Argos, immediately south and west of the Argolid.

TRICCA (I). North of the Pindus and the Peneus River, Tricca is located in the northwestern corner of Thessaly.

WALL OF HERACLES (III). The low coastal mountain range which separates the Plain of Ilium from the coast. The southern tip of the Wall slopes down to Besika Bay.

XANTHUS. See SCAMANDER.

ZACYNTHOS (I). The island of Zacynthos is due east of Elis in the Ionian Sea. Dulichium and Ithaca are located to the north of Zacynthos.

ILLINOIS SHORT FICTION

Crossings by Stephen Minot
A Season for Unnatural Causes by Philip F. O'Connor
Curving Road by John Stewart
Such Waltzing Was Not Easy by Gordon Weaver

Rolling All the Time by James Ballard
Love in the Winter by Daniel Curley
To Byzantium by Andrew Fetler
Small Moments by Nancy Huddleston Packer

One More River by Lester Goldberg
The Tennis Player by Kent Nelson
A Horse of Another Color by Carolyn Osborn
The Pleasures of Manhood by Robley Wilson, Jr.

The New World by Russell Banks
The Actes and Monuments by John William Corrington
Virginia Reels by William Hoffman
Up Where I Used to Live by Max Schott

The Return of Service by Jonathan Baumbach
On the Edge of the Desert by Gladys Swan
Surviving Adverse Seasons by Barry Targan
The Gasoline Wars by Jean Thompson

Desirable Aliens by John Bovey
Naming Things by H. E. Francis
Transports and Disgraces by Robert Henson
The Calling by Mary Gray Hughes

Into the Wind by Robert Henderson
Breaking and Entering by Peter Makuck
The Four Corners of the House by Abraham Rothberg
Ladies Who Knit for a Living by Anthony E. Stockanes

Pastorale by Susan Engberg
Home Fires by David Long
The Canyons of Grace by Levi Peterson
Babaru by B. Wongar

Bodies of the Rich by John J. Clayton
Music Lesson by Martha Lacy Hall
Fetching the Dead by Scott R. Sanders
Some of the Things I Did Not Do by Janet Beeler Shaw

Honeymoon by Merrill Joan Gerber
Tentacles of Unreason by Joan Givner
The Christmas Wife by Helen Norris
Getting to Know the Weather by Pamela Painter

Birds Landing by Ernest Finney
Serious Trouble by Paul Friedman
Tigers in the Wood by Rebecca Kavaler
The Greek Generals Talk by Phillip Parotti